D1522209

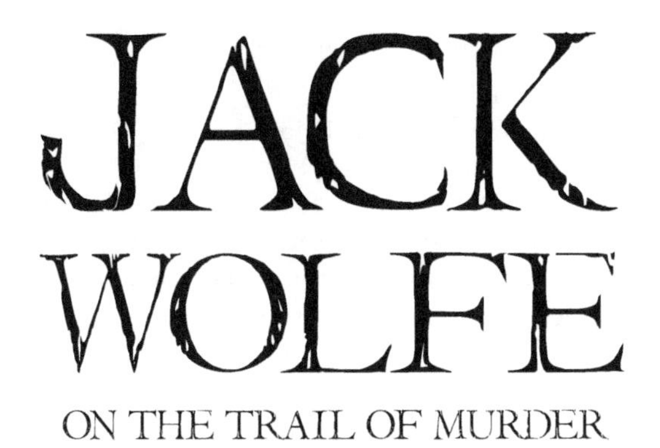

JOHN SAXXON

This is a work of fiction. All of the characters, names, incidents, organizations, and dialogue in this novel are either the products of the author's imagination or are used fictitiously.

ISBN: 978-1-4834-7897-5 (sc)
ISBN: 978-1-4834-7896-8 (e)

Library of Congress Control Number: 2017919838

Lulu Publishing Services rev. date: 5/11/2018

You never know what you can accomplish unless you try.

To my parents, who have always been there for me;
To my son, Jack, just because I can;
And to my best friend for all the great support and encouragement.

ACKNOWLEDGEMENTS

I'd like to thank Diana, without whose help this book would never have been written. She was the driving force behind encouraging me to write it and at every stage thereafter. And also, the Windsor VT American Precision Museum for helping me with information on munitions in the 19th century. Finally, I'd like to thank David for his useful insights into life during the American Civil War.

PROLOGUE

20 September 1854
The Romanian–Bulgarian border

It was after midnight as the man moved stealthily down the main street of the small village. He did not pause, but continued to the last lane of crumbling houses, where the poorest villagers lived. The most vulnerable, the women among them, were his prey of choice. Covered from head to foot in dark clothing, Casper Bogdan was a despicable little man. A cold-blooded killer, rapist, and petty thief, he didn't value human life at all. He crept from house to house in the darkness, furtively peering in every available window. Finally, he found what he was looking for. A lone woman sat sewing by the faint smoky light of a tallow candle.

Bogdan's blood started to flow faster as he crept down the deserted side alley of the house, preparing himself for what he was about to do. Trying the handle on the back door, he found it unlocked. Quietly letting himself in, he continued silently moving toward the room where the young woman sat. It was easy to be quiet on the packed earth floor – no squeaky floorboards to give him away. Apart from the glow of the candle, the house was in complete darkness. The woman had no idea he was there until he grabbed her by the throat and pulled the chair over backward. The back of the woman's head hit the packed earth with a sickening thud, temporarily knocking her out as the chair hit the floor. The force of the momentum threw her skirts up, exposing her legs.

Bogdan licked his lips. This was going to be easier than he thought. Usually he preferred them to struggle a little but he wasn't about to let that stop him here. Not wasting any time, he rolled her off of the upturned chair. Pulling open her legs, he ripped off her underwear, undid his trousers, and violated the unconscious woman. Finishing, he closed up his trousers and tightened his belt. He smiled to himself.

He was about to leave when he became aware of feeling a curious lack of satisfaction. He still had a burning inside him that wasn't fulfilled. The woman hadn't screamed, hadn't struggled. She'd just lain there as he'd taken what he wanted. He realized that what excited him most was to see the fear in their eyes as what was happening finally dawned on them. He felt cheated. It hadn't been enough. He needed more. In frustration, he kicked her in the side. She let out a faint moan but didn't open her eyes.

This was too slow. Going into the small kitchen, he found a jug of water. Bringing it back into the room, he emptied its contents onto the woman's face. The cold water revived her, and she started to sit up, spluttering. As her eyes came into focus, she could see Bogdan kneeling in front of her. She started to scream, but he backhanded her across the face.

Her head whipped viciously sideways, and she could taste blood in her mouth. "What do you want?" she asked shakily in Romanian.

Replying in the same language, Bogdan cruelly told her he didn't want anything. He'd already got what he wanted. That was when the woman realised she was practically naked from the waist down. The horror of what he had done drove her into a frenzy. Pulling down her dress to cover herself, she tried to move backward away from him, but didn't get far. Feeding greedily on her fear, Bogdan pounced on her. Terror filled her eyes, and she started to scream again. Bogdan clamped a dirty hand over her mouth.

"That's better," he said. "I like it when you struggle."

The woman continued to fight, even though it seemed hopeless. She managed only to free her arm and scratch him down his face.

Enraged by the pain, he roared, "You're going to regret that!" With his hand still clamped over her mouth, he pushed her head sideways. Lowering his mouth, he brushed his lips up her fully exposed neck and whispered maliciously in her ear, "Time to die, *kuchka*."

Terrified, the woman made one last, desperate bid to escape her fate, but Bogdan was too quick. He moved his mouth back down to the side of her neck and bit down hard. The soft flesh yielded. He bit harder. He could now feel the jugular vein through the sinews of her neck, feel the woman's blood pumping through the vein inside his mouth. His excitement was becoming almost too much to contain. With one last effort, he sank his teeth even deeper and shook his head from side to side like a dog. Hot blood filled his mouth and splashed over his face. He swallowed. He felt so alive. His mouth filled again. Again, he swallowed and then opened his mouth and pushed the woman away, watching in fascination as the last of her blood disappeared into the dirt floor.

Bringing his hand up to his mouth, he wiped at the blood. Holding his hands out in front of him, he rubbed the blood between them, enjoying its warm stickiness. He started laughing uncontrollably. This was it – the feeling he'd been searching for his whole life. Nobody was going to stop him now. He felt invincible. Without a second glanc at his hapless victim, he left by the same door he had entered only a few minutes earlier. Bogdan then stood for a few moments in the rear garden. A faint moon cast a pale glow. Looking down at his hands, he saw they had turned black. The moonlight had altered the colour of the blood. Confusion filled him and then turned to wonder. His hands looked like death. He liked that. He was death.

CHAPTER ONE

25 October 1854
17th Lancers of the Light Brigade, somewhere near Sevastopol or, more exactly, Balaclava

Misery. The dead and dying lay everywhere. The screams of men and horses could be heard from all directions. Those left alive took small comfort in having faithfully followed their orders in the face of overwhelming odds. The only problem was the orders were wrong. From the time the orders left command to when they finally ended up on the front lines, they had been misinterpreted, ordering an attack on the wrong target. What was supposed to be a mission to harass a fleeing Russian artillery battery instead became a full-frontal assault on a heavily armed and well-entrenched artillery position. The main problem was that the Light Brigade, made up of five regiments, including the 17th Lancers, was not at all prepared to attack cannon. Designed for speed and lightly armed with only lances and sabres, the mounted soldiers were meant to scout targets and attack infantry or other cavalry units.

On this fateful day, 670 brave men of the Light Brigade had

ridden their horses into a valley of death. Cannon, occupying the high ground to the left and right, spewed deadly cannon balls and grapeshot. Refusing to be deterred, the Light Brigade had fought their way through the Russian riflemen to the front, and then continued on to their ill-fated target, the artillery at the head of the valley. With their speed and agility, many of the men actually made it through the Russian lines, and even further on, killing any artillerymen who hadn't already fled their positions. But although they had managed to break through, they now found themselves surrounded by enemy fire and clearly had no possible way to hold the position. The order to retreat was given. That meant retracing their route back the way they had come. By the time they had retreated to the line of Russian riflemen, the gunners at the head of the valley had retaken their position on the cannon and were firing indiscriminately into friend and foe.

Four hundred and twenty-three human casualties were sustained, and more than half the horses were slaughtered. Out of the five regiments, the 17th Lancers, suffered the greatest tragedy. Of the 145 men who went into battle, only 38 answered the roll call the next morning.

Remnants of the 17th Lancers, Battle of Balaclava

Turning his back on the battlefield, Jack Wolfe led his tired horse toward the encampment. A lieutenant in the 17th Lancers, he was a heroic officer who stood up for his men. In turn, he was well liked and respected by them. Standing six feet tall, with broad shoulders and tanned features, he cut quite an imposing figure. He was a kind but hard man who could put the fear of God into you with one stare from his piercing blue eyes. He was not the sort of man you argued with. But, even at six feet, he seemed dwarfed by the horse he led. His mount was a Belgian Black he had raised from a foal and brought with him to the Crimea. Although not bulky enough to be classed as a heavy horse, the breed had strength enough to have carried armour-clad knights into battle in times gone by. He had named her Skeiron, for the God of the northwest wind, taken from Greek mythology. She had good breadth of chest and was sure-footed and nimble, the perfect animal for a cavalry charge over muddy and uneven terrain. Jack was glad to have her. They had both been to hell and back many times. Today was no exception.

The fight had left Wolfe with three separate wounds from a bullet, some shrapnel, and a sabre. The bullet wound to his upper arm had only grazed the muscle but the shrapnel had impacted with his side. The only reason it hadn't killed him was because the lump of metal had lost most of its momentum as it passed through his canteen before glancing off a rib and exiting throught the flesh in his side. The last and most serious wound was a sword slash from one of the Russian riflemen. This had come across his upper thigh and had continued, slicing into the neck of his horse. They were both bleeding profusely from this shared wound. He had managed to bandage his own leg but was struggling to keep enough pressure on his horse's neck to stem the flow of blood. If it didn't stop soon, she could die.

"Lieutenant Wolfe, sir?"

"What is it, trooper? I'm afraid I can't stop. I need to get my horse to the vet." Wolfe kept up his slow but steady pace, forcing the young man to follow.

"What are your orders, sir?

"Where's your sergeant?" Wolfe replied.

"It was Sergeant Smith, sir, but he's dead. Cannonball took his head clean off. I was riding right next to him." The trooper's eyes were downcast as he relayed the brutal memory.

"What's your name?" Wolfe paused, taking his gaze off Skeiron's bleeding neck and turning to acknowledge the young man.

"Cartwright, sir," the lad replied, his pale face and tattered, muddy, blood spattered uniform grim evidence of his part in the day's tragedies.

"Jesus, what a mess," Wolfe cursed. "Have many of the men reported back?"

"Not yet, sir, but there's a call to muster for oh seven hundred tomorrow."

"Then orders are for the men to regroup at camp, see to the horses, check over their gear, and get some food inside them."

"Yes, sir!" The boy snapped to attention, giving him a smart salute.

"All right, Cartwright, that will be all."

Cartwright hesitated a moment. "Glad to see you made it, sir."

"Me too trooper, me too."

With another quick salute, Cartwright left. Standing there for a few more moments, Wolfe surveyed the destruction behind him. Dead bodies of men and horses were tangled together like grotesque monsters. Most had limbs missing or were disembowelled. The stench was already nauseating. A faint breeze carried the smell of gunpowder across the field and the rancid combination was something he would never be able to forget. He started walking again. As he limped back into camp he saw the back of a familiar form.

"Bull!" he shouted.

Bull, otherwise know as Sergeant Major Mathews, turned around at hearing his name. He was a large man, taller than Jack, standing six feet two with a barrel chest, brown eyes, and a mop of shaggy black hair. His nickname fit him perfectly. With a relieved grin on his face, he strode over to Wolfe.

"Holy shit, sir. I wasn't sure I'd be seeing you again! The last thing I saw was you heading through the Russian lines with your sabre dancing like you were fighting off the very devil himself. After that, the world turned upside down, as I got my mount shot out from under my sorry arse. I went over the top and was lucky not to break my neck, never mind getting crushed to death, as the damn beast nearly rolled on top of me. I only got out of there alive because I managed to get hold of a stray horse from some poor sod that wasn't so lucky. You look like you didn't get through exactly unscathed yourself." Bull trailed off looking at all the blood on Jack's uniform.

"Yeah, it got pretty hairy for a while. What the fuck were we doing attacking those guns? I mean seriously, they had cannon on three sides. I'm surprised anybody got out alive."

"Word has it that the orders got messed up, and we attacked the wrong target." Bull's bleak features belied the casualness of his reply.

"Bloody hell! It's hard enough to stay alive out here without being sent on a suicide mission. Have you heard any reports of numbers yet?"

"No, sir. The roll call is in the morning," he looked at the blood seeping from the wound on Jack's thigh and Skeiron's neck, "Do you need help seeing to those wounds, sir?"

"Thanks, Bull. I'll be fine for a bit longer, but any idea where the brigade's vet is? I need to get Skeiron looked at right away."

"Last I saw him he was over by the trees." Bull pointed beyond the main camp to another smaller cluster of tents set in a clearing in the woods.

Wolfe eyed the seemingly deserted veterinary area as he tried to keep enough pressure on his horse's neck wound. "I could maybe use a hand ..."

"My pleasure, sir," Bull said, falling into step beside him as they started to make their way over.

"I keep telling you, Bull. When we're on our own, call me Jack. We can ditch the formality." Wolfe clapped him roughly on the back." We've been through enough of this war together that we're practically brothers. I think it's safe to say we've saved each other's lives more times than either of us would care to remember."

"Yes, sir," said Bull, as he jokingly stumbled forward from the force of the slap. They trudged over to the vet's tent trading stories of past escapes, the seeming normality a welcome antidote to the tension of witnessing the horror of the battle, a tension that threatened a man's sanity.

As they walked along, Wolfe realised just how cold it was. He was covered in sweat from fighting, and with the wind starting to pick up, the temperature was dropping. The stress and exertion of the last few hours were catching up with him. He inwardly shivered. It was not hard to imagine that winter would be descending upon them soon. He needed to get Skeiron patched up and his own wounds tended to as quickly as possible so he could collapse in front of the campfire and eat something hot.

When the two men got into the trees, they could see a picket line of horses. Most had their heads down, looking dejected, hardly bothering to shake off the flies crawling on their wounds. Before they had time to wonder at the dismal sight or look for the vet, their attention was drawn to a gunshot in the distance at the other side of the wood. The loud crack reverberated off the surrounding hills. Continuing along the track that cut through the vegetation towards the sound, Wolfe and Bull approached the group of canvas tents.

"Hello," called out Bull. "Anybody here?"

From off to the side, they heard twigs snapping and leaves crunching underfoot. A man appeared wearing an army uniform with a bloody apron over the top, a rifle held loosely at his side.

"What do you want?!" came the angry voice.

"Major Colbert, sir!" exclaimed Wolfe, as both he and Bull snapped to attention. "I need some help. My horse has been wounded."

Stopping and turning, the vet gave Skeiron a cursory glance. Observing the large amount of blood running down her neck and on her front leg, he merely said, with a wave of his hand.

"Tie her over there with the others."

"It can't wait, sir. She's bleeding quite heavily and needs to be sewn up now."

"I can see exactly what's wrong with your soddin' horse, lieutenant. I'm the vet, not you. Now put the damn animal over there and let me get back to work."

"With all due respect, sir, she'll probably die if she's not treated immediately," Wolfe responded, refusing to back down.

"I'm sorry to tell you, lieutenant, but the beast will die anyway. I have my orders. All animals that come through here needing anything more than minor attention are to be released. Command has deemed we can't afford the drain on our already depleted supplies for any animals not fit for service, as we are coming into winter. The winters up here are brutal. Only the fittest men or horses will survive. In its infinite wisdom, command has deemed that we need to concentrate our efforts on keeping healthy horses alive and not wasting time and resources on the rest. It's a damn shame, but it's just the way it is. We're overwhelmed. They won't give me the time or supplies to do my job any better. It's that simple. I'm disobeying orders by even shooting them. Damn waste of good horses if you ask me, but the most humane action in the circumstances. I'm not prepared to just release them. I've seen what these barbaric Zouaoua do to the horses they catch. It's not a pretty sight. He trailed off, his eyes focused on some distant point on the horizon over Jack's shoulder."

"Then I'll sew her up myself," Wolfe responded flatly, his mouth set in a stubborn line.

"Are you stupid, man?!" Colbert blurted in exasperation, looking back at Jack. "Did you not hear what I said?" His gaze moved to the large blood-oozing slash on Skeiron's neck. "There's no anaesthetic or disinfectant available for treating the horses. Aside from the certainty of an infection settling in the wound, the moment you put a needle anywhere near that wound, the pain flare-up alone will terrify your horse, causing her to kick you, most likely resulting in your own death!"

"As you say, sir, you're the vet, but my father being a teamster for the last thirty years means I see things a bit differently. In his line of work, losing a horse to an injury or healing that horse can mean the difference between a good living and the workhouse – not somewhere you ever want to be. Your horse is your lifeblood. I worked with him for nearly twenty years. In that time, we built up quite a big business with a lot of horses. I started out in the stables, worked my way up to running several teams myself. I know how to keep horses healthy. I also know how to patch them up if they get injured. I have some medical supplies I brought with me," he gestured to the gear on Skeiron's saddle, "I just thought you could do a better job with the stitches. But if you're too busy, then I'll fix her up myself." Jack wound up his explanation hoping he'd said enough to convince him.

"No matter how good you think you are," said the vet, "you're still going to risk getting killed doing it. But maybe that's a better way to go than at the hands of the Ruskies," he added shaking his head in disgust.

"I don't care." Wolfe turned to look at Skeiron's wound seeping blood from under his hand as she gazed at the other horses. She was starting to sweat from shock, and there was now a slight tremble to her body. "I'm going to try, and nobody's going to stop me. She's not just a company horse, sir. She's mine. Bought and paid for. I've ridden only her from the start of this bloody war, and she's brought me back every time."

The major seemed about to argue again but paused, seeing the determination in Jack's eyes. "Okay, sonny." He gave in, sighing heavily. "I can see there's no talking you out of it. I'll give you what I can spare, but then I have to attend to my other duties. Our commanding officer has ordered me to report to him by seventeen hundred hours, and I'm already going to be late." With that, he ducked quickly into the nearest tent. When he came back, he had a few items in a bit of clean cloth. "This is the best I can do. There's a disinfected needle, some thread and a square of clean linen. Just be careful. And good luck." And with that, the vet walked off to his meeting.

"Thank you, sir!" Jack called to the major's rapidly retreating back. Standing there, he looked at Bull with a wry grin. "Well I guess we better get on with it. Seems she's not gonna stop bleeding on her own."

"Any idea how you want to do this?" asked an apprehensive Bull.

"First, give me your whisky." Bull's eyebrows arched as if to deny he had any. "I know you have a flask over your heart in that breast pocket. I just don't know if its to stop bullets or for liquid courage." Jack winked. When Bull still didn't hand it over he added, "I won't use it all and you can have the first swig." With that Bull was convinced. He took out the metal flask and had a long draw. Handing it to Jack, he wiped the back of his mouth with his grimy sleeve and smiled.

"That was much needed! Now, where were we?"

Jack poured a good dose of the remaining whisky onto Skeiron's wound, quickly handed the flask to Bull and stepped back holding her head down to protect the wound from opening as she danced in place from the sting of the alcohol. "Easy girl, it'll pass." He stroked her nose and placed a hand on the top of her neck. He then folded the linen into a square the size of the wound, placed it on top and put pressure with his hand to slow the bleeding. Bull watched the proceedings a bit morosely, sorry to see the loss of his precious whiskey on a horse's hide.

"Now I say we take her into the trees to a quiet clearing where she'll feel less vulnerable. She's trained to lie down on command. Once she's on the ground, you hold her head and neck down so we can keep her somewhat still. This will give me the best chance to get her stitched up and hopefully get that bleeding stopped."

With a raised eyebrow, Bull set off through the woods. Jack followed, leading Skeiron. When they found a clearing, he stopped in an area of soft grass and began to quietly speak to her, rubbing her neck and muzzle. After a few minutes she seemed to calm, letting out a deep fluttering breath through her nostrils in a long snort, and lowering her head. Jack lightly touched her shoulder below the wound, and she folded her legs, sinking gracefully to the ground. Once Skeiron was lying down, Jack kept talking to her in a quiet voice and nodded to Bull, who moved into position to hold her head in place. Reaching into his own medical kit, Jack removed a round metal tin. Opening it, he scooped out some paste.

"What's that?" asked Bull.

"Anaesthetic," replied Wolfe, spreading it around the wound.

"But I thought the vet said he didn't have any?"

"He didn't, but I do. It's cocaine based, something my father taught me. You just take some cocaine powder, mix it with water, and apply it to the area. Numbs it pretty good for a while, certainly long enough to put these stiches in."

Taking his time and continuing to talk in soothing words, Jack started stitching up the gash in her neck as neatly as he could. He was glad the thread was silk. It allowed him to put in lots of small stitches, and in his personal experience this technique would leave less of a scar and hold better against the stitches ripping out. Hopefully it would work for Skeiron too. After an initial attempt to lunge to her feet when he started stitching, she lay still, flinching only when the needle went a bit deep. The area had become partially numb from the trauma of the wound, and adding the cocaine paste almost numbed it completely. Once he'd finished stitching, he again reached into his medical kit and removed a small cylinder. It contained cayenne pepper, which he used as a coagulant. Removing the lid, he shook the reddish powder onto the wound. After a few minutes, it had congealed and dried. He gave Bull a nod to release his weight from Skeiron's neck and let her stand. When she was up on her feet Jack surveyed his work with satisfaction. The wound had stopped bleeding completely, and the stitches looked like they would hold well enough.

He stroked her soft muzzle, relief flowing through him in a wave. "Looks like you'll be with me a while longer, old girl. Thanks," he added, turning to Bull.

"Glad I could help. But after what the vet said, I'd thought there was no way we were going to manage that without at least one of us getting seriously injured. How come she didn't move?"

"Well, I think there are several reasons. Firstly, she's a Belgian Black. They were originally bred to be used by knights hundreds of years ago and are renowned for being rock solid when it comes to anything that would spook another horse. I'm counting on this calm demeanour to also work to keep her quiet so the stiches have the best chance to hold and knit the wound together. Another reason is that me and Skeiron have been together for about six years now, and, well, we've formed a special kind of bond. We both trust each other and, ultimately, take care of each other. The last, and probably most likely reason she didn't move is she couldn't get up for your fat arse lying on her."

"Now the last one does sound the most likely," agreed Bull with a grin. "Can she walk?"

"Yeah, she'll be fine, and she won't have far to go any time soon. I think after today's debacle, they won't be sending us back out for a while. With some rest, she should heal pretty quickly. Talking of which, I better go get her bedded down and see the doc. I need to get stitched up myself." With that, they headed off to the main camp, keeping Skeiron to a slow pace.

When they got to the first line of military tents, they parted ways. Jack towards the stables and Bull headed off to his tent in happy anticipation of enjoying some comforts of home. He was in the lucky position of having his wife with him. Not many men were so fortunate, but Mary had wanted to come when the 17th Lancers deployed, and the regulations allowed it, so here she was. She had her own general jobs around camp, along with tending to her husband's needs. Wolfe, being his commanding officer and friend, benefitted also, as she would wash and mend his clothes and most often cook for both of them too.

After seeing Skeiron settled for the night and surviving being patched up by the brigade doctor himself, who was unfortunately more of a butcher than a doctor, Wolfe finally returned to his tent. It was next to Bull's, which made life a lot easier for meals. It meant only one fire out in front of both tents for cooking and warmth when they were sitting and eating together. Mary, was tending the fire and cooking pot. As soon as she saw him, she came running over and started fussing around him.

"I'm okay, Mary," said Jack, "just a few scratches. Nothing a good plate of your stew won't cure," he added with a wink, hinting broadly.

"You're sure you're okay?" she persisted, knowing Jack's tendency to play down any danger to himself.

Jack nodded as he gently moved past Mary and sat down next to

Bull in front of the warm fire where his personal camp chair had been set up. He loved his chair. It had a collapsible wooden frame and a canvas back and seat. He slid down into it now and rested his feet on a nearby crate. There were times when he'd even managed a few hours sleep like this. Looking into the fire, he felt grateful for Mary's help. If she weren't here, he would have to find wood and light his own fire. She had everything done so well. There were stones round the base to keep the fire contained and to soak up the heat. Then, when the wood was running low, the stones could still radiate some precious warmth. The metal tripod with the stew pot was already bubbling, its aroma chasing away any lingering traces of the acrid smell of blood and death. Jack could also see through the open flap of his tent that clean clothes had been laid out on his cot. Mary gave Jack a concerned look as she ladled out stew.

"I'm fine," he said, smiling reassuringly and patting his bandages. "The doc gave me light duties for about ten days. By the time that's over, me and Skeiron will be out of the woods, so to speak."

She nodded, relieved, and handed them both a plate of steaming food and then left to carry out some of her other chores.

"Mary," Jack called.

She stopped and looked back.

"Thank you, for caring. Also, for everything you do around here. We'd be lost without you."

Mary just smiled and left.

"I never knew your dad was a teamster?" said Bull, breaking into the comfortable silence that had settled in the wake of Mary's departure.

"Yeah, he's been running horses for over thirty years. Really knows how to care for them right proper," Jack said, his voice laced with irony. "He cared for those horses better than he did me."

"How do you mean?" asked Bull, intrigued by this statement.

"When I was a kid, things seemed fine. He took me out with him to do most things. He was a drinker, but I never saw it as a kid. What I didn't know was that he was beating my mum when I wasn't around, often after I'd gone to bed. I sometimes think that's what killed her in the end. Then, when I grew up and started to run a team of horses myself, he started drinking even more and beating me instead. I think he hated the fact I was getting stronger than him and could handle a team of horses as well if not better. I just wish my mom had been there to see me when I first handled a team on my own. She would have been so proud."

Bull stared into the fire, imagining the painful disappointments of Jack as a young man. Changing the subject, he asked, "What did the major mean by what he said about what the Zouaoua do to horses?"

"The Zouaoua," explained Wolfe, "are Algerian and Moroccan tribesmen. They fight alongside the French troops. From all accounts, they're pretty aggressive, if not reckless fighters. Because they're from Africa, they have a completely different way of eating. Any of the horses that get released risk being captured by them, killed, and eaten. The trouble is, they will either hack the animal to death or start hacking lumps off it while it's still alive, in the mistaken belief it keeps the meat fresher. They're totally barbaric. I guess the major just couldn't stand the thought of that cruel end for Light Brigade horses."

The two men fell back into silence again for a while longer. Watching the flames flicker and listening to the wood crackle was mesmerizing.

It was Bull who spoke first again.

"I've been thinking," he began.

"That can be dangerous," countered Jack.

Bull was quiet for a few seconds.

"I almost bought it today, having my horse shot out from under me. Seeing all the dead and dying men around me, I got to thinking. If something happens to me, I want you to make sure Mary's okay and gets back to England safely."

"Nothing's gonna happen to you, Bull. We're both gonna make it through this, and then you'll be able to take care of her yourself."

"I'm serious, Jack," Bull said quietly. It was the first time he had ever used his friend's name. "I want you to promise me you'll look after her."

"Are you sure that, when your horse went down, you didn't land on your head?" Jack asked flippantly. "It won't come to that. But if it'll keep you happy, I swear, that if anything happens to you, I'll make sure Mary's safe. She's like a sister to me."

"Thanks," was all Bull could manage, swallowing hard.

Finishing their food, they sat there warming themselves from the fire trying to get some heat back into their bones after the chill of being constantly soaked in mud and water.

"We lost so many good men today," Jack said, attempting to slouch farther back into his chair despite the protests of his wounds, "and all for nothing. We didn't gain a single inch of ground. It was totally senseless."

"War generally is senseless," said Bull, gazing into the flames.

"Are we the lucky ones? Or are they?" mused Jack. "Their fighting is done. The pain is over. How many more years is this gonna go on? How many more men will be buried? Will we end up crazy from all the death and destruction?"

"We can only do what we're ordered. At least you and I have an edge that most other men don't. When we go into battle side by side, we don't think about our own safety. We fearlessly attack the enemy because we know that we have each other's back. I've seen the terror it creates in the eyes of our enemies. How would you react facing an enemy with no fear?"

"Since when did you turn into a philosopher, Sergeant Major Mathews?"

Bull laughed. "It's the downside of being around you. Before I met you, I just followed my orders and didn't question anything or look for a better way. You get me thinking."

"Hmmmm," said Jack. "Well, I've been doing a little more thinking of my own. I know we're supposed to only carry lances and sabres, but today's battle got me wondering. When we made it all the way to the enemy cannons, most of the men were fleeing. If I'd had a musket, I could have stayed there and shot them from a distance. Instead, I could only watch until we were ordered to retreat the way we had come. As soon as we started to fall back, the fleeing gunners turned around and ran back to their guns. They then opened fire on us. I think that must have been when you lost your mount and we got seperated. It was a total slaughter. If I could have shot even some of them, it would have saved so many of our men and their horses."

Jack fell quiet, musing on how he would proceed with his idea. If he bumped it up the chain of command, his request would be refused out of hand, as a musket wasn't part of his allocated equipment. If he got his hands on one himself and it was discovered, he could be written up for breaking protocol. He would have to proceed very carefully. The last thing he wanted was for an over officious officer to see him with a musket and write him up on a disciplinary. These officers loved nothing more than to exert their authority on the lower ranks. If Jack did get a disciplinary on his record, he risked being moved to another unit and his men would then be commanded by someone else. He couldn't allow that to happen. His men were too important to him. He would have to be very careful indeed. Jack's deep thoughts were interrupted by a loud belch.

"That's better," stated Bull.

"I'm sure it is," replied Jack. "Sounds like it came right from the soles of your boots."

"Nothing like a good belch after a fine meal. In some cultures, it's deemed a compliment to the chef."

Jack just raised his eyebrows. "Well, on that fine note, I'm going to hit the hay. It's been a hell of a day, and I'm done in." He stood and started for his tent.

"See you in the morning, Bull."

"Good night, Jack."

CHAPTER TWO

Waking the next morning, Wolfe started to dress. His large frame and wide shoulders filled the tent making it necessary for him to crouch down as he put his clothes on. Women seemed to like his broad shoulders. They liked his piercing, blue eyes too. At six feet, he was taller than most men. His close-cropped brown hair gave him a more severe, menacing look than the longer styles favoured by current fashion. However, past experiences had taught him that women like a man with an air of danger. He never went looking for trouble, but if justified, he wouldn't hide from it either. When he'd first joined the Lancers, he had spent many months at their base with the other men training to be soldiers. The local town was always a popular escape to forget about a hard day's drills. As with all towns that had military men based near them, conflict between the locals and the outsiders had been inevitable.

Wolfe was no stranger to these disagreements. He never started them but invariably found himself the only man standing once the dust had settled. It was after these disagreements in particular that there would be several women trying to attract his attention and seeking him out the next time he was in town. Every time the fights would break out, a crowd would gather. For these women, it was like a moth being drawn to a flame. They just couldn't stay away. He would never totally understand the other sex but couldn't say he minded their company at all when the occasion presented itself. The solitary, nomadic nature of his life meant he'd never let anything get too serious. Those were complications he didn't need.

His wounds protested at his movements, bringing his attention back to the present. They had stiffened up in the night, restricting his mobility somewhat, but it didn't seem like there was any infection. Finally dressed, he picked up his jacket, left his tent, and slowly started walking to where Skeiron was stabled. The cold morning air had the feeling of a long winter as Jack shrugged himself carefully into his jacket. The soggy ground squelched under his boots with each step. When he entered the dimly lit stable area, Skeiron spotted him and gave out a soft nicker. Jack strode over. Seeing his horse made him forget about his own injuries. He spent a few minutes stroking her nose and talking to her as she nudged him for treats. Glancing down at the wound on her well-muscled neck he could see that the stitches had held during the night, and there was no new blood. This was a good sign. He ran his fingers lightly over the area, checking for heat, but he detected nothing out of the ordinary. She seemed in good spirits too.

Spending a few more minutes, he gave her some food and then left reluctantly. He wasn't looking forward to the next part of his day. The roll call had been ordered for oh seven hundred, and it was fast approaching that time now as Wolfe made his way towards the parade area. Other soldiers were already milling about, and Jack was shocked at just how few men were there. He spotted a few familiar faces and nodded to them. The order was given to form up. The men made parade lines and stood to attention further highlighting their pitiful numbers. The roll was taken, and then the commanding officer came forward.

He stood on a makeshift podium to address the men. "You should all be proud of how well you handled yourselves yesterday. It was a trying time, but you showed great bravery. Lord Cardigan has heard of your bravery and has sent his regards and gratitude."

Jack could hear quiet mutterings from the ranks. He could make out the odd word – "toff," "bastards," "shit."

The men's mutterings didn't sound encouraging, but the officer droned on. "The British people will hear of your heroism, how you fought tenaciously in the face of the enemy. It will give them a great sense of pride. You will all return as heroes."

Jack could hear more mutterings, slightly louder this time.

The officer must have sensed the troops' disapproval, as he quickly finished his pontification and, duty fulfilled, left to return to his comfortable tent.

The order was given to fall out. Men gathered round in small groups talking among themselves. Wolfe could now hear what the men were saying and was in agreement, even though he couldn't publicly support them. The problem the men had with what the officer had said was that they didn't believe any of it. Yes, they had fought bravely but they didn't need an officer, who hadn't even been there, to tell them that. They had been in the thick of it and knew exactly what had happened. Lord Cardigan sending his gratitude was more of an insult than something to be proud of. The men would much rather he sent them more food and decent equipment. And as for the British people hearing about their bravery, they probably would eventually. But it was doubtful the British public would care too much what had happened in a place so removed from their daily lives. They were, understandably, too busy with their own struggle to be worried about strangers thousands of miles away riding into battle. For a large majority of them, trying to earn enough money to buy the food they needed to stay alive took up all of their time.

Wolfe left the area, nodding to several men on his way, and headed over to check in with his superior officer about any specific orders he might wish him to carry out. He was also hoping to try to find out more information about what had happened with the previous day's battle.

Arriving at the closed flaps of the Captain's tent Wolfe called out. "It's Lieutenant Wolfe, sir."

"Enter," was heard from inside the tent.

Wolfe parted the canvas opening and stepped inside. It was a much larger tent than the simple sleeping quarters of he and his men. It had a cot along one side but there was also a large wooden desk, stacked with papers, which Jack's superior officer was sitting behind.

"Captain Sibbert, sir," said Jack, coming to attention and snapping a salute. "What are your orders?"

The captain said nothing for a moment, keeping his head down as he finished scribbling something onto the bottom of a piece of paper. He looked up at Wolfe with a tired expression on his face.

"Privileges of rank!" the captain exclaimed.

"Excuse me, sir?" said a confused Wolfe.

"Writing letters to the families of the men we lost. I have to tell each and every one how grateful we are that their son gave his life fighting for his country. It sickens me how many men have died." The captain paused as if lost in his own thoughts. "I'm sorry, Lieutenant, what did you ask me?"

"What are your orders, sir?"

"Just make sure that that the men we have left are ready to move out once we get fresh orders. I expect it will be a move towards Inkerman to provide support for other units."

"Yes, sir," said Jack. "If that's all, I'll get back to the men?"

But before Jack could turn to leave, Captain Sibbert stood up from behind his desk and moved next to where Jack was standing.

"Listen, Lieutenant," the captain said in a low voice. "I'm telling you this because you're a good officer, and I trust you. We did attack the wrong target yesterday. I've not been privy to how the order got screwed up so badly, but there is a rumour doing the rounds that the officer in charge attacked the wrong target on purpose as an opportunity to try out some new battlefield tactics he'd been working on."

Jack was dumfounded at what he was hearing. Such a senseless loss of life and for what? He could see by the look on his commanding officer's face that he too was truly disgusted with those higher up the chain who had ordered a charge that had resulted in this horrific loss of life.

"Thank you, sir," said Jack. "I appreciate your candid comments."

"Well I better get back to my letter writing," he said in a resigned voice. "They aren't going to write themselves." The captain turned and returned to his desk to carry on with his unpleasant duty.

Jack saluted again and departed to go back to his quarters, mulling over the new information. So many thoughts were running through his head, not the least of which was why all those men had been allowed to be slaughtered on someone's new idea. Wolfe was angry. It had cost too many of his men's lives and almost Bull's and his own. Too angry to go straight back, he went to check on Skeiron again.

Finally feeling somewhat restored from the familier routine of caring for his horse, Wolfe headed over to his tent. The fire was lit, and Mary was busy boiling some water. At his approach, Mary looked up with a smile, bidding him good morning. He returned the pleasantries and sat down in his chair by the fire to try to get some of the morning cold out of his bones. Lost in his own thoughts, he wasn't aware of Bull sitting down next to him until he spoke.

"A good morning to you, sir. Did the captain say anything interesting?"

"Morning, Bull," Jack replied, pulling himself from his thoughts. "No, he didn't say too much. I actually think he's at a bit of a loss about what we're supposed to do until reinforcements arrive. We lost a hundred and nine men. With only thirty-eight left, we're not much of a fighting unit any more. He did mention there was going to be a push towards Inkerman, but other than that, he gave no more details."

"So, we're not going to take Sevastopol?" asked Bull.

"No, it seems the army is going to put Sevastopol under siege, and we will continue around to Inkerman."

Mary came back, made them both coffee, and gave them biscuits. They sat there, enjoying the feeling of the warm liquid.

"What are your orders for our men?" asked Bull.

Jack leaned forward in his chair and cradled his coffee in his hands, thinking. "I'll need you to get me a total number of how many of our section are left and how many of those are able to fight. I also need a count of how many horses we have. Tell the men to resupply themselves with what food and water they can find. They should also scavenge around for better boots."

Bull nodded. Everyone knew the boots supplied by the British army were generally too small, and after about a week, the mud sucked the soles off. In desperation, many of the soldiers had taken to wearing the boots they acquired from dead Russian soldiers. The more their men could take away with them now, the better.

Six days after their ill-fated Sevastopol foray, the orders were received from further up the chain of command that they were, indeed, to move out towards Inkerman, although word was that they would be kept in reserve.

The roads they were travelling were surprisingly good, especially for the time of year and considering the recent rain. The wagons carrying their supplies got stuck only a few times. At one of their overnight stops, they were met by a detachment of reinforcements, swelling their severely depleted numbers to a fighting force to be reckoned with once again. On the third day, they reached Inkerman. It was a small but ancient town, tucked below some cliffs, overlooking an inlet. The looming presence of a cave monastery and medieval fortress on the top of those cliffs combined to make it an imposing sight despite its size. Setting up camp within sight of the town but well out of cannon range, they went about their standard duties while waiting for orders. Clean blue tunics glared in contrast against the soiled, tired uniforms of the existing lancers. It was easy to see who the new men were.

Jack had ridden Skeiron. Her wound continued to heal well, but he wasn't confident she was ready to ride hard into battle. He feared the extra exertion and any sharp movements would open up the stitches. He himself was also well on the mend. His arm was fine, and he had only minor pain in his side. The slash to his leg was still sore but had finally healed over enough in the last few days so that it no longer restricted his movement.

The next morning, orders came to move up towards the front lines and wait for more orders. Out of concern for Skeiron's wounds, Jack took one of the spare horses. They set off in total darkness. When dawn finally arrived, a heavy mist blanketed the area. Visibility was down to about twenty yards when they reached their new position.

As the morning wore on, the sounds of battle could be heard in the distance, but, with the fog still so thick, it was difficult to know properly where the sounds were coming from. A lone man on horseback came riding into their midst. Relaying his message to Wolfe, he disappeared back into the soupy fog.

"We're moving out, men!" Jack called.

The men started to mount their horses. Trotting his horse over to Bull, he leaned across to his friend. "The Russians have attacked Home Hill. They've sustained heavy casualties, but the British commander fears they'll counter-attack and has called for reinforcements. That, as you may have guessed, is going to be us."

As the men moved out, it wasn't very clear where their designated point of attack actually was, with visibility still virtually impossible. Despite this, they rode on up the valley as instructed to their staging area. The closer they rode, the louder the battle could be heard still raging over the next rise. The 21st Regiment of Foot was inflicting heavy casualties on the advancing Russian forces but was in danger of being out flanked. Wolfe and his men were ordered into the fray to attack the Russian flank and drive the Russians back into the centre of the line, where the British gunners could do more damage.

Riding abreast, the 17th Lancers formed a line and advanced at a trot. It wasn't easy to see where the enemy was, as the fog kept swirling in and out. One second, you could see fifty yards; the next, you could hardly see the man riding next to you. From the far left, the order to charge was given. As Wolfe dug his heels into his mount, he could see Bull do the same from the corner of his eye on his left and he wondered what they would be riding into after the last debacle.

They shot forward as a line, some screaming battle cries and others remaining silent. Wolfe was the silent type. They crested a small rise, and the fog seemed to lift. Spread out in front were the Russian riflemen. They were out in the open and slowly advancing through the muddy ground. Before most of them had a chance to react, the 17th was upon them. It was a grim sight to see a lance rammed through the midsection of the enemy. It was also a great feat of skill to do this to an enemy while still remaining mounted and able to pull the lance out and attack the next man. Wolfe, a great horseman himself, found a lance too unwieldy, preferring his more nimble sabre. You had to get closer to the enemy but everything was much more in control. Or at least, that was the theory.

Today, Jack wasn't quite so confident, as he was riding a strange mount. Down into the Russian soldiers they thundered. Bull smashed his mount through a group of soldiers. Two were trampled to death instantly. Bull got one with his sabre. The other two threw themselves to the side, only to end up in the path of the advancing Wolfe. Like Bull, Wolfe aimed his horse at them. One fell to his sabre, but the other dove to the ground to avoid his charge. Wolfe pulled his horse round in a tight circle and went back after the one who had escaped. Just as the Russian was getting to his feet, Wolfe closed in. With one sweep of his sabre, he separated the man's head from his body. Turning back around once again, Wolfe joined the rest of the men. When their unit had made it through the Russian lines, the order was given to charge back the way they had come with the intention of inflicting more misery on the Russian soldiers who, it was assumed, would now be in total disarray.

They charged back. Unfortunately, the Russians seemed well prepared this time and immediately opened fire with their muskets. Musket balls could be heard whizzing past, but the musketeers were mainly firing blind, as fog had enveloped the area once again. Wolfe came out of the fog in a gallop and was on top and through the Russian lines before he knew too much about it. He still managed to hit two of the enemy, who both went to the ground dead or mortally wounded.

Just as he was clearing the battlefield, he thought he heard Bull call out his name but couldn't be sure. In the maelstrom of battle, it was sometimes hard to recognise distinct sounds. He might not have even heard anything. Slowing his horse, he waited for the rest of his troop to regroup.

One by one, they emerged from the fog. They were a sorry looking bunch. All were covered in mud; some had blood mixed with the mud, but it was hard to know if it was their own blood or the Russians'. Two of them, though, were clearly wounded. One was hanging over his horse's neck, missing the lower part of his arm. As each man rode past, he would nod to Wolfe, too exhausted to even think about saluting. To his relief and surprise, they had all made it – apart from Bull.

Wolfe instantly made his decision. He sent the rest of the troop back to the staging area for any needed medical attention and to await further orders. He alone would go back and look for his friend. After the rest of the men departed, Wolfe sat there a moment, thinking on his next move. He decided stealth was the best option. Dismounting, he dropped his horse's reins to ground tie him and proceeded on foot. Bull couldn't be that far away, as he had heard his friend call out his name. Approaching the top of a small rise, Wolfe lay flat on his stomach, sabre ready at his side. Peering into the fog, he could barely make out several forms walking around. Unable to make much sense of it, he stood up and continued on.

Walking past several dead Russian soldiers and still under the cover of fog, Wolfe sheathed his sabre and picked up a Russian musket. He looked it over and found that the mechanism was damaged. He discarded it and picked up another. Making sure it was loaded and in working order, he walked on. Passing several more dead Russians he picked up two more muskets. He had realised that, if he had to start shooting, he probably wouldn't have time to reload. This way, he could just drop the empty gun and pick up the next.

As he picked up the last gun, the tendrils of fog had begun to lift once again. In the distance, about fifty yards away, Wolfe could now make out the distinctive shape of Bull. He was obviously a prisoner, as there was a Russian soldier either side of him.

Taking up a prone firing position, Wolfe readied himself. If this were to work, he would need to be quick. He cocked the two spare muskets and carefully placed them on the ground next to him. With his third and last musket tight in his shoulder, he regulated his breathing, took aim, and gently squeezed the trigger. The hammer fell. There was a flash of gunpowder and then a blast of smoke from the end of the barrel. The noise was deafening. Without looking to see what damage he had inflicted, Wolfe was already reaching for the second gun. With the hammer ready and cocked, he tucked the musket firmly in his shoulder and pointed it towards where he had last seen the enemy. As he had hoped, only one Russian was still standing. Taking the time to ensure an accurate shot, he aimed at the last Russian and pulled the trigger. Once the smoke cleared, Wolfe could see Bull standing there alone.

Last rifle ready, he waved his arm and shouted for Bull to come to him. The shock was plain to see on Bull's face, quickly followed by delight at both being free and seeing his friend. Bull hotfooted it across the open space while Jack continued to scan for enemy soldiers. As he got close, Jack jumped up, and they both raced back to Jack's waiting horse. Grabbing up the reins, Jack mounted and pulled up Bull behind him, and they set off at a gallop back towards their lines.

"Jesus Christ," said Bull. "I thought I was a goner for sure."

"Yeah, you didn't look like you were having too much fun."

"Thanks, Jack. I'd say you saved my life."

"Nothing you wouldn't have done for me."

"True enough," replied Bull, "but possibly not with that much efficiency. Where did you learn to shoot like that?"

"My father took me out hunting all the time when I was a kid. Near our farm there were about a hundred acres of fields and woods that the local landowner let us hunt on. We would go out shooting rabbits and the like. I just seemed to have the knack for it. Never shot a person though, until today."

Riding back through the fog, they could hear the moans of the wounded or dying soldiers. Every now and again, people could be seen carrying stretchers. The battlefield was slowly being emptied of its suffering cargo.

"I hope you know where you're going," said Bull, his voice laced with humour.

"So do I," replied Jack. "This fog seems to be getting worse. If we are going the wrong way, you may end up in the record books as the only British soldier to be captured twice in the same day."

"I guess I deserved that," said Bull.

"By my estimations, we should—"

Jack's words were cut off by a terrible scream.

"What the fuck was that?!" exclaimed Bull.

"I'm not sure I want to find out, but it sounded like it was just up ahead."

They trotted through the fog and the mire in the direction of the scream, with only the odd moment of visibility when the breeze picked up and dispersed the banks of fog. It was during one of these reprieves that Jack and Bull glimpsed a stretcher-bearer in the distance kneeling by a soldier. Oddly, upon hearing their approach, he quickly turned and scurried away and was swallowed up by the grey mist. They plodded on until they came to where the man had been kneeling. Looking down they could see it was a one of their own lancers. His clean blue uniform also marked him out as one of the recently arrived reinforcements. He was lying on his back. His lifeless eyes were wide open, obviously dead, but there was something odd about him. Jack jumped off the horse. Kneeling by the man's side, he looked him up and down, studying him.

"What is it, Jack?"

"I'm not sure. Something doesn't seem right. It looks like this guy's only been shot in the leg. I don't know why his neck and chest are covered in so much blood. Taking a rag he wiped at the area of his neck. There was nothing – no bullet wound or sword marks. Turning him slightly, Jack could now see the other side of his neck. There was an area of torn flesh with blood oozing from the wound. "Jesus!" exclaimed Jack. "There's a bite mark on his neck."

Bull jumped off the horse and knelt by Jack's side.

"What could have done that?"

"I'm not sure. Maybe a wolf or some other wild dog. Since this war started, the wolf population has exploded with all the dead horses to feed from. They've never been fatter. Maybe one just happened by, and this unfortunate sod was too incapacitated to fight it off.

"But what was that other guy doing?"

"I'm guessing," said Jack as he started to check the pockets of the man's uniform, "he was looking for soldiers to help. This guy was clearly beyond help, so he moved on." He pulled out some money from the man's pocket and then replaced it. "At least he wasn't looting."

"Well, we may have just spooked him a bit before he had the chance. He did seem to be acting a bit weird, spending too long with a soldier who was obviously dead."

"I thought so too. But who knows? Maybe if we spent all day picking up screaming soldiers, we'd be a bit weird too."

With that, they mounted Jack's horse and continued on to camp.

Once there, Jack went to return the borrowed mount, while Bull went to requisition a new one. The latter was gaining quite a reputation for losing horses. Finding himself with some free time, Jack went over to where Skeiron was stabled. He fussed with her for a while, grooming her coat to a gloss, checking her feet and legs for heat, and even dressing her hooves with some oil. Her wound had healed up nicely, and he carefully removed her stitches. She would carry a scar from the charge at Sevastopol, but many would consider that lucky. She seemed to enjoy the attention and kept nuzzling his pockets hopeful for treats as he worked. He felt himself unwind a little. The familiar routine reminded him of a time before the war when things were normal. Normal – he wasn't sure he would ever see normal again. The war would end – that was inevitable – but after the horrors he'd seen, would the world ever look normal to him again?

After bedding Skeiron down and feeding her, he left the makeshift stable and made his way back to his tent. Bull was already there good-naturedly teasing Mary with a swat or pinch everytime she walked too close.

"It's good to see you two having fun."

"It's the only thing keeping me sane," said Bull.

"You're a lucky man to have such a good wife."

Warming himself on the fire, he began to think about his day. It had been quite eventful – the blind charge into the fog, shooting the two Russian soldiers who'd taken Bull prisoner, and then the dead British soldier with his throat ripped out. The thought came to him again. He really needed to get his own firearm. He'd been plain lucky to survive the charge and then find loaded weapons on the field today. He couldn't count on just luck again.

"Hey, Bull, do you know any of the soldiers from the 21st Foot?"

Bull paused in his horsing around and pulled Mary onto his lap. "Yeah, I know a few of them. I played cards with them before we shipped out. Why?"

"I need to get their opinion on muskets. If I'm going to get one, then I want it to be the right one."

"Then I'd say you should speak to Corporal Black. From what I've heard, he's about their best shot. If anybody can tell you about guns, it's him"

"Thanks," said Jack. "I'll be back in time for dinner, Mary," he added with a wink as he walked off in the direction of the 21st camp, "in case you're tempted to give my portion to that blighter."

Headed over to where the 21st was camped, he could feel the cold starting to creep into him. It wasn't far, but after leaving the warmth of his own fire behind, he quickened his pace in the hopes of generating some body heat but also to beat the setting sun. It was already low enough that long shadows were starting to form from the line of trees he was walking parallel to. Another, more pressing factor for his haste was self-preservation. Approaching an unfamiliar camp in the dark carried the serious risk of being shot by a nervous sentry. The battle had been won, but the enemy was still close enough that you could see the glow of their campfires several miles in the distance. He hoped that these enemy troops had stopped only to regroup before they continued to retreat in the morning. He did not relish the thought of going into battle again so soon. He slowed his pace to greet a pacing sentry.

"Good evening, Private"

"Good evening, sir," replied the private, coming to attention.

"Can you tell me where I might find Corporal Black?"

"Yes, sir. He's over in the medical tent." He pointed towards a large military-issue canvas structure.

Wolfe thanked the soldier and walked over. On his way, he passed several rows of smaller tents all perfectly laid out with exact spacing – nothing like the arrangement of the 17th Lancers, who pitched theirs in a haphazard but efficient pattern. *The 21st Foot commanding officer must be a real stickler for the rules and regulations,* he thought.

"I'm looking for Corporal Black," announced Wolfe as he entered the large tent.

"That would be me, sir," replied a soldier lying in a military cot to his left. As Wolfe approached, he started to try to raise himself up.

"Lie easy, soldier," said Wolf. "Where are you wounded?"

"I took a bullet in the shoulder, sir," he answered. "Fortunately, it went through clean without hitting the bone. Just waiting for the surgeon to patch me up. I'm a long way down the list of casualties to be seen. There's a lot worse in front of me."

"I feel your pain. I had to wait in line a few weeks ago when I took a sword slash to the leg. Took them a few hours to get to me too."

"But you're an officer. Wouldn't they have seen you straightaway?"

"Yes, but I chose to wait for an opening according to the severity of my injuries just like everybody else. I don't believe I deserve special treatment because I'm an officer. My men are just as important as I am. I'm guessing by the look of your camp," said Wolfe gesturing towards the tent opening where the meticulous layout of the surrounding tents could be seen, "that your commanding officer is of a different breed?"

"Yes, sir. He has all his servants with him, if you know what I mean."

"Indeed I do," said Wolfe. "It has come to my knowledge, corporal, that you are reputed to be the best shot in the 21st Foot?"

"I might be, sir," said a wary Black.

"Don't look so worried, man. I'm just looking for some information about muskets. My unit is the 17th Lancers. As you may be aware, we carry only lances and sabres. About a week ago, I was in a situation where a musket would have come in handy. I just want to know which one is the best one for the job."

"Have you ever fired a musket before, sir?"

"Yes, I've been hunting on and off for years in my civilian life. Then today I found myself in need of one on the battlefield. Luckily, I was able to pick one up from a dead soldier, but I find I'm reluctant to trust my luck the next time."

"Chances are, you've been using smooth-bore muskets. Most of the men will be carrying the 1842 smooth-bore musket. What our regiment has are 1853 Enfield rifled muskets. This means they fire a shaped, not round, shot, and the barrel has grooves cut into it to make the shot spin. This gives us greater accuracy over longer distances."

"Thanks, Corporal. That sounds like the weapon I need. Any idea where I might pick one up?"

"If it wasn't for our commanding officer, I'd give you one of ours. However, with the nature of this war, I'd say you should easily find one lying on the battlefield. Just look out for one with three straps fastening the barrel to the stock. That'll be the Enfield."

"I will do that. I hope you get patched up soon and you stay safe."

"Thanks, sir," replied Black.

Wolfe started to walk away, but Black called him back.

"Did you say you're with the 17th Lancers, sir?"

"That's right," replied Wolfe, pausing mid-stride and turning back to listen.

"I'm just thinking. Do you have a blacksmith with you for fixing horse shoes and the like?"

"We do, why?"

"A musket's a long weapon. When we're in battle, we stand in rows of two. The second row have their barrels pointing over the heads of the first row. The main reason it's so long is because a shorter barrel would deafen and burn the soldiers in the front row when fired. With you being on horseback, you won't need such a long barrel. You could get your blacksmith to just cut off some of the barrel. You'll lose a bit of range, but it will be much more manoeuvrable. You also might consider getting him to manufacture some sort of scabbard so you can carry it on your back, out of your way until you should need it."

With a smile on his face, Wolfe said, "You're a genius, Black. The next time my sergeant is over this way playing cards, I'll get him to bring you a bottle."

"Thank you, sir."

With that, Wolfe turned to leave the tent. A medical orderly was walking past leaving the tent, his arms and apron covered in blood. "Goddam dirty bastard wolf," he muttered as he exited.

Wolfe grabbed the man's shoulder, spinning him back around to face him. “What did you call me, soldier?” growled Wolfe, squaring up to the man.

The man looked up at Wolfe with confusion on his face. “I didn’t call you anything, sir.”

“You called me a dirty bastard. I heard you.”

“I said dirty bastard wolf, yes, sir, but I meant the beasts. This is the third soldier brought through to me with only minor wounds but his throat ripped out by wolves. They could have been saved if it wasn’t for those stinking animals.”

Wolfe turned and walked away, leaving the confused orderly standing in dazed silence. He couldn’t be bothered explaining why he thought he’d been called a dirty bastard. All he wanted now was some food and his bed. It had been a long day.

CHAPTER THREE

The next morning, Jack woke early, as was his norm. He found the fire already lit and a pot of water boiling for their coffee. It didn't seem to matter how early he woke, Mary was always up first. Leaving his tent, he plonked himself in his chair by the fire. The winter was fast drawing in. The cold night had left a thin covering of frost on everything. This change was not surprising, as his blanket hadn't seemed to be doing much good at keeping the warmth in during the night. He poured some of the boiling water into a cup and made himself some coffee. Taking his first sip, he grimaced at the bitter taste as he warmed his feet by the fire. The coffee couldn't be roasted and shipped out to the men dry, as it would go bad. They shipped green coffee beans instead. *What he wouldn't do for a decent cup of properly roasted coffee.*

The swish of Bull's tent flap opening made him look up. Once Bull had gone through the same ritual as Jack, they both sat there in comfortable silence for a while. Finished with his coffee Jack went to check on Skeiron and then to go see the company commander for the day's orders. After checking on his horse and talking to the commander, Jack returned to their camp to relay the orders he'd received to Bull.

"It seems we have a scouting mission. Our unit will be away for two nights and travelling light so no need to pack tents. We'll find barns and the like to sleep in on the way. We leave within the hour."

With that, Jack ducked into his tent, gathered up what he'd need for the mission, and went to saddle his horse. When Skeiron saw him carrying the saddle, she whinnied, very excited, and pawed the ground as he tacked up. It had now been several weeks since she'd been out with Jack. Walking her out of the stable, he mounted, and she sprung into a lively trot until they reached the staging area to await the rest of the men.

Looking over at their camp, Jack could see Mary and one other woman. The only other person left in camp was a wounded trooper. Jack grinned to himself at all the fussing that the young trooper would have to endure from the two women.

The mission, as it turned out, was suprisingly easy. They were to scout ahead in an attempt to assess the total numbers of soldiers the Russians had and how well dug in they were. On the first day of their reconnaisance, they came upon a Russian cavalry unit. They had barely spread out their formation and prepared to charge, unfurling their company colours, when the Russians turned and ran. It was to be a familiar tale throughout the rest of their mission, and, the war. It seemed their ill-fated charge at Balaclava had had one redeeming factor. The Russians who were there had spread the tale of how fearless the men of the 17th were. Several more times on their scouting mission, they came upon enemy cavalry, but each time they encountered the same result; the moment the colours were shown, the enemy ran.

By the morning of the third day, they had gathered all the information needed and started to make their way back towards base camp. The pace picked up the closer they got; all were eager to get back to familiar surroundings and the warmth of a fire. The barns they had stayed in had been decent enough, but fires hadn't been allowed for fear of giving away their position.

The rest of the day proved to be uneventful and with the winter sun fast approaching the horizon, the 17th Lancers finally sighted their tents. Weary from three days in the saddle, the men plodded into the stabling area. After quickly putting their horses away and seeing to their needs, Jack and Bull were some of the first few to walk back into camp.

"There are no fires lit," observed Jack.

Bull grumbled. "Mary knows we were due back today. I hope we're not out of wood again? I'm sick of having to scavenge around like a beggar."

"This doesn't feel right," said Jack as they got closer. "There's nobody here."

"*Mary*!" shouted Bull. But there was no answer. "Maybe they had to go over to the command tent."

"It's possible," said Jack. "I'll go and ask the wounded trooper. He'll know." Jack strode quickly over to where the injured trooper was camped. Opening the tent, he could see him asleep on his cot, lying on his side with his back to Wolfe.

"Trooper," Jack called softly, not wanting to alarm him and have him reopen his wound. The trooper continued to sleep. Jack bent over and gently shook his shoulder.

"Trooper."

Still nothing.

Wolfe shook him more vigorously, the motion causing the trooper to roll onto his back to face Jack. "Where's Bull's wife?"

That was when Jack noticed the glazed look in the trooper's eyes. Reaching down, he felt for a pulse. He needn't have bothered. The trooper's skin was freezing to the touch. He had obviously been dead for some time. Not consciously knowing why he did it, Wolfe took hold of the trooper's chin and tilted it towards him. There, for all to see, was the bite mark that had taken his life. His adrenaline racing, Wolfe ran from the tent.

"*Bull*!" he shouted, panic starting to rise within him at the thought of what might have happened to the two women who were also in camp. His panic escalated when there was no immediate reply. Jack raced back across the camp to Bull's tent. Opening the flap, he saw Bull. He had Mary cradled in his arms. The inside of the white canvas tent was covered in blood, so much blood that Wolfe knew Mary was dead. He also knew there was no point going to his friend. Bull would need to be alone. Wolfe would just wait until he came out of the tent and then help him in any way he could.

The truth began to crystallise in his mind in bits and pieces. Wolfe now knew that this was no animal attack – that all those men on the battlefield had not been killed by rogue wolves. He also realised that the killer was one of their own, no Russian enemy, but a British or allied soldier fighting on his side. That sent a chill down his spine. Not wishing to leave Bull, he sent one of his men to inform the commanding officer of the tragedy. He also got the men to search the rest of the tents for the other woman they had left in camp.

The other woman was found in the same condition as the trooper and Mary – her eyes open and her throat ripped out. Even after living through battles, Jack was shocked by the amount of blood found in the macabre death scenes. The murderer, whoever he was, must be covered in blood. How could someone not have noticed? How could he just walk away and not be stopped and questioned or even seen? It didn't make any sense.

Such was the horror of the event that outside help arrived in the form of a senior officer sent to take charge. It wasn't Jack's captain but Jack's captain's commanding officer. At least, Jack thought, it seemed the army was taking the threat seriously. Jack walked over to where the man was standing.

"Major Walker, sir," Jack said, snapping a salute. "I'm Lieutenant Wolfe. One of the women who was killed was married to my sergeant. Is there anything I can do to help?"

"You can start by removing these tents and getting the blood washed off them," was the curt reply.

"Yes, sir." Wolfe started to respond to the command, although he was slightly puzzled by it.

The officer continued, "It's such a tragedy what happened." Wolfe started nodding his agreement. "To be attacked in their own tents by wild animals is so unfortunate."

At this, Wolfe stopped nodding and looked over at the officer, confused. "But, sir, these were not animal attacks. These people were murdered."

The officer moved in closer to Wolfe and lowered his voice. "Do you have any proof of this?"

"Not yet, sir," replied Wolfe.

"Just as I thought. Then, as we don't have any police or resources to investigate these deaths, they will be deemed animal attacks."

"But, sir!" protested Jack.

"Are you questioning the judgement of a senior officer, lieutenant?" asked the now irritated major.

There was a tense moment as Wolfe met Major Walker's eyes and stared him down, but then he decided it was the wrong time to stand his ground. "No, sir," replied Wolfe in a voice taut with frustration.

"Then we will write this up as animal attacks. Could you imagine the panic that would ensue if we said a murder was loose among our men? The morale of the entire army would decline. If word got out of the details, it would leave a stain on the reputation of this unit. I won't let that happen. You're dismissed." As an after-thought he said, "Give my condolences to your sergeant."

Wolfe stood there, rage building inside him, looking at the officer's back as he walked away. He shouldn't have been surprised. The army and this toff officer were covering their own backs as usual regardless of the cost to others. If the men knew what had really happened, they would be able to stay vigilant and hopefully stop it happening again. As for the reputation of the unit, that was just crap. Major Walker was more worried about his own reputation than anything else. The bottom line was that the major wasn't prepared to do anything and for Wolfe that just wasn't good enough. He vowed to investigate the horrific deaths and track down the killer. He owed it to the dead soldiers, to Mary, and certainly to his friend.

For the rest of the day, Bull was practically catatonic. He had stayed in his tent, holding onto Mary until the medical orderlies, under the instruction of Major Walker, forcibly removed her body from his arms. Bull had then wanted to continue to stay in the tent the two of them had shared, but Major Walker had once again stepped in and had the tent burned. He clearly wanted this business behind him as quickly as possible, a point about which he and Jack were in total agreement for the moment. The hours wore on in a mundane progression of tasks, each of which slowly took away all evidence of the tragedy. *I suppose that's a specialty of war,* Jack thought to himself, *the ability to once again restore order and carry on as normal after unspeakable tragedy.*

By late evening, Jack had finally managed to persuade Bull to rest on an extra cot that had been put in Jack's own tent for the night, but he suspected Bull had agreed only because he was asleep on his feet already and wanted someplace to be alone. In respect Jack, took himself off and busied himself with all the chores he could think of but eventually ended up simply loitering with Skeiron until he was too tired to keep his own eyes open. Hoping Bull was sleeping, he made his way back to the tent and settled into his cot as quietly as possible. Of course, despite his exhaustion, once he lay down, his mind wouldn't shut off.

Jack lay awake for some time, trying to piece together all the information and also trying to come to terms with the loss of Mary. She was such a lovely woman. He could only imagine the pain that his friend was feeling. After a while, he realised he could hear Bull fidgeting around. It appeared rest wouldn't come to him either. However, at some point, they must have both fallen asleep because, the next thing Jack knew, the light coming through the cracks in the tent flap told him it was dawn, and he could hear the rhythmic breathing of Bull across the tent. Unfortunately, as Jack rolled over in his cot, the wood creaked loudly enough to rouse Bull from his sleep, but Bull didn't' react. He just lay there looking up at the canvas above him.

"I'm sorry, Bull," said Jack breaking the silence. "I can't imagine what you're going through. If there's anything you need, you know you only have to ask."

Bull was silent for several minutes. "I just don't understand how this could have happened? Wolves have never come near camp before, let alone entered a tent. What sort of freak of nature could have caused one to lose all its fear and attack three people like that?"

Jack was silent, trying to figure out how to tell Bull what he really thought had happened. He knew Bull would rightly want justice for Mary, but he also knew his friend could be hot-headed. The last thing he wanted was for Bull to go and see Major Walker and demand something be done. The major would refuse, and Bull would probably hit him. Bull would then most likely face a court martial.

Jack couldn't seem to find the right words, but he also couldn't let his friend believe a lie about something so important. He decided to just tell him and then try to control the fallout.

"It wasn't nature, but it was a freak," Jack started into his explanation. In one fluid motion, Bull swung his legs off the side of the cot and sat straight up, staring at Jack. Jack continued, "After what we've seen on the battlefield and talking to one of the medical orderlies, I believe this was carried out by a man – a very sick and twisted man but a man nonetheless." Jack sat up also. "You're right when you say no wolf would enter camp and certainly not a tent. I truly believe it was that same man we saw on the battlefield. The one who had been leaning over the body of the soldier the day when we were coming back towards our lines through the fog. We thought there was something wrong at the time, but we just put it down to the strains of war."

He watched carefully as Bull let this information sink in. Then, as expected, the floodgates opened. "Do you know who he is? Have you told anyone? Is there anybody investigating this? Why did he do it?"

Bull paused for breath and Jack took advantage of his pause to try to answer his questions. "I know as much as you do of the man we saw on the battlefield. And, yes, I told Major Walker. He says I don't know what I'm saying. He shut me down because he believes it would cause panic and ruin the reputation of the unit if the truth got out. Ruin his reputation more lik," he added in disgust.

"Bloody bastard!" was all Bull could say, getting more agitated by the moment

"As for anybody investigating this, it's going to be down to you and me and must remain between us. Major Walker will inflict serious punishment on anyone caught looking into this. As for why this man did what he did, I just don't know. Maybe he's crazy, or maybe he's evil. Either way, we have to find him and stop him."

"What do you mean by stop him?" Bull asked.

"We track him down, make absolutely sure we have the right person, and then kill him," said Jack matter-of-factly.

Bull didn't move for a long time except to drop his gaze to the ground. Jack could only imagine his friend's thoughts but he just hoped they did not include Bull confronting a senior officer. He tensed, ready to stop his friend from any rash action. To his immense relief Bull didn't make a move for the tent opening but instead took a deep breath and lay back down on the cot seemingly satisfied with the plan. Hands behind his head he spoke to the roof of the tent in a deathly, determined voice.

"Good, that fucker needs to die."

CHAPTER FOUR

Bull's wife was buried in a local cemetery. There was no way to get her back to England. It was a small, simple ceremony, made all the more painful with the knowledge that her final resting place would mean Bull would most likely never be able to visit her grave once the fighting was over in the area.

The army did move on eventually and life with it. For Jack and Bull the remaining sixteen months of the war all merged together into one long, miserable mess. They fought battles with the enemy while also fighting cold and hunger. Bull disappeared into himself. It was understandable. The loss of Mary had taken a heavy toll on him. Jack himself would never be the same. The one thing that kept Jack and Bull going was their mission to find retribution for Mary. They were constantly asking other soldiers from different regiments if they had seen or heard anything. The story always came back the same – dead bodies and vague information. They never gave up but kept pressing, and eventually, little by little, the bits and pieces started to form a disturbing picture of unrestrained senseless killing.

By the time the war finished, Jack and Bull had a good idea of who they were after. Every time attacks had taken place, there was a Bulgarian regiment close by. It was the only constant that had any meaning. The other thing Jack had untangled was the reason nobody had reported seeing the killer. In the end, lots of people had seen him, including Jack and Bull. They just hadn't realised it at the time. The man Jack and Bull had seen leaning over the soldier on the battlefield when they'd responded to the terrible scream came to his mind again and again. The killer, Jack deduced, had to be a medical orderly. It was the only identity that fit. An orderly who collected the wounded from the battlefield was the one person you wouldn't look twice at, even if he were covered in blood.

They were closing in on which unit the man was from when the war came to an end, making them most likely the only soldiers to have mixed feelings about the army being withdrawn. The war ended too soon for their quest to find the killer, but they were grateful to leave the slaughter of the battlefields behind them. With the army moving out, Bull and Jack parted ways. Bull had heard his father was ill and so was anxious to return home as quickly as possible. He remained with the unit, travelling by ship to England and then by train to his parents' cottage back in Lancashire.

Once back, he went to see Mary's family to give them the sad news in person. It was a visit made more difficult by the fact that they had been against her following him from the start.

Jack had decided to stay in Europe. He couldn't go back to civilian life until he had cleared his head of the endless days of battle. Besides, he didn't have anything to go back to. His mother had died several years earlier, and he had never really got on with his father. The closest thing he'd had to a family had been the time in camp with Bull and Mary. He decided to stay in the area to see if he could track down her killer and finally get some justice. Even though Bull had seemed ready to let go of his vengeance when the war ended Jack knew the man would never have peace while his wife's killer was still walking the earth. To this end, he meandered around Eastern Europe, earning his way by defending livestock and villagers from the increased wolf population. Every time he heard of a wolf attack on a human, he would go to the village where it had been reported, always wondering if he would find the aftermath of a real wolf attack or the grisly work of the man who had become his personal nemesis.

He had taken Corporal Black's advice – found an Enfield rifled musket and gotten the barrel shortened by a blacksmith. The blacksmith had also willingly sold him an eight-inch bowie knife, which Jack now wore on his belt. He'd held onto his sabre, but it was more for sentimental value, as he found he didn't have much call for it after the war. It was just too cumbersome to wear and use. The Enfield proved to be very accurate, furnishing a decent living for him as he made his way across southern Europe collecting the bounty on rogue wolves that were killing livestock.

He was following one such lead on a hot dusty summer's day three years on when he came across an isolated farm about twenty miles outside the town of Buzau in Romania. It was in a desolate farming community, with many small farms and very little money. These people scratched out an existence to keep themselves alive, with nothing much left to sell at the local market. This farm consisted of three buildings – the farmhouse, with a red tile roof, whitewashed walls, and chimneystack with smoke lazily rising; a small outbuilding to the side; and a larger barn in need of some repair across the yard. There was also a skinny horse with its head held low tied to a rail near a drinking trough beside the barn. Its skin was covered in sores and stretched over ribs and jutting hip bones. The animal was in such a sorry state Jack wondered how it was still standing. It reminded him of the condition of some of the mounts from the war after the hard winters.

Hopeful of watering Skeiron and also getting some food himself, he approached the farm. Nothing looked out of the ordinary as he entered the yard, and he made his way towards the barn. Closer inspection of the horse revealed it to be healthy enough, just starving. Reassured, he let Skeiron drink from the trough as he surveyed the area with a soldier's eye. *Once you've had people trying to kill you, you never look at anything the same again*, he thought to himself. Satisfied that there were no high vantage points from which he could be attacked and all the doors and windows were closed, he allowed himself to relax a little. He splashed some water on his face and dried it on his sleeve. Dipping his bandana into the trough, he rung out the excess water, and tied it back round his neck. It was cooling against the fierce summer heat. He then tied Skeiron's rein to a hitching post out of sight of the road, in the shade of the barn. He wasn't taking any chances on her being easily spotted by a passer-by. Satisfied she was as safe as possible, he made his way across the yard to the little farmhouse. It looked quite well cared for, with a dry-stone wall around the front garden that had been planted up in neat rows of vegetables. They had just been watered, and the smell of damp earth was a welcome change to the dusty road. He opened the small picket gate and smiled to himself. Well oiled. Somebody had made an effort.

Just then, a sharp scream pierced the air. Without stopping to think, he burst through the front door and was confronted by a woman lying motionless on the floor, covered in blood, with another woman, holding a watering can, standing over her. The woman with the watering can turned, and he saw she looked ready to scream again. Jack stayed where he was and started to slowly raise his arms, palms out, to show the woman he meant no harm. That was when the heavy piece of wood connected with the back of his head, and the world went black.

When Jack came round, he was lying on the stone floor of the farmhouse in a small pool of his own blood. Trying to get up, he stumbled against the wall. His fingers felt the back of his head, and he winced. There was a large gash on his scalp. As he was removing his hand, he heard a moaning noise coming from across the room. His vision started to clear, the girl who he had seen earlier covered in blood was still lying motionless on the floor. Jack studied her for a moment. He could now see she was dead from having her throat torn out. The similarity to Mary's death made his skin crawl. The same woman who had been standing over her was now sitting beside the still body, holding her knees to her chest and rocking backwards and forwards, her hands clenched. She seemed not to notice Jack, too caught up in her own misery.

"Are you hurt?" he managed to ask. The woman continued to rock back and forth, not responding. Jack asked again, this time in Romanian and the woman looked up at him. Tears filled her eyes

"No, not hurt," she replied in broken English. "My sister!" she wailed, breaking down again.

"Who attacked me?" the question came out in a half groan as he steadied himself on his feet.

"Bad man. He did this … My sister!" She pointed to the woman on the floor.

Knowing there was nothing that could be done for the dead woman, he asked, "Any idea where he went?"

"To north," was her only reply.

Jack gritted his teeth against the pain and strode towards the door. Over his shoulder, he called, "I'll come back."

Once outside, he broke into a run across the yard towards Skeiron, but a wave of dizziness hit him and made him stagger. The wound to his head and loss of blood must have been worse than he thought. Slowing down, Jack leaned against the wall of the barn. As he tried to get his bearings, he noticed that Skeiron's rein had been untied and was hanging loose. If the situation hadn't been so grim, Jack would have smiled to himself. When he had trained Skeiron for riding, he had also trained her to not be ridden by anyone else. They could get into the saddle or even try to lead her, but she wouldn't move. Being without a horse during the war or even now could mean the difference between life and death. The man who had struck him over the head must have tried to steal his horse instead of the poor animal he was riding but then given up when she wouldn't move.

Being careful of his wound, he mounted Skeiron, and they set off in pursuit. Jack wasn't sure how long he'd been knocked unconscious for, but it probably hadn't been too long. The blood was still flowing from the wound on the back of his head. If he had been unconscious for any length of time, it would have started to congeal. This also meant he probably had no business being on his horse in the state he was in, but he'd never let that stop him before and even the hounds of hell couldn't stop him now.

Pushing Skeiron on, he went north and up the ridge at the back of the big barn. He wanted to get to some high ground. As he crested the rise, he slowed the pace to better scan the area. Once at the top, he could see for quite some distance. The terrain was undulating, but the mostly bare hills and valleys weren't steep. With few trees to obscure his view, his position afforded him a good field of vision. He saw no signs of his quarry, and thinking his target might have doubled back, he started to change his direction. At that very moment, a movement caught his eye, and he looked to see a lone horseman ride out of a small copse 800 yards away.

His adrenaline kicked in. Years of hunting could soon be at an end. He could finally get Mary some justice. Jack put Skeiron into a full gallop. The sure-footed horse ate up the distance between the two riders, but Jack could feel himself losing consciousness again. The edges of his vision were going black, so he eased up the pace a little, in the hopes of keeping his focus. It helped, but he and Skeiron were no longer gaining ground. In a desperate attempt to slow the man down, Jack called out. His plan worked. The other rider turned around, and what Jack saw made his stomach churn. From this distance, he could see that the man was quite small, but the thing that Jack couldn't take his eyes off of was the blood. It covered the front of his clothes and most of his face – so much so that it gave the gruesome impression he was wearing a red mask.

Jack felt himself involuntarily recoil, his triumph of discovery quickly replaced with horror. Nothing on the battlefield had prepared him for the sick twistedness of the sight. Between the neck wound on the girl in the farmhouse and the gruesome sight before him, Jack now had no doubt he'd found Mary's killer, but there was no time to relish having finally tracked down his quarry. By slowing the man down, Jack had gained the distance he needed. Shaking off the horror, he reined in his horse to dismount.

Thinking Jack was giving up, his nemesis slowed his horse with a smug grin. In one fluid motion, Jack dismounted and started to lower onto his knee and pull the Enfield off his back. When the other man saw what Jack was doing, the smile fell from his face, but he still hesitated. When he had first called out the man was just over 300 yards away. As Jack reined in his horse and dismounted, his target had kept riding and was now approaching 400 yards.

Obviously, the man thought himself safe at this distance, as he didn't make a move to try to gallop away. Jack readied himself just as another wave of dizziness hit. With his peripheral vision going black, he tried to regulate his breathing to stave off the impending unconsciousness as he aimed the rifle. He fired and felt some satisfaction, for the last thing he saw before he passed out was the man being thrown from his horse.

Some time later, Jack gradually came to with the pressure of Skeiron nuzzling at his cheek. His eyes focused on clear blue sky. An unknown bird flew overhead. He became aware of the ticking of a beetle somewhere in the grass around him. Slowly sitting up, he then steadied himself against Skeiron to get back to his feet and stood there for a few seconds, regaining his balance. When he gingerly touched the back of his head, he found the blood on the wound had finally congealed. Taking his canteen off his saddle, he took a few sips. It seemed to help, so he took a few more and then emptied the contents over his head in an attempt to cool off and revive himself more.

Feeling more alert, he surveyed his surroundings. Nothing was moving. Reloading his gun, Jack climbed up on Skeiron, and they headed to where he had shot the man. He found the spot easily enough. From the signs, he could see where the man had fallen and also the blood that had been spilled on the earth. What Jack couldn't see was a body but judging from the amount of blood on the ground, the man had taken a solid shot. Jack looked around some more and could see where he had got back on his horse and ridden off. Following the hoof marks, he kept scanning the horizon for any signs of him, but about thirty minutes later the dizziness started to creep in again. Realising that night was falling and not wanting to ride into an ambush in his disoriented state or leave the poor woman to deal with her deceased sister alone, Jack set off back to the farm.

This time when he returned, he put Skeiron in the barn after letting her drink from the trough. Feeling she was still a bit hot from the ride, he quickly brushed most of the sweat off her coat with some twisted straw to keep her from cooling down too quickly and stiffening up. The last thing they needed was for her to be injured as well. Satisfied she was taken care of, he walked over to the farmhouse and tentatively pushed open the door. The body was still on the floor but had now been covered by a sheet. The sister was nowhere to be seen. Jack went over to the body, pulled back the sheet and examined her neck.

"She's not the first you know."

Jack almost jumped out of his skin. The girl had been in the kitchen, and he hadn't heard her approach.

"The first what?" Jack replied in native Romanian to her local dialect.

"The first murder like this. It happened many years ago. A woman was attacked in her home, raped, and her throat bitten. Then there were a few more before it stopped and we started to forget. Now it's started again."

"This isn't the first victim I've seen either," said Jack. "I fought with the British in the war. We had many soldiers with the same wound.

My best friend's wife was also killed by him. I think he's Bulgarian and was serving in the army as a medical orderly. I've been trying to find him for the past three years."

"Did you kill him?" she asked. "I heard a shot."

"I'm not sure," said Jack, regretfully. "I did hit him, but then I passed out. When I came to, there was a mark where he'd fallen and blood, but he must have managed to get back on his horse and ride off. I tracked him for a few miles but then felt like I might pass out again so I returned here."

"Let me look at your wound," said the girl.

Jack was too tired to argue so sat in a chair and let her tend to him.

"It will need a few stitches. I can do it if you want. The nearest doctor is a day's ride."

"Yes, please," said Jack. "That would be most helpful."

Jack stayed at the farm for the next few days, resting up. He wanted to go after the murderer but was sure his head wound would benefit from not being jostled around on a horse and hoped he might hear word that his shot had killed, or at least injured the evil little man. He also felt an obligation to this poor girl who'd lost her sister. While there, he helped the woman dig a grave. They buried her sister in a family plot next to the farm, bringing back for Jack the painful memories of Mary's burial. He wondered how Bull was faring in England. Communication between them had been sparse in the last few years. He thought of writing his friend a letter to say that he'd finally tracked down the killer. He wrote a note and had it in his breast pocket when he took the farm girl into the local village so she could report what had happened. But in the end, that was as far as it got. He rode by the post office without stopping. The murderer could still be free, and the news of the encounter would only bring up painful memories for Bull.

The girl wanted to stay and run the farm, so Jack did what he could to be sure she had what she needed before setting off to once again hunt his quarry.

When a year passed with no more wolf attacks of the animal or human kind, Jack deduced that his bullet must have done enough damage to eventually kill the man. The wolf population also seemed to be more under control. With nothing left for him to pursue on the continent, Jack decided to head back to England. Not wanting to see his father and explain where he'd been, he decided to make his way to Lancashire to find Bull. Before they'd parted Bull had given him an address where he could be contacted. With a new purpose in his life, Jack set off for England.

CHAPTER FIVE

Late August 1860
London, England

Jack couldn't wait to get off the ship. He hated ships. He loathed everything about them – the way they moved, the way they smelled, and especially the way they creaked. He wasn't a good swimmer, and the thought of the boat possibly sinking filled him with dread. *There would have to be a very compelling reason for him to ever set foot on another ship*, he mused to himself. Standing at the railing, he kept a tight grip on the weathered wood as he surveyed the coastline. They had entered the Thames estuary some time ago, and the channel was now getting narrower as they approached London.

Sadly, the city wasn't a very welcoming sight from the water. Hulking warehouses lined the docks, looking dismal – their faded, crumbling brickwork a contrast to the wealth of fine goods that passed through them on a daily basis. Behind them, row upon row of terraced brick houses crowded their way up narrow streets, each one billowing out black palls of coal smoke. The place would reek of sulphur, he thought. It already tainted the breeze that filled the ship's sails. Jack took some comfort from the thought that, even as foul as it was, it could have been much worse. Two years previous, in 1858, the government had issued new rules regarding the disposal of sewage. Until then, everybody had just dumped it in the Thames. By the summer of 1858, the place had been awash with such a huge amount of human waste that it had become known as "the great stink," the smell so bad even parliament had to be closed. Well, now it smelt of sulphur. Maybe it always had, but previously the smell of shit had overpowered it. Whichever was the case, he wanted off the ship and out of London as fast as he could manage.

The boat moored next to some old rotting pilings, and passengers started to disembark. Jack made his way below decks and into the cargo area. Passing several large crates marked Bordeaux Vintners, he smiled to himself. Not many people knew what the word *vintners* meant, clearly not the crew. If they did, he imagined the contents would have mysteriously disappeared long before they were ever unloaded. Sailors seemed to be a thirsty lot. Continuing on, he came to a large wooden door. Removing the bolt holding it closed, he eased it open. Once his eyes adjusted to the gloom, he could make out Skeiron. She nickered a greeting.

"Okay, girl, let's get you and me get off this death trap and onto solid ground," he said as he fumbled around in the dark for her bridle and saddle. No lamps were allowed in the livestock area because of the high risk of bedding straw catching fire. Such a fire could have devastating consequences on a wooden ship.

Once he had her tacked up, Jack led her out of the stabling area to a ramp that led up and over the side of the ship. The sure-footed Skeiron negotiated its slippery well-worn surface alongside Jack down onto the wooden jetty to the harbour side. Finally on solid ground, he mounted up and they headed north. He could sense Skeiron wanted to gallop but held her in check until they were out of the bustling harbour area.

"Easy, girl," he said giving her neck a pat. "I know. I want to get out of here too."

Trotting along, Jack couldn't believe the state of the British Empire's capital city.

"What a shithole!" he muttered to himself. There was filth and squalor everywhere. It was the middle of the day, but the coal smog hung so heavy it seemed as if the sun was setting and nightfall was close. As soon as the crowds thinned he pushed Skeiron into a lazy gallop. The sooner they were out of this cesspool the better!

After what seemed an eternity, they reached the outskirts of London. Trees and open fields started to replace the houses and factories. The sun was also making a brave effort to shine through the cloud cover. Jack felt good. Back out in the countryside the fresh breezes blew in his face as Skeiron's long stride easily ate up the miles beneath them. He felt alive again.

He entered a wooded area, brought Skeiron back to a steady trot, and breathed in. Finally, the air felt clean. Too many years of death and destruction had tainted his sense of smell. He hadn't been sure he would ever smell this again. He brought his horse to a halt. Looking around, he had to smile. The woods were the one place he truly felt at home. He was roused from his thoughts by movement to his left. A man had appeared from behind a tree.

"'Scuse me, sir," said the scruffy dirty man. "Can you spare some food?"

Jack had spent too many years fighting for his life to allow himself to be totally distracted by the man. Glancing over his right shoulder, he saw two more similarly dressed men approaching from behind. *Welcome home*, he thought wryly. These men were about to try to rob him. He dug his heels into Skeiron's side, and they sprang forward. The lone man was taken completely by surprise as Skeiron's right shoulder crashed into him, sending him sprawling to the ground. Jack pulled her round in a tight circle and charged straight for the other two men. With shock on their faces, they both turned and ran. Jack kept after the one on the left, and as he drew level, he pulled his foot out of his stirrup and kicked the man in the back. The would-be thief went down hard and didn't move. Swinging around once more Jack sought out his remaining quarry. The last man had changed direction and was running back down the track on which Jack had entered the wood. Spurring Skeiron on, man and horse chased down the terrified man. Once again, as they drew level, Jack gave a good kick to the man's back. This one wasn't as lucky as his companions had been. He stumbled once, caught his footing, and then ran headlong into a large tree. With a sickening thud, the man bounced off the tree and fell to the ground, unmoving. Sitting there, Jack surveyed the scene with a sense of satisfaction. He had defeated yet another enemy and hopefully made the area safer for other travellers.

Swinging Skeiron back in the direction they were going, Jack continued on towards Lancashire.

He travelled at a steady pace over the next few weeks, while being careful not to over tax Skieron. They camped out under the stars and occasionally asked a farmer to use his barn. The money he had earned from the wolf bounties was keeping him and Skeiron fed, but life on the road was still hard. The good news was they had almost arrived at their destination – that was presuming Bull was still there, of course. It had been over four years since the two men had parted company. Jack was a little apprehensive as to how he would find Bull but also excited about seeing his friend. The last time he had seen him, he was still mourning the loss of Mary and heading home to look after an ailing father.

Once he'd reached Lancashire, he stopped in a small market town called Garstang to ask for final directions. He was told the village he was looking for, Calder Vale, was about six miles away into the hills. He set off on the final leg of his journey with renewed vigour. Approximately six miles later, he reached the top of a hill overlooking a valley. Stopping to give Skeiron a rest, he surveyed the terrain. Beyond the valley, it was quite bleak – tufted sparse grass enclosed by drystone dykes receded into heather moor as far as he could see. Below him, a single cart track led down the side of the hill into woods surrounding the village. He could see rooftops and smoke from some of the chimneys lazily rising into the blue cloudless sky. The clatter of machinery in the distance echoed off the hills. It would appear he had arrived.

Making his way down, he followed the steep track until he eventually came upon a uniform row of terraced sandstone houses. He looked for anybody he could ask as to the whereabouts of his friend. However, upon finding not a soul around, he concluded most everyone must be at work. Not wanting to cause any problems, he decided to find somewhere to wait until the millworkers finished and hopefully spot Bull. He continued on and turned right onto a bridge. The huge brick mill loomed up on his right and another row of sandstone houses was backed against the far side of the small valley. Next to the mill and in front of him now was a church. It occurred to him that the vicar would surely know the inhabitants of this small village. With this in mind, he tied Skeiron to the rail out front, climbed the steps and pushed on one of the large double doors. It swung open smoothly and Jack went inside, his booted feet ringing loudly with each step on the rough flagstone floor. It was nice and cool in the building after the summer heat. He sat in one of the pews and took out a handkerchief to wipe the dust of the road from his face. Looking down at his dusty boots and clothes, he realised he must look quite a sight but figured they'd have to do as there wasn't much that could be helped there. He heard a noise behind him and glanced up to see the vicar approaching. He looked to be a man in his sixties, wearing a long black robe with a white collar.

"Can I help you, my son?" the vicar asked.

"I'm looking for a friend of mine."

"Well if he lives here, I'm sure I'll know him. Calder Vale is a small community."

"Bull …" Jack started to say. "I'm sorry. That was his nickname. Ian Mathews is his name."

The vicar smiled. He had a friendly face but looked like he had the weight of the world on his shoulders. "Ah yes," replied the vicar. "I know Mr Mathews, although not as well as I do the other parishioners. He's not very forthcoming when it comes to religion."

"Well, when you've been through what he has and seen what he's seen, you tend to think that God doesn't exist."

"God moves in mysterious ways."

"I'm sorry," said Jack. "If your God is so mighty and powerful, then why does he let such misery and suffering happen?" The vicar opened his mouth, but before he could answer, Jack held up his hand. "I'm not interested. I don't want to hear what you have to say. It's just words. You can't prove any of it. It's all myth and superstition. What I've seen in my life is real. I mean no disrespect. You have your beliefs, and I have mine. Can we leave it at that?"

The vicar looked like he wanted to press the point but saw the look in Jack's eyes. It was a look of dissociation. It appeared as if Jack was looking not at the vicar but a thousand yards past him. He gave up the argument. *Shame*, he thought. *These are the men who could probably most use God's solace.* But out loud he said only, "Your friend is working in the mill and won't be finished till six this evening. You're welcome to rest here for as long as you want."

"Thanks. I appreciate the invitation, but I think I'll take a look round and then come back tonight." Jack left the church.

Back in the sunlight, he mused on what to do. He walked over to where Skeiron was tied up, checked her over and made sure all his gear was still secured. Although it didn't look like much, it held everything he needed – his bedroll with his sabre stashed inside; the Enfield rifle he'd used to hunt wolves; one waxed cotton bag with ammo, and another with food. A small tin box encased in leather held his medical supplies. He also had a water canteen.

About to swing up into the saddle, he glanced over the top of Skeiron at the mill. Three men were standing on a loading dock looking in his direction. One, dressed in a suit, looked like he was in charge and was animatedly giving the other two instructions. The two men broke away from the third and jumped off the loading dock, heading in Jack's direction. They wore wool jackets and pants and heavy leather boots. He also noticed they had small wooden clubs hanging from their belts. Taking in the scene, he recognised it immediately. The muscle was being sent to check out the stranger. Not alarmed by this but on alert, patiently he waited for their approach.

"What's your business here?" the first and bigger one demanded gruffly.

"Good afternoon to you too," replied Jack.

The man was slightly taken aback at the casual flippant response. "You think you're a funny man, do you? I asked you what you're doing here."

"Minding my own business, and I suggest you do the same."

The two men, probably not hired for their brains, didn't know quite how to react to Jack's brush-off. Usually their bully tactics worked, and their victim answered and complied with their wishes. They looked back at the third man, who was still standing on the loading dock, for direction. He pushed out his hand impatiently, indicating they should carry on.

The bigger one of the two took another step forward while releasing the wooden club from his belt. "You're going to tell me one way or another what you're doing here," he said menacingly.

Jack had now taken several steps away from Skeiron. He didn't want any stray blows to hit her. "Are you sure you want to do this?" asked Jack of the man who was still approaching.

"I'm through talking nice to you. There's two of us, and you're going to answer my question." He smugly raised his club above his head. As he did, Jack stepped towards him, not away, as the bully expected him to do. With his arm raised in the air he had left his ribcage fully exposed. Jack threw a sharp punch to this exposed area. The welcome sound of a grunt and a slight snapping sound greeted his ears. The man's arm came down to protect his side from more damage, a pained expression on his face. The second man now entered the fray. Seeing his partner disabled so easily, he approached with more caution.

"We don't have to do this," said Jack. "You could just walk away."

This seemed to only enrage the man, whose response was to swing his club wildly at Jack's head. Jack rolled back out of the way and then punched the man in the side of the head as the momentum of the swing unbalanced him. Both men were now bruised and a little wary of Jack, but there was no way they could back down with their boss watching. Separating, they came at him from both sides. After a swift assessment, Jack decided to take out the smaller man first. He was more mobile than his bigger partner, and Jack didn't want to get caught out. The bigger man, he suspected, now had a broken rib. *Learning to fight on the battlefield is completely different from a civilian fist fight*, he reflected, and he'd learned that when your life was at stake a quick unexpected attack was usually the most effective way to gain the upper hand. With this in mind, he leapt forward and punched the smaller man in the jaw. While the man was still stunned, he followed it up with a kick with the flat of his boot at the man's knee. The knee gave way and he collapsed to the ground, howling in pain. Jack now turned his attention to the other man, who was looking more uncertain by the second. Jack grinned at the man. It had the desired effect. In a complete rage the man charged. Jack sidestepped this basic manoeuvre and punched the bully in the ribs in the exact same spot as last time and felt the man's ribs crunch under his fist. The man, now doubled up in pain, was labouring for breath.

"You come at me again," Jack said in a quiet menacing voice, "and I'll punch your ribs right into your lungs, and you'll die."

The man swayed for a second and then sank to his knees in defeat.

With the momentum now in his favour, Jack decided to push his advantage. He despised bullies and, even more, the cowards who hid behind them. Jogging over to the loading dock, he leapt up onto the platform. The man in the suit seemed frozen to the spot. Getting a better look at him Jack could see he couldn't be the owner. His clothes were ill fitting, showing signs of wear. He obviously had some authority but was not in charge. Offering his hand to the man to alleviate his fears and put him off guard, Jack continued to approach. The man, seeing this as a sign of weakness, seemed to grow in stature and confidence. The man held out his hand also, now with a slight sneer on his face. As Jack took hold of the man's hand he pulled him in and headbutted the bridge of his nose. Not used to physical violence, the man immediately crumpled to the ground, his nose spewing blood over his face and white shirt. Keeping hold of his hand, Jack yanked the man back to his feet. With tears and blood streaming down his face, the man glared balefully at Jack.

"Next time you want to ask a man a question, do it yourself. Don't send your gorillas. It's less painful."

With that, Jack jumped off the loading dock, strode over to where Skeiron was quietly waiting, and swung up onto her back. Riding out of the village, they passed the rest of the afternoon alone up on the moor. It was liberating to be in a wide, open place with fresh air. He let Skeiron nibble away at the sparse grass while he lay on his bedroll, both of them soaking up the sunshine. Enjoying the space, Jack began to realise it wasn't as empty as he'd first thought. There were also quite a few rabbits and hares. He decided these would be a welcome addition to Bull's larder. Using his rifle, he bagged four of the animals and slung them on his horse.

As the afternoon turned to evening, he made his way back into the village but now decided not to go up to the front of the mill to meet Bull as he'd originally planned. He didn't want to risk getting his friend mixed up in the trouble he'd been a part of earlier that afternoon. Watching the entrance to the mill from a distance, he saw Bull appear, easily recognisable by his large frame. He seemed to be walking with a woman.

Following their progress from his vantage point, he saw them both enter one of the sandstone houses that he had ridden past earlier when he had first arrived. Jack smiled to himself. It was good to see his old friend and also that he seemed to have left the past behind him and started a new life. He made his way to Bull's house, tied Skeiron to the rail at the end of the row of houses, and then knocked on the door and waited.

The door was opened by a pleasant-looking young woman. "Can I help you?" she enquired.

"Can I speak to Ian Mathews please?" asked Jack.

"One moment." She turned and re-entered the house.

Jack took a step to the side and leaned against the wall, so Bull wouldn't be able to see him in the doorway. The door creaked open, and the familiar form of Bull stepped out.

"What's for supper?" asked Jack.

Bull whirled round and came face-to-face with his old friend.

"Well I'll be damned!" said Bull.

Jack held out his hand. Bull ignored the hand and instead enveloped Jack in a big bear hug. When the life had almost been squeezed out of Jack, Bull released him.

"Bloody hell, it's good to see you!" said Bull.

"You too, Bull."

"What are you doing here? Sorry. Where's my manners? Come in, come in!"

Jack stepped inside with Bull. It was a simple place, sparsely furnished but spotlessly clean.

"Elly!" called Bull. "Come see who our visitor is."

Elly came from a side room.

"Elly, I have the pleasure to introduce Lieut … Jack Wolfe, my good friend and former commanding officer. Jack this is my wife, Elly."

They both exchanged pleasantries.

"I've heard a lot about you from Ian," said Elly.

"It's all lies," said Jack good-naturedly.

Elly laughed. "I'll leave you two to get caught up. I have laundry to bring in."

"Please, sit down," said Bull as Elly left out of the same side door she had come in.

They both sat beside the fire.

"What brings you here?"

"Well, after the war I stayed in Europe for a while longer, just didn't feel I was ready to come back. I earned money by shooting rogue wolves that were troubling farmers and villages. I then slowly made my way back when I felt the time was right. I always kept your address, so when I came back, you were my first port of call."

"You haven't been home?" enquired Bull.

"No, it just doesn't hold anything special for me. The only people I considered family were you and Mary."

At the mention of his murdered wife Bull looked sad. "Hardest decision I ever made to let that go and come back here. Did you ever get any closer to finding the bastard who killed her?"

"As you know, we were getting it narrowed down pretty close just as the war ended. When everybody was sent back to their countries or disbanded, I lost the trail for a while. Luckily, hunting wolves, I kept coming across victims that could have been his work. I followed every lead. One day, I was entering a farm where an attack had just happened. He knocked me out while making his escape. When I came to, I followed his horse tracks. I was pretty dizzy, but I wasn't going to let the bastard get away. I got close enough to shoot at him. I hit him pretty good but then blacked out. When I came to, he was gone. I stayed around the area but never heard of any more attacks. I don't know if he's dead or not, but I certainly hit him. Sorry, I can't give you better news Bull."

They sat in silence for some time, each lost in his own thoughts.

Elly came back into the room carrying a basket full of the clean laundry.

"Will you be staying for supper, Mr Wolfe?"

"Please, call me Jack."

"Yes, he will," said Bull shaking off the memories. "And if he doesn't have lodgings, he will be staying the night too."

"That would be most appreciated," said Jack. "I can contribute to your food. While I was on my way here, I shot some rabbits and hares this afternoon. The game is outside on my horse. I'll go get it." Jack stood to go and get the animals.

Elly nodded, "I'll gather some fresh herbs to make a stew." Smiling she continued upstairs. "I'll come with you Jack," said Bull. Stepping outside, the two men made their way to Jack's horse. As they walked past the other houses, Bull asked, "How long will you be staying?"

"I haven't decided. I'm not sure. It's so different now. Or maybe it's just me. I don't know where I fit in anymore. What I do know is that I need to find a way to earn some money."

"They're always looking for people to work in the mill. I'm an overseer there so would be able to get you a job," Bull offered.

Jack started to laugh. "Em, there may be a problem with working at the mill. I had a run-in with a few of the men down there this afternoon, and things got a bit messy."

"That was you?" asked Bull, grinning. "It was you who kicked their arses and broke the nose of one of the watchmen?"

"Guilty as charged," said Jack, holding up his hands to show his damaged knuckles.

"Well this could just be your lucky day. The owner found out what had happened and fired all three. He said he wouldn't tolerate that sort of behaviour. You could apply for the job."

"As a watchman?"

"No, as sort of a head watchman. We've been having problems with shipments getting hijacked and equipment smashed. The owner thinks it's a local rival mill owner but can't prove it. You did a great job investigating Mary's death. This would be easy in comparison."

"It's not a bad idea," said Jack.

"It's settled then. I'll get you an introduction in the morning."

"Thanks, Bull."

"You don't have to thank me. I think I probably owe you from now until doomsday for all you've done for me."

"I only brought you some rabbits and hares for supper," said Jack, laughing.

But both men knew what the other meant and so left it at that. They continued past the houses to where Skeiron was tied up.

"You've gotta be kidding me," Bull exclaimed. "You've still got her!"

Bull patted Skeiron on the neck, tracing the faint scar from the sabre wound at the Battle of Balaclava. She snorted in recognition. "This brings back some memories of us riding into battle."

"Sometimes it seems like yesterday and the next, a lifetime ago. She brought me back through situations no man should have gotten through. Do you have anywhere can I put her for the night?" asked Jack.

"There's a stable the mill uses for its draught horses. You can put her in there. I know the night stableman. He'll be fine with it."

Jack and Bull took Skeiron to the mill stables. As Bull had predicted, the man was happy to accommodate the extra horse, so Jack unsaddled her and gathered up his things to take to the house. They then both walked back to Bull's in anticipation of supper.

The supper conversation consisted of Jack and Bull catching up with what they had each been doing. Jack told of his exploits across Europe, while Bull's stories consisted of his family and working life in Calder Vale. It turned out that Bull's father had eventually made a full recovery. When Bull had first arrived home from the Crimea he had found his father still seriously ill but being nursed back to health by his wife and another lady from the village who knew how to use herbs to make remedies. The lady, a neighbour, had brought his father fresh remedies every few days. Her name was Elly. Bull had fallen head over heels in love with her. She had not only been instrumental in healing his father but had also helped Bull get over a broken heart. They had now been married for eight months.

After the supper pots had been cleared Bull informed Jack that, as the mill started at six, he would be heading off to bed. Jack thanked Elly for the delicious supper and thanked them both for letting him stay the night. After they had gone upstairs, Jack unrolled his bedroll in front of the dying fire, lay down, and was soon fast asleep.

The creaking of floorboards from above roused Jack in the early morning. He was clearing away his bedroll as Bull came down the stairs.

"Sleep well?" Bull asked.

"Like a log. First time I've slept in a house since I don't know when."

"Yeah, I usually sleep pretty well here too," said Bull. "Everybody works a twelve-hour day, so by the time night comes, you're about done in."

They grabbed some bread and an apple from the kitchen and headed out the door. Elly would follow later, but Bull wanted to show Jack around before they went to see the owner.

"What exactly do you do here?" asked Jack.

"I oversee all the workers to make sure they are doing their jobs and everything runs smoothly."

"Sounds like how it was in the 17th. You always could get the most out of the men."

"You'd be surprised at just how similar it is," said Bull. "These weaving looms are dangerous pieces of machinery. If not maintained properly and operated by competent people, they can kill. The mill just downstream loses at least one worker a month due to neglecting maintenance to save pennies. It's brutal how the owner there treats his workers."

They entered the large brick building. The mill was still in full operation even though a stream of workers was just coming off the night shift. The two twelve-hour shifts ensured continuous operation. Bull showed Jack around the many different parts of the mill, starting with the carding room. After that, they made their way through the spinning, winding, and weaving work areas, with only a quick foray into the weaving shed, as the clatter of the looms there was almost unbearable.

Once the tour was finished, Bull took Jack up to the owner's office.

He knocked on the door and waited. Someone shouted, "Come in," and they entered an outer office.

A light came from the rear office, so Bull and Jack kept walking until they stepped through the second doorway. It wasn't a big office. Books lined three of the walls, and the fourth had two windows. A man in a dark well-tailored suit sat behind a large wooden desk that was littered with more books and papers, his head bent over a ledger lit by a brass lamp.

"Mr Owens," started Bull, "sorry to bother you, but there's someone I'd like you to meet."

Owens looked up at Bull's words, his thick silvery grey hair lending him a distinguished air. Dark brown eyes met Jack's, assessing him.

"Mr Owens," Bull repeated respectfully, "I'd like you to meet Jack Wolfe."

Owens stood and extended his hand to Jack. They shook. Although several inches shorter than Jack and tending toward portly, he had a firm handshake. Jack was starting to like the man already.

Bull continued with his introductions. "Mr Owens, I know from what I heard yesterday that you fired your head watchman and his goons. I'm not sure if you're looking for a replacement, but if you are, may I recommend Jack?"

Owens didn't reply but just looked Jack up and down.

"Take a seat, gentlemen," he said, waving at the two green leather armchairs in front of his desk.

Once they were seated Owens addressed Jack directly. "What makes you think you'd be a good head watchman?"

"To be perfectly honest, sir, I'm not sure I would. It was Ian's idea. I was in the war in the Crimea and had to do some investigative work regarding problems we were having. Ian thinks I was rather good at it."

Owens showed no reaction and just sat there, his gaze still evaluating Jack. "What sort of investigating?"

"Well, there were some unexplained deaths. Everybody attributed them to animal attacks, but I turned up evidence to suggest it was actually a Bulgarian soldier."

Owens now seemed to be impressed as he considered Jack's words. He spoke, "As you may have already heard, some of our shipments have been getting stolen and our machinery damaged. You say you were a soldier. Do you think, if the need arises, you can protect my property?

"Yes," was Jack's quick one-word answer, followed by a wry smile.

"I like that, a man with confidence. However, just for arguments sake, can you justify that answer with any skills?" There was an amused look on Owens' face too.

"Well," said Jack, any humour now gone from his voice, "I can ride a horse better than most men. I'm a trained hunter and tracker and can kill a man at over 600 yards with my rifle." He let that last statement hang in the air for a moment before continuing, "If I may ask you a question, do you think your previous head watchman and his henchmen could protect your property?"

Owens sat there quietly thinking for a few minutes before answering. "I think my former head watchman, while not being able to fight himself, thought he could manage his help into accomplishing his and my goals. In truth, I was getting fed up with his ineptitude and was about to fire him. As for his two henchmen, as you called them, I had heard they were pretty handy with their fists and were quite intimidating." Owens paused. "I don't like fighting Mr Wolfe. I don't expect my employees to fight either unless it is absolutely necessary. I do, however, expect my property to be protected with whatever force is necessary. I paid them better wages than most for the job they were doing, and they still failed miserably. If I do employ you, I will pay you well. The average weaver gets forty-five pounds per year. As my head watchman, your wage would be considerably more than that."

Jack decided to let the talk of money end there. He didn't want to appear as if money was all he was after. "Then I should tell you, Mr Owens, that I have the same philosophy. I will avoid trouble where I can, but if forced to, I will defend myself – with lethal force if necessary.

If I do have to defend your property, I will do so as if it were my own property. In return, I expect you to defend me should the authorities become involved. From what I've heard, it sounds like your main protagonist is a rival mill owner. If I do protect the shipments and others get hurt, I don't want to be left to deal with the police without your support."

Owens looked Jack in the eyes. "I see honesty in you, which I like. You're not afraid to speak your mind either. I'll need to think it over but will have my decision made by lunchtime. How about you come back then?"

"Yes, sir," said Jack. "I'll do that. By the way, I'm not sure if it matters, but you should know, I was the one who fought with your watchmen yesterday."

"I know," was all Owens said, an enigmatic smile on his face, before returning his attention to the papers on his desk. Jack and Bull stood and left. They closed the door on the way out and made their way to the ground floor.

"Well, what do you think?" asked Bull.

"I like the guy," replied Jack. "I could see myself working for him. We'd have to discuss details, but all in all, he seems like a good guy. How do you think it went? Oh yeah, and how the hell did he know it was me who had slapped around his men?"

"In answer to your first question," said Bull, "I think it went well. He admires honesty. And you were painfully honest! And the second is that, although Mr Owens isn't a particularly religious man, the vicar usually comes 'round to the mill every other night, and they talk. This way, Mr Owens hears if any families are having problems and can try to help out. I'm guessing it was the vicar who told him of your exploits."

CHAPTER SIX

Jack and Bull left the mill.

"Well I guess I've got a few hours to kill before I come back to see Mr Owens at lunchtime," said Jack. "Where's the other mill located, the one where all the problems seem to be coming from?"

Bull started to shake his head. "You just can't stay out of trouble, can you?" he said with humour in his voice. "It's about two miles downstream. The owner is a guy called Charles Smythe. A miserable bad-tempered fat bully of a man with as bright a red face as you ever saw. You can't miss him. Struts around his mill like an emperor. He rules his employees the same way. Not afraid to dish out a beating." He paused and waited until Jack looked at him, expecting more information. Bull gave him a sarcastic grin. "If I haven't put you off, take the dirt road that runs past the stable where we left Skeiron last night. It will take you right there."

"Okay. Good. I'm just going to have a little look. Get the lay of the land. I promise I'll be good, Mom." Jack slapped Bull on the back and headed for the stable.

He found his horse happily munching hay, groomed, and in a clean stall. The stable boy must have taken care of her along with the mill's draft horses, he thought. He'd have to make it a point to look for him on his return and thank him.

"Sorry old girl, I'm going to have to interrupt your breakfast," he joked as he grabbed the saddle and bridle and brought them into the stall. Once Skeiron was tacked up they set off at a brisk trot down the dirt road outside the stable.

Jack felt good. He had a new challenge in his life again. He didn't have the job yet but had a feeling he soon would. He could investigate the hijackings and smashed equipment and also get to spend some time with his friend. The countryside around Calder Vale was pretty enough too, and unlike London, the air was clean. With renewed vigour, Jack urged Skeiron into a canter when the road came alongside the river.

The River Calder, wasn't what you would call a big river. It wasn't deep either. It was more like a large stream. However, the constant flow was still enough to fill up the mill ponds. When directed through the sluices to the water wheels, this steady supply of water powered the machinery in the mills. Most importantly, the high average rainfall in Lancashire meant the stream never ran dry. He was drawn from his thoughts when the dirt road narrowed to barely the width of a wagon as he entered into the tree-lined valley.

The farther he got the denser the understory became, filled in with rhododendron bushes on both sides of the track. The lack of openness gave him a slight feeling of wariness. The large overgrown bushes could easily hide any number of enemies. Fortunately, he encountered no trouble, and the first indication he had that he was approaching the other mill was the sharp clattering noise of its belt-driven machinery carried on the gentle breeze blowing up the valley. Jack slowed his approach. Up ahead, through the trees, he could now see the outline of the building. It was similar to the shape and size of the mill in Calder Vale but didn't look as well kept. The mill sign hung skewed from a rotted timber, and even from the distance, he could see the woodwork needed painting.

Breaking off from the track, he headed up to higher ground, found a suitable vantage point, and dismounted. He then tied Skeiron to a tree out of sight and walked a bit closer. Lying on his stomach, so his head just cleared the rise, he made himself as comfortable as possible and surveyed the area. From here, he could see the whole of the mill and some of its outbuildings, even the houses that the workers stayed in. Jack also noticed there were four horses tied to a rail in front of the mill. He smiled to himself. This could bode well for his investigation if they belonged to the men he was looking for. Happy he had a found a good concealed place from which to observe his potential adversaries, Jack settled himself in to watch.

He saw several workers moving from the mill to the outbuildings. They were clearly carrying items to and fro, but there was something about them that gave him concern. They all seemed to be wearing very old, worn out clothing and were walking like they were exhausted. As Jack was watching, four men exited the mill. Two of them walked up to the horses while the other two approached one of the workers carrying a small wooden barrel and stood in his path. As the dishevelled man approached them, he slowed and started to go around. Jack could see he kept his head down, obviously afraid. One of the men then pushed the unfortunate worker, causing him to drop the barrel. As he bent to retrieve it, the other man kicked him, and he fell to the ground, at which point both men stood over him and started shouting. Jack couldn't tell what they were shouting but he figured it wasn't anything good. After a few minutes, the man slowly got to his feet, picked up the barrel, and continued on his way. The two men continued to berate him until he entered the mill, and then they walked over to the horses and rejoined the others.

With his attention focused on the two who had attacked the worker, Jack hadn't paid much attention to the others. He now looked them over and quickly recognised them. It was the two watchmen he had fought the previous day. Jack grinned to himself. It looked like this would go some of the way toward explaining the recent misfortunes of Mr Owens's mill. It now appeared to have been an inside job. These two must be the culprits, informing Smythe when and where loads would be transported and smashing the equipment. The unfortunate thing was it also meant that, as soon as Jack showed his face at the rival mill, he would be recognised. He'd originally thought to infiltrate the mill as a prospective customer, but a second plan was now called for. Pleased with the results of his first foray, he dusted himself off, mounted up, and headed back for his lunchtime meeting with Mr Owens.

Back at the Calder Vale mill, Jack stabled Skeiron and headed inside. He knocked on the office door and was invited to enter by a female voice. Opening the door, Jack was greeted by an older lady. She wore a tweed jacket and long skirt with a mannish air, and her greying hair was tied up in a bun. Jack told her of his lunchtime appointment with Mr Owens. She asked him to sit down and then disappeared into the other office, returning a few minutes later to usher Jack in.

"Please sit down," Mr Owens said, waving to the chair across from his desk. Jack sat and waited as Owens continued, "I've been thinking over what we talked about this morning, and I'm sorry to say that I cannot offer you the job. Whoever I hire as head watchmen will need to be someone I personally known and trust implicitly." He leaned back in his chair watching Jack. He placed the pen he had been holding back on the desk with a shrug.

"Unfortunately, you are an unknown entity. I know Mr Mathews vouched for you, but I just don't know enough about you. If I get this wrong, it could ultimately cost me my business and the livelihood of all the people who work for me. It's just too big a risk."

"I appreciate your honesty," said Jack, hiding his disappointment. "It's something I value highly myself. As you may have already heard, I rode downstream to the other mill after we met this morning to have a look around. Even though I won't be working for you, I think you should know what I found. The two watchmen who I had the run in with yesterday, who you subsequently fired, appear to be working there.

In fact, they seemed to be very at home at the other mill." Jack stood and calmly held out his hand. "Thank you for your time."

Mr Owens didn't move to get up. Instead he leaned forward to place his hands on the desk and motioned for Jack to sit back down. "I'm sorry to say I've been a little devious."

Jack just raised an eyebrow.

"What I said about needing to trust you and if I got it wrong losing my business and my workers' livelihoods was true. I pretty much decided the moment you left this morning I would offer you the job. I like to think I'm a pretty good judge of character, and you seemed like an honourable man. The last test was to see was how you would react if I didn't give you the job. Needless to say, you passed with flying colours. The job is yours if you want it."

At these words Jack took his seat once again as Owens continued, "There would normally be a house that goes with this position, but your predecessor has unfortunately made something of a mess before he left. He managed to set two small fires and broke all the windows. I will get it repaired as soon as I can, which hopefully won't take too long. I'm sure you must be curious about money. I said yesterday that I would pay you well. I will be offering you a salary of 200 pounds per year. How does that sound?"

Jack almost fell off his seat. It was far more money than he had ever earned as a soldier, and now he would have a place to live. With as straight a face as he could manage, he accepted the amount, and he and Mr Owens shook on it.

Owens continued, "Now that we have that out of the way, how do you propose we deal with our problem?"

"We will have to proceed with caution. If I'm spotted near the other mill, they will be suspicious. Also, we should keep our plans to ourselves. These types of people are bullies. They could try to intimidate any of your workers into giving up information on what we are doing. If you're in agreement, only you, Bull, and I will be in on any plans."

"Bull?"

"Oh sorry. Ian Mathews. Bull's his nickname from when we served together"

"Why would you bring him in on it?"

"Well, I'll need an extra man to work with me and I've trusted him with my life many times and he's come through, so I know he wouldn't do anything against me. He's also got first-hand knowledge of the workers. He would be able to spot anything out of the ordinary and let us know. I'm hoping one of the workers does get approached. We can then feed them misinformation and lay a trap for the hijackers."

"It sounds like a good enough strategy. I'll see that Mr Mathews is given some free time to be able to assist you as necessary."

"Thank you," said Jack. "If there's nothing else, I'm going to inform Bull of what I found and then work out a more detailed plan."

With that, Jack left Mr Owens's office, nodding to the secretary on the way out, and set about finding Bull. After locating him, Jack explained that Mr Owens had indeed offered him the job. He also mentioned the short-term lack of accommodation. Bull insisted that Jack was to use his front room until the house was ready. Jack readily accepted the offer, and then, making sure they weren't overheard, he explained his initial plan for stopping the thefts. It was simple. For now, all he needed Bull to do was to watch the workers for suspicious or out of the ordinary behaviour and let him know if he saw anything.

Work at the mill continued without any incidents for the next few weeks. Bull looking out for anything unusual, and Jack planning for what would happen once they had a suspect. Jack rode the trail on which the wagons had been hijacked several times and located a few likely ambush points. He also identified places from where he could ambush the ambushers, a thought from which he derived much enjoyment. There was great satisfaction to be found in trying to outwit your opponent.

Three weeks into Bull's watch on the workers, he came to Jack with a suspect. It was one of the weavers who had been at the mill for just over a year. He'd been struggling to make ends meet to support his wife and five children. Now with another on the way, he was an easy target for bribery from the robbers. He had also been overheard asking when the next shipment of raw cotton was due to arrive at the mill. This was none of his business, which was why Bull's suspicions had been aroused. With this new information, Jack's plan was put into motion.

The following day, Bull let slip the information about the next shipment in front of the worker. After the shift at the mill was over, Jack kept an eye on the suspect. When he went off into the woods instead of going straight home, Jack followed, keeping his distance. The worker stopped at a big oak tree. Jack watched as the man picked up a rock and placed it in a hole at the base of the tree. The man then turned 'round and went back to his house. Jack left also, as there was nothing to be gained from staying. He would, however, be back the following night after the man's shift was over to see if he returned.

The next night, about an hour before the mill shift was over, Jack made his way into the woods and took up a position that gave him a good view of the oak tree. Settling into some cover, he waited. He didn't have long to wait as two men rode up the valley and waited by the tree. The millworker appeared shortly after. Jack was too far away to hear the conversation, but the millworker was obviously intimidated by the two thugs. They finished and as the millworker turned to leave, they kicked him in the back. He went sprawling to the ground.

"If you fuck us over, there's a lot more where that came from!" one of the thugs said in a loud menancing voice. "We know where you and your family live!"

With that they got onto their horses and set off back down the valley.

Jack waited until everybody was out of sight before heading back to the mill. He wanted to see if Mr Owens was still there so he could let him know what was happening. As he approached the mill, he could see a light in Mr Owens's office. Climbing the stairs, he walked up to the office door. He knocked once and continued into the office.

"Mr Owens," started Jack.

Owens looked up and waved a hand at the seat opposite.

Jack sat down. "I've just come from the woods. There I saw one of your weavers having a covert meeting with two other men who came from downstream. The meeting was very secretive. From what I've concluded, I now believe your rival has the information for the next shipment."

"How sure are you about this?" asked Owens.

"About as sure as I can be without giving the game away. One of your weavers was asking some strange questions about the next shipment. I asked Bull to let slip the next delivery information, seemingly by accident, in front of the suspect worker. Right after the weaver overheard this, he met with these men in the woods. I couldn't hear most of their conversation, but I did hear them threaten his family."

"And what do you propose we do with this information?"

"Am I right in saying that, when the other shipments were hijacked, the driver wasn't hurt?" Jack asked.

"That's correct," confirmed Owens.

"Then I say we prepare to receive the next load on schedule. The only difference is that we have something valuable put on the load that the other mill owner will want. I'm hoping that, when they get the load back to the mill, they will unload it and find the valuable item, and he will put the item in his office. If it's just the load of cotton, then they will put the cotton in the warehouse, and he could deny all knowledge and blame his workers. If the item's in his office, then we have him, and your troubles should be over."

"Hmm, it's an ingenious plan." Owens put his elbows on the desk and tapped his index finger's together and stared into the distance. "Charles Smythe outed for the scoundrel he is....." He looked back at

Jack and dropped his hands to the open ledger in front of him. "What sort of valuable item do you propose we put on the load?"

Jack thought for a moment. "Would I be right in assuming he has a safe?"

"Oh yes. Charles makes sure that nobody can steal from him."

"Good," replied Jack. "Then the item needs to be the right size to put in his safe. That way, he can't say he didn't know anything about it."

Owens looked worried. "I do know something that will have Charles foaming at the mouth. Can you promise me with absolute certainty that you will be able to get it back?" He leaned forward in his chair and raised an eyebrow in challenge.

Jack looked him in the eye and nodded, "I will ensure it comes back into your hands."

Owens relaxed, leaning back again and regarded Jack intently before he continued, "Yes, I believe you will," he paused, "Have you ever heard of Tyrian purple?"

"No," said Jack.

"It's also known as royal purple. It's a cloth dye, a very expensive cloth dye. It comes from sea molluscs, a lot of molluscs and a it takes long time to harvest them. In the past, it was only the royals who could afford such luxury. It predominantly still is although some wealthy landowners are using it now to show their status. A few years ago, I was commissioned to produce some purple cloth and had to purchase the dye. It nearly bankrupted me at the time, but the job paid handsomely and gave us access to a wealthier clientele. I would be willing to purchase a bit more if it means catching him in the act and putting a stop to my cotton shipments being stolen. If Charles could get his hands on some of the dye for free, there's no way he wouldn't put it in his safe."

"It sounds perfect," said Jack.

"All right, then. If you're sure we can retrieve it, I'll arrange for a small amount to be on the next load."

"Make certain," said Jack, "that whoever sends you the dye ensures it's identifiable as your property, and we shouldn't have any problems." He thought for a moment. "Do you want to know the details of my plan?"

"I know enough. I don't think I need to know more – not unless you need my help with anything?" replied Owens.

Jack shook his head, "Nothing more for now. The only time I will need you is when we call the police to open Smythe's safe. You should be there to identify the dye as yours so he can be arrested immediately. I'll let you know when that will be, but you might have to move very quickly once I give you the word. We wouldn't want to give him the chance to remove the evidence."

Owens nodded. "I can do that."

With nothing more to discuss, Jack left the office. He went to find Bull and told him about the meeting he had witnessed between the weaver and the thugs in the woods and his subsequent conversation with Mr Owens. Bull listened intently, occasionally interjecting with some ideas of his own. They agreed on a basic plan, in which they both would shadow the shipment from the supplier. Then, assuming the cargo was hijacked, they would follow it to make sure it arrived at the rival mill and stay to observe the area to get as much information as they could. Once they were sure the trap was well and truly set, Bull would ride to get Mr Owens, while Jack continued to watch the mill to make sure the cargo stayed on the premises.

With the shipment due the following night, Jack decided he would make camp in the wood near the other mill and study everything that happened there. He needed to establish which office was Smythe's and then watch his movements. As the two previous shipments had been hijacked at night, Jack saw no reason why this wouldn't be the case this time. He hoped the thieves would continue with this pattern, as it would afford him and Bull the best chance of shadowing the shipment without being seen.

Packing up his gear and some food that Elly had given him, Jack saddled Skeiron and rode out, taking a circuitous route to the other mill, just in case anybody was watching. He felt alive again. The game was on. The skills he'd learnt as a soldier and some of the hunting skills his father had taught him would all come into play. He made camp in the same spot from which he'd watched the mill before. Skeiron was tied to a tree a few yards away with a grain bag and water.

Jack opened his bedroll, laid it on the ground, and took up position to begin his observations. It was a slow and mostly boring job, but he knew he would need the additional information if he and Bull were to be successful. He could hear the clatter of the machines and also the occaisional raised voice berating someone. Every hour, two men would make a cursory walk around the outside of the mill and then disappear back inside. Jack deduced they were some sort of watchmen patrol.

At one point, another man was talking to them. From how Bull had described Smythe, Jack knew that this was his man. After a long afternoon of boredom and being bitten by midges, Jack watched the daylight start to fade and lights come on in the mill. The reflection of the window glass in broad daylight had prevented him from actually seeing inside the offices. Now with dusk falling he pulled back a bit from the rise to stay hidden and knelt while he extracted his pocket telescope, a pen and paper from his saddlebag. Lying back down, he used the telesope to survey each of the now brightly lit windows. On his fourth pass, he located the window he was looking for. It was a large window on the second floor, almost directly level from where Jack was lying. Smythe was sitting behind a sumptious desk more suited to a bank. Behind the desk he could see a wall safe. This was where Mr Owens would take the police and confront Smythe. Jack felt another part of his plan beginning to form. With careful attention to detail, he sketched the layout of the office.

The rest of his evening was taken up monitoring the mill's activity.

At 6.00 p.m. the shift changed, with people coming and going for about ten minutes. With lots of shouting, and some shoving, the new shift was herded into the mill. Things quietened down after that, except around 9.00 p.m., at which point the emperor, as Jack had now nicknamed him, left his office and headed off in a carriage. The watchmen patrols continued every hour but now with two different men whom Jack recognized as the ruffians who had formerly worked for Mr Owens. Jack guessed that, on the night of the hijack, all four watchmen would be at the mill, along with Smythe. This meant the odds were slightly against Jack and Bull, but the element of surprise would still be on their side. They would also have the police to do most of the work. Happy with his plan, Jack decided to get a few hours' sleep and then observe the mill again at the next shift change.

The early dawn light had just started to creep into the valley as Jack once again took up his vigil. He had managed about five hours' sleep. The clatter of the machines had kept him awake for a while, but then its steady rhythm had eventually lulled him to sleep. At 6.00 a.m. people were once again coming and going from the mill. It appeared the shift pattern was the same at both mills. He continued to watch until all was quiet again. At around 8.00 a.m. a carriage appeared and Smythe got out and strode into the mill. Satisfied that he had seen enough, Jack packed up his gear and rode Skeiron back up the valley. Putting her once again in the mill stable, he located Bull, and they both went to see Owens.

After knocking on his door, they entered, were invited to sit, and Jack began to lay out the rest of his plan. Bull and Owens, both already familiar with the first part, listened intently as Jack explained the additional steps he had worked out the day before while watching the rival mill. Jack told them how Bull and Mr Owens, along with the local constabulary, would enter the mill and go up to Smythe's office. There they would force him to open the safe and give up the dye. Mr Owens would then prove that it was his, and Smythe would be arrested.

"Will you not be coming into the mill with us?" asked Owens.

"I think I'll be of most use outside. I've found a vantage point on the knoll above the mill, where I can see what's going on in his office and what's happening in the mill yard." He looked at Bull. "I'll show you where I'll be watching from." Turning back to Owens, Jack continued, "The other reason I won't be inside is three-fold. First, the police know you, and Bull has worked for you for several years. A stranger in their midst might distract them, which could be bad. Second, the two watchmen I slapped around might cause more trouble if I'm there. But most importantly, if anything does go wrong, I'll be able to sneak into the mill, while all the attention's on you, and take them by surprise."

"That seems to make sense. Sounds like you've got all the angles covered," said Owens.

"How long will it take from Bull getting back here to you being able to arrive with the police?" asked Jack.

"I've been thinking about that," said Owens. "It would usually take about two hours, but I've been a bit sneaky. Knowing the load is due in tonight, I've invited the local chief of police for dinner. He will bring along at least two of his constables to drive his carriage. This means we can be there in about twenty minutes from when Ian lets me know."

With a smile on his face, Jack leaned back in his chair, "You would have made a fine commanding officer with those tactics."

"I like to think I'm capable of coming up with some good ideas from time to time." Owens smiled back.

"One more thing; do you trust your driver?"

Owens paused, "Yes, I think he is trustworthy, but I see where you're going with this. I could take steps to ensure his absolute loyaty." He rubbed the fingers and thumb of one hand together in a gesture for money.

"I think that would be smart. We don't want him injured so he should give up the wagon without being too obvious and prepare to walk back to Calder Vale. Jack paused, "I think that is everything."

Owens nodded, "I'm in complete agreement. I think this is going to work."

Jack stood up, "I'd like to take Bull out of the mill at about three this afternoon. We need to head down the trail to start following the load. Will that be okay?"

"Oh yes, absolutely fine."

"He will need to borrow one of your horses, too."

"Yes, of course, just see the stable boy and tell him I said to find an additional mount for you."

Jack and Bull left the office and headed outside the mill, where nobody could overhear them. They worked out a few small details and then arranged to meet at the stable at three. Jack went back to the house and spent some time there going over the plan in his head as he cleaned his rifle. He oiled the leather sheath to his bowie knife and checked the blade. Satisfied he was prepared, he strapped the knife to his belt, grabbed his rifle and went to the stable early. Once there, he spent time with Skeiron brushing her and checking over her legs and hooves until Bull arrived right on time and they saddled up the horses.

"Let's hope you bring this one back," Jack quipped, reminding Bull of his poor record of returning horses during the war.

"In my defence, there were people shooting at me." Bull grinned leading his horse as he followed Jack and Skeiron out into the stable yard where they mounted.

"Once more unto the breach," Jack said as they started down the road towards the supplier's warehouse. They rode in silence for most of the way, as they were riding hard. When they could hear the workings of the other mill they took side trails to give a wide berth to the wagon's route and to be sure they wouldn't be seen in front of the shipment and inadvertently alert the thieves. Intersecting the main track an hour before dark, they cautiously surveyed the area. They could see the recent deep wagon tracks in the soft earth. There was also fresh horse manure.

"Looks like we're not far behind," Jack observed. "Keep your eyes peeled. We don't want to run into the wagon or the hijackers."

Bull just nodded in silence.

On they rode, now closing the gap separating them. As they crested a rise, the light was starting to fade, but about a mile in the distance they could still clearly make out the tree-lined banks of the River Calder. Halfway between where they sat and the trees, the wagon could be seen still making its way up the valley.

"Looks like perfect timing," said Bull. "That wagon is going to reach the trees just as it's going dark."

"Yeah," Jack agreed with a wry smile. "The dopey bugger on the wagon couldn't have timed it any worse to get hijacked. He should have a sign saying, 'Please rob me.'"

They sat for a while, watching the wagon's slow progress and giving their mounts a rest after the hard riding of the past few hours. A few minutes after the wagon disappeared into the trees, they urged their horses into a brisk pace up the valley. Upon entering the treeline, they slowed once again to a walk and went on high alert. This was dangerous territory. They were certain there were armed men hiding along the trail waiting to ambush the shipment. If they got too close to the wagon, they risked becoming the target themselves. But lag too far behind, and they might miss the ambush and lose the shipment to the thieves.

After another hour of riding, they could see Smythe's mill through the trees. Jack guided his mount next to Bull's and leaned over so he could speak quietly.

"When I scouted the trail a few weeks ago, I thought there were three areas they might hijack the wagon. The first one is in a few hundred yards. However, if it were me, I'd pick the second one. It doesn't afford the best cover, but it's the easiest place to get the wagon turned around back towards Smythe's mill. I'd say we should arrive at that second area in about thirty minutes."

"When do you want to get off the trail?" asked Bull.

"We need to make sure the wagon's been taken before we do that. With it being so dark in here, we shouldn't have to go far off the trail to be hidden, so we can leave it to the last minute."

As they got closer, their adrenaline kicked in and sweat began to trickle down their backs from anticipation of the action. They stopped their mounts every few minutes to listen until they could hear shouting in the distance. As it was so dark Jack made a quick decision. Without the added bulk of his horse to hide he could get a lot closer. He dismounted and got Bull to ride the horses a short distance into the undergrowth.

Jack was still moving up the trail when he heard horses' hooves approaching. Ducking behind a tree, he watched as two riders appeared and then disappeared down the trail, closely followed by the hijacked wagon and then another rider leading a spare mount. The game was definitely on!

Jack recognised all four men as the watchmen for the other mill. After they had passed him by, he sprinted back to where Bull was hidden. Mounting their horses, they followed the stolen load. When it turned off towards Smythe's mill, Jack and Bull rode their horses up towards the vantage point that Jack had been using for his initial surveillance. Once they arrived, they dismounted and tied the horses to some trees. They then crept up to the rise and lay down on the hard ground in silence to wait for the wagon to appear. What seemed only moments later, it pulled into the yard and was swiftly escorted into the mill through a set of large wooden double doors. The minute the wagon was inside, the doors were quickly closed, effectively concealing the crime.

Watching from their vantage point, the time seemed to drag on as they waited.

"What is taking him so long?" Jack muttered.

Bull blew out a long breath, echoing his impatience, "They must be unloading the cotton. They'll need to get rid of the wagon."

Another twenty long minutes went by before the light came on in Smythe's office, and he appeared carrying a small wooden box. Jack picked up his telescope to get a better look. Charles Smythe was sat at his desk. In front of him was with the box they had planted in the shipment. He opened it and took something out. Jack couldn't see what it was, but by the animated way in which the man jumped up and practically danced about his office, he knew it was the expensive Tyrian dye. Little did Charles know, this was about to be his best and worst day all rolled into one.

Quickly replacing the dye, Smythe spun around and went over to the big safe. He reached next to the safe and took a lone book off a shelf; opening it, he withdrew a key.

"Sneaky bugger," Jack said under his breath. "Must be hollowed out."

"What's hollowed out?" Bull demanded. When Jack didn't reply, Bull nudged him in the ribs, "C'mon, man, what's going on?"

"Smythe is unlocking his safe. He's placed the box inside …" He paused. "Now he's locked it and replaced the key where he's hidden it in a hollowed-out book on the shelf next to it. He lowered the telescope and gave Bull a satisfied smile. Looks like he's taken the bait. That's your cue to ride for Mr Owens and the cavalry."

Bull wasted no time in mounting his horse. He trotted down the incline to the road before breaking into a fast gallop back to Mr Owens' house.

Jack kept watch from his vantage point. Just after Bull left the empty wagon pulled out with one driver and a saddled horse tied to the back; it looked like he was going to dump the wagon somewhere and ride back. Nothing much happened for the next thirty minutes. Nobody else left the mill, and Smythe stayed in his office. Eventually the lone rider appeard again and Jack wondered where he'd left the empty wagon and team. The man tied his horse out front and went into the loading area. Just when Jack was beginning to think something had gone wrong with Bull's ride back, a carriage came barrelling into the yard and pulled up to the front of the mill, along with a man on horseback. Jack instantly recognised Bull as the horseman. As the carriage came to a stop, Owens and three police officers got out. They all entered the mill by the loading dock.

A few minutes later, Jack saw them appear in Smythe's office. He could only imagine the conversation, but the mannerisms of the people in the office were plain to see and spoke volumes. Mr Owens was pointing at the other mill owner, no doubt accusing him of stealing his wagon. Smythe was sitting there with his arms wide apart, pleading his innocence. They seemed to be at a stalemate. Then Jack saw Owens point at the safe. He must have dropped the bombshell about the box of dye because Smythe stood up so quickly he knocked over his chair, clearly indignant at being accused of such a thing. It looked like his time was running out, thought Jack.

One of the policemen stepped forward and looked like he was trying to calm down the situation. Jack could see him pointing at Owens and the safe. Smythe turned around, pointed at the safe and shrugged his shoulders. Bull then stepped forward and took the book off the shelf and opened it. Smythe looked like he was going to explode. Holding out his hand, Bull gave him the key and stepped back. Smythe turned to the safe, inserted the key, and opened the door. But instead of turning back to the room with the box of dye, he had a pistol in each hand. One was pointed at Bull while the other was pointed squarely at Mr Owens. With one fluid motion, Jack laid down the telescope and picked up his rifle. With his experience in the war and hunting the wolves afterward, he was at one with his rifle and felt totally at ease. Settling the gun into his shoulder, he cocked the hammer and took aim. He regulated his breathing, and as he was exhaling for the third time, he squeezed the trigger. Picking up the telescope again, Jack could see a hole in the window and no sign of Smythe.

Without wasting any time, he reloaded the rifle and made his way down to the mill. If Smythe's henchmen hadn't been alerted by the arrival of the carriage, the boom of his gun would certainly have made them aware something wasn't right.

When Jack was halfway across the mill yard, one half of the double doors opened, and two men stepped out. Jack instantly recognised them as Smythe's men. Dropping to one knee, he took aim and shouted a warning for both men to surrender. When neither obeyed, Jack opened fire, killing one of them instantly. The other man then ran back inside, leaving the door partly open.

Jack reloaded again and cautiously approached the partly open doors. Every fibre of his being screamed danger. Trusting the warnings, he picked up the body of the dead man and carried it in front of him to the doors. As always, his instincts were right. The minute he stepped into the gap with the body in front of him, the darkness inside erupted into several spits of flame. Jack felt the impact from the bullets as they hit the dead man. Throwing the body to the side he fired at where the spits of flame had originated and was rewarded with a sharp cry of pain. Moving further into the darkness, he found cover behind some bales of cotton and stayed completely still, listening intently for any sound that might alert him as to where the remaining two men were hiding. Crouching in the dark, Jack realised that he could no longer hear the clatter of the looms. The brick walls and the heavy doors had deadened the sounds of the mill machinery.

"Hey, mister," a voice called out. "Don't shoot. I wanna surrender."

Jack knew these were not honourable men, so he was expecting a trap. He did, however, need to resolve this and if the man really was prepared to surrender then he should give him the chance.

"Step over to the door unarmed and lie on the floor," Jack ordered.

He heard the noise of a man walking to the door. A faint glow of moonlight was coming through the door, and he could just make out the shape of the man doing as he had instructed.

"Where's the other guard?" Jack asked.

"He took off when the shooting started. I'm the only one left."

Jack decided it was too dangerous to stay where he was, as he had now given away his position. Quietly, he made his way down the side of the warehouse loading area – not headed for the front and the surrendered guard but towards the back. He wanted to be sure he wasn't being set up. He soon found the rear wall and continued, moving across the back and then up the opposite side boxing round towards the entrance.

The entire time he was repositioning himself, he heard no other sound apart from the guard lying on the floor complaining about what was taking so long. Jack stopped, crouched down once again, and listened. He didn't move for a few minutes. He then heard a faint noise on the other side of the room at almost the exact spot where he had taken cover. Jack now had a decision to make. If the guard lying down had lied about the other guy taking off, it raised the question of what else had he lied about? Feeling around on the dirty wooden floor, he found a small stone. Tossing it across the room to the approximate location where he had previously been taking cover, he heard it clatter to the floor. The guard who had been creeping up on where Jack had previousely been fired his weapon at the noise. The flash of the powder igniting lit up the area and Jack saw the silhouette of the man. Jack fired at the spot and heard a grunt and a body hit the floor. With satisfaction, he now knew there was only one guard left – the one lying on the floor at the entrance.

Preparing to move to a new spot, Jack felt a searing pain across his chest. A split second later, he heard the loud roar of a gun being discharged and realized he'd been hit. The guard by the door had used Jack's own tactics against him and fired at the area of light that had been created when Jack had shot the other guard.

Fortunately, his aim wasn't as good as Jack's. Crumpling to the floor, Jack lay there for a moment to assess the damage. His left arm was useless, but judging from the pain, he also had several broken ribs. He surmised the bullet had passed through his upper left arm, probably breaking the bone on its way. It then must have glanced off his ribs and continued on in a slightly forward angle because he could tell it had entered his chest muscle high on the left side. Feeling around, he couldn't find the hardness of the bullet in his skin. That was good. It had most likely continued through, embedding itself in the crate behind him. The pain was excruciating. He was losing blood, but he knew he could still function on the adrenaline that was now starting to kick in.

However, knowing that would give him only a temporary reprieve from the pain before his body went into shock, he realised he would have to bring the fight to a fast conclusion if he wanted to survive. He managed to get to his feet, leaving his rifle where it had fallen. It would take him far too long to reload it one-handed, and he wasn't even sure he would be able to fire it now. Reaching across his belt, he withdrew his eight-inch Bowie knife. He knew the guard at the door had heard him fall. For what he planned next, he hoped he was right about a couple of things. First, that the guard had only one gun and was now standing but still in the same location as where Jack had last seen him. And second, he wouldn't expect Jack to be charging at him.

As it turned out, luck was on his side, and both his assumptions were correct. Like an express train, Jack came out of the darkness and hit the guard. Even in the dim light, the look of horror on the guard's face was one that Jack wouldn't forget for some time. Already wounded and not wanting to take any chances, he sank the blade up to the hilt in the man's chest as they hit the hard-packed dirt with a dull thud. The man didn't make a sound or move again.

Untangling himself, Jack stood on now shaky legs. The adrenaline was starting to wear off. Leaving the warehouse, he headed for the loading dock, crossed it, and entered the mill. Inside, the workers could still be seen going about their business. It seemed that either the noise of the machines had drowned out the sound of the gunfight, or the brick walls and heavy doors of the warehouse had contained the noise. Struggling up the steps, Jack continued single-mindedly towards Smythe's office. Working out the location from counting the windows he passed, he leaned against the wall and pounded on the closed door.

"Bull!" he called.

"Jack!" was the excited reply.

"You mind opening this door? I seem to be leaking."

The door was yanked open, and Bull's body filled the frame.

"Jesus Christ!" exclaimed Bull, grabbing hold of Jack and steering him into the room. Seeing how unsteady he was on his feet, he lowered Jack into a chair.

"Is everybody okay? Where's Smythe?" asked Jack.

"All the good guys are fine. The same can't be said for the emperor. He's over in the corner with a sheet covering him."

Just at that moment Mr Owens face appeared. "Jack, my boy, how badly hurt are you?" he asked.

"I think my arm's busted, and I broke some ribs. I need to stop the bleeding soon, or I'm in trouble."

Bull pulled out his ripper's knife and started to cut away Jack's clothing. The knives used in the mills for the rippers to cut the cloth were always kept razor-sharp. After the jacket and shirt were cut away, the full extent of the damage could be seen. Bull quickly bound the wound with the remnants of Jack's shirt to stop the bleeding.

"We need a doctor," Bull said to no one in particular.

Owens turned and ordered one of the police officers to go and bring the doctor to the main house, as that was where they would be taking Jack. The officer left in a hurry.

"Did everything work out?" asked Jack.

"Your plan was perfect, especially with you being outside. If you had been in the room we would have all been under his gun. I truly believe he was about to fire when you shot him through the window. I owe you my life, young man." Owens finished gratefully.

But Jack didn't respond to the thanks. In fact, Jack didn't remember anything more that night, as he thankfully passed out.

CHAPTER SEVEN

Jack woke with a start. He sat bolt upright and was immediately hit by the pain. He looked down at his body. He was bound up like a mummy around his ribcage, and his arm was in a sling. The memories came flooding back to him – the mill, the shootout, being shot. Taking in the dimly lit surroundings, he lay back on the pillows again and tried to remember where he was. He had a vague recollection of Owens sending for the doctor and getting him brought to his house. He must be at the big house. The bed was certainly comfy enough. He looked towards where a faint light was coming from. As his eyes fully focused, he could see heavy drapes were pulled across a window. He wondered what time it was. He was feeling hungry, so it must be getting late in the day. Jack threw back the covers and tentatively swung his legs over the side of the bed. Feeling the cool air hit his skin, he looked down and realised he was naked. He glanced round the room but couldn't see his clothes anywhere. He remembered Bull cutting off his jacket and shirt to dress his wounds but that was all. Where were his damn pants?

Well, he wasn't about to sit there and wait. He tentatively stood. Everything felt a little sore but otherwise seemed okay. Walking towards the window, he kept one hand against the wall for balance. Reaching the heavy drapes, he grabbed one and pulled it back. Sunlight filled the room, temporarily blinding him. The warmth, however, felt good on his body. He wanted to keep standing there soaking it in but just then he heard a faint noise behind him. Turning, Jack saw a fairly tall young woman standing in the room with a jug in her hand. She was staring at him open mouthed and looking a little embarrassed but seemingly frozen to the spot. Jack took her in. She didn't look like a maid, judging from the expensive-looking dress and well-styled long brown hair. The dress fit her frame perfectly, showing off just enough skin to tantalise without being cheap. She was also strikingly beautiful. They stared at each other for a few moments, her face growing pinker under his assessing gaze.

Recovering from her embarrassment, she said, "You're not supposed to be out of bed."

Not too impressed by her bossy tone, Jack just stood there in front of her, suddenly not caring that he was naked. "I seem to have mislaid my pants," he said, "I was feeling hungry but thought I should put on some clothes before looking for the kitchen. I see, though, that you don't seem to mind naked men, so maybe I'll just go like this." He gave her a challenging glare.

It didn't seem possible, but the young woman's face turned an even brighter shade of red in response to his caddish remark, and she gasped. Realising how unladylike she was behaving and embarrassed at being called on it, she turned and fled the room, slamming the door on the way out. Jack chuckled to himself. That had been a most unusual encounter. Now to more pressing matters; he was still naked and still hungry.

Spotting a wardrobe on the far side of the room, he ambled over. He was relieved to notice that, after a few minutes on his feet, his balance now seemed fully restored. Opening the door, he found several different items of clothing. Unfortunately, none of them were his. Picking up the first pair of pants and inspecting them for size, Jack put them on. It was no easy thing one armed, but he managed, and they fit well enough. Picking out a loose shirt, he slipped it over his head and put his good arm through the hole. That would have to do. Now, food.

Jack left the room by the same door the fleeing woman had exited. Stepping through, he found himself in a long corridor with several doors on either side. Wood panelling came halfway up the wall to meet expensive wallpaper. A plush red patterned carpet running down the centre felt cosy on his bare feet. *So, this is what rich feels like*, thought Jack. At the far end of the hallway, he could see a fancy carved bannister leading to a staircase. Jack headed for this and descended gingerly to the lower floor, sliding his hand on the polished wood for balance, each step reminding him of his broken ribs. He could smell food, and his stomach began to rumble. Following his nose, he was soon standing at the kitchen door. Two women were working at the stove. Not wanting to startle them, Jack cleared his throat. The elder of the two women turned.

"Good day, sir," she said with a slight curtsy.

Jack walked into the room.

"You don't have to 'sir' me," he said with a smile. "Is there any chance of some breakfast?"

The two women nervously looked at each other.

"Erm, sorry, sir. But its two o'clock in the afternoon," one said.

"Ah," replied Jack. "That'll be why I'm so hungry then. Do you have any bread I could possibly eat?"

"I'd hope we could do you better than that, sir. You've been in bed for two days," said the younger girl.

"Polly!" admonished the older woman.

"Two days?" Jack raised an eyebrow and leaned his good shoulder against the door frame. "It's okay, Polly. I didn't mean to get you in any trouble. An apple maybe?"

"Please," said the older woman, waving Polly away, "take a seat over there. It's just we aren't used to guests coming into the kitchen. It's usually the servants who go to the guests."

"I'm not really a guest," said Jack, walking towards the huge wooden table in the middle of the kitchen. "I actually work for Mr Owens just like you. I'm here only because I got wounded at the mill, and I was brought to the house for the doctor to take a look at my injuries."

"We know all about you, sir," said Polly, giving him a flirtatious smile. "The news is all over the village." She paused as she walked by him and lightly touched his arm. "We hear you were quite the hero."

"Polly!" admonished the older woman again, but slightly louder this time. "I must apologise for my young helper, sir. She forgets herself sometimes. If you take a seat at the end there, I'll bring you a bowl of stew and some bread."

"You're a lifesaver," said Jack sitting down on the wooden stool at the end of the table. A bowl of stew and large chunk of bread were placed in front of him, and the two women got back to their chores. With each delicious mouthful, he could feel the energy creeping back into his body. Finished, he picked up his bowl and made his way over to the sink, preparing to wash it. There was a slight commotion between the two women, and Polly came dashing over.

"I'll take that for you, sir."

Jack reluctantly handed her his bowl, "It was very tasty. Thank you."

Polly blushed.

Jack turned to the older woman "Thank you, Mrs?"

"Newton," the lady replied.

"Thank you, Mrs Newton. I appreciate the hospitality. Would it be possible for you to point me in the direction of the garden? I feel a walk in the sunshine would do me some good."

"This way, sir," said Mrs Newton, walking towards the back of the kitchen and opening a big heavy metal clad door.

"Much obliged," said Jack. Then, with a smile to the still blushing Polly, he left the house. The gardens were vast and very tidy, the borders immaculate. He walked over to one particular flower bed that caught his attention. It was a unique kidney-shaped bed that looked like it was used for cut flowers. The scent emanating from the flowers was tantalising to the senses. The adjacent bed also caught his eye. It was packed full of different herbs. Jack bent and touched some of the leaves, slightly crushing them in his fingers and smelling their scent.

"Do you know flowers and herbs?" said a gentle female voice.

Jack turned and came face-to-face with a distinguished-looking woman of about fifty.

"I know some of them," he replied. "My mum loved her garden. She would rhyme off all the names when I was growing up. Some of the names have stuck with me."

"I'm Judith Owens," she said extending her hand.

"I'm sorry," said Jack with a smile, taking her hand. "I'm forgetting my manners. I'm Jack Wolfe."

"Oh, I'm well aware of who you are, young man," she said with a warm smile. "From what I can gather, you're the only reason I still have a husband today."

"Your husband had everything under control. I just helped out a little."

"If you say so," she said with a knowing look in her eye. "If I may ask, why did you come over and look at these two areas?"

"I'm not sure," Jack said. "There was something about them that stood out from the rest. I just seemed drawn to them. They are exquisitely maintained."

"You've just made an old lady very happy. These two beds are my pride and joy. Only I look after them. My husband James has several gardeners, but I won't let them anywhere near these." They continued to walk around the garden with Judith pointing out the most unique or rare plants that were growing there. As they started back towards the house, she turned to him. "Would you care to join me for some tea?"

"I'd be delighted," said Jack, "but maybe I should put on some boots and tidy myself a little?"

"Nonsense," she replied. "If you're comfortable as you are, then so am I."

Jack offered her his good arm. Taking it, she guided him towards two glass doors that were wedged open. They entered a large conservatory, and Judith rang a bell to call for a servant. A footman appeared. "Yes, ma'am?"

"Colin, we'll have tea for two in the conservatory."

When the footman left, she gestured towards several chairs set around a small wrought iron table under the large palms on the side. Jack gingerly lowered himself into one of the chairs.

They had been sitting only for a few minutes when footsteps were heard and Polly came into the room carrying a large tray. She gave Jack a surprised look but quickly busied herself with the tea service. Setting the tray on a side table, she brought them the cups, saucers, sugar, and milk. She then filled the cups with tea.

"Thank you," said Mrs Owens.

"Thank you, Polly," said Jack.

Polly, blushing, collected the now empty tray and left. Mrs Owens gave Jack a quizzical look. With a grin Jack relayed how he'd woken hungry; headed to the kitchen; and, after a little persuading, had secured some stew.

"You must be quite a charmer," said Mrs Owens.

"I must?" enquired Jack.

"Mrs Newton is well known for being a stickler for her rules in the kitchen. I've never heard of anybody getting food out of her unless it was at a set mealtime. I'd say you must have made quite an impression."

Just then Jack heard voices. Mr Owens and the young lady he had seen earlier in his room entered the conservatory. Jack stood.

"Amanda," said Owens with a broad smile, "I'd like you to meet the man who saved my shipment and quite possibly my life. Jack, my daughter, Amanda."

Jack stood up slowly, took her hand and bowed slightly, as much as his tight bandaging would allow. *This is an interesting development*, he thought, with a wry smile. "It's a pleasure," he said, winking at Amanda, whose cheeks immediately turned bright pink. He was tempted to tease further with an innuendo about their earlier encounter but suppressed the urge.

"Please, sit down." Owens waved his hand at the chair behind Jack. "I hope you are feeling somewhat improved? I see you've already met my lovely wife."

"Yes, the Dr. did an excellent job of patching me up. I woke earlier and feeling a need to stretch my legs I took a walk in the fresh air of your garden where I was fortunate enough to bump into her. I had been enjoying the sun from the window in my room but was interrupted," Jack glanced at Amanda as he took his seat again, taking in her panicked look, and gave her a mischievous smile before continuing. "Your gardens are very impressive!"

"Thank you," replied Mr Owens. "We do try to keep things looking nice."

"Clearly, you have succeeded." Jack glanced at Amanda who was suddenly very busy with the items on the tea tray before eventually settling into one of the chairs.

There was a pause in the conversation while they drank their tea. Jack finished his and set the cup down in the saucer.

"If you don't mind me asking in front of the ladies, how did everything go at the mill after I left? Were the police satisfied with the evidence that it was Charles stealing your shipments?"

"After Charles pulled those two pistols on us all, I don't think there was any doubt in the chief constable's mind as to Charles's guilt. The icing on the cake was the evidence he had in his safe. He was a little bit perturbed that he had nobody to arrest. It seems Charles's hired muscle also failed to make it out of the mill alive."

"You don't say?" Jack shared a conspiratorial glance with Owens before continuing. "You didn't happen to find a rifle lying around in the warehouse by any chance. I'm not in much shape to use it at the moment, but I would hate for it to be lost."

"All taken care of," said Owens with a smile, "found it during the clean-up, along with a big knife that was a little more difficult to retrieve. I have them both in a safe place. Just let me know when you want them back."

"Greatly appreciated," replied Jack, sitting back in his chair. "So what will happen now?"

"Well, some changes for the good of all I think. I have some very exciting news. The morning after our encounter, while I was in my mill office, Charles's wife came to see me. I was very surprised. It had been only a few hours since his death but it appears she wasn't overly mourning his passing. In fact, she hated him. He treated her no better than he did his millworkers, and we've all seen how he handled his business there. It seems she dislikes living in Lancashire, as she originally comes from London and misses her family and friends. She offered to sell me the mill. I think she wants to leave as soon as possible so I got it at a very reasonable price. I am now, short of all the paperwork and having to talk to the lawyers, the proud owner of two weaving mills.

They all sat there in stunned silence at this unexpected news. Mrs Owens was the first to react. She leaned over and gave her husband a kiss on the cheek. Amanda stood, and with a warm smile, walked over to hug her father. She left her hand on his shoulder, while her parents held hands. They were all smiling. Jack felt touched by the show of family warmth, but also saddened. It had been a long time since he had felt that himself.

CHAPTER EIGHT

Over the next two months Jack was encouraged to stay at the big house as he recovered. To be truthful he hadn't taken much persuading. The bed was certainly comfier than a bedroll on the floor at Bull's. His wounds continued to heal, and after six weeks, his broken arm was almost fully mobile. From what the doctor said, he'd been very lucky. Nevertheless, after the first two weeks he had been feeling more restless than lucky. Resuming some of his watchman duties at the mill had helped, even though he'd still been in some pain and sporting some very colourful bruises. However, with Charles and his cohorts dead, protecting the mill wasn't much of an issue anymore, and the lack of activity meant Jack was starting to get bored and found himself entertaining thoughts of the possibility of a new challenge.

Initially, he'd thought the flirtation with Amanda might go further, but after their first encounters, she seemed to go cold towards him. He kept catching her looking at him with interest in her eyes, but if he ever tried to approach her, she would give him a look of disdain and move away. It appeared she was nothing more than a silly rich girl who didn't know what to make of him. This had been going on for several weeks now, and Jack had had enough of the games. He promised himself the next time he caught her watching him he would make sure she didn't get away.

One chilly morning in late November, Jack was summoned to the mill for a meeting with Mr Owens. He entered his office and took a seat.

"Jack," began Owens, "with the two mills now running at full capacity, I'm beginning to see the need for more cotton. The way Charles ran his mill was disgusting. The way he treated his employees was nothing short of criminal. Since I took ownership and made Ian the new overseer, the machines are much better maintained and the workers are happier. The changes have led to an increase in production, but unfortunately, I have now created a shortfall in the raw material.

To make matters worse, I'm hearing rumours from the colonies about a possible war of Northern aggression, and I'm worried it might affect our supply. With our security issues out of the way and you almost fully healed, I'd like you to travel to America as my representative to secure an increased supply of raw cotton. The suppliers in Charleston were set up by my father many years ago, but I think it would be beneficial if you could rattle their cages a little and get me more raw materials at a better price. What do you say?"

Jack mulled over this new offer. The assignment would relieve his bordom but he wasn't thrilled about getting back on a ship. He mused that he should be careful what he wished for. As he thought more about it, he felt the familiar pull of excitement. A chance to experience a bit of the new raw land of America first hand made an uncomfortable sea journey seem worth the trouble. With his decision made, he told Mr Owens he would be happy to represent him in the colonies. They agreed to discuss it further the following day and work out all the details. Jack left the office to go and find Bull.

He found him supervising the loading dock of the Calder Vale mill and told him his news.

"When do you leave?" asked Bull.

"I'm not sure. I think in the next few weeks. As I'm fully healed, it could be anytime. But I guess it depends when a ship will be sailing. I'll most likely leave from Liverpool and land in Charleston."

"It sounds like a proper adventure," said Bull enviously. "I wish I was going with you. It's a nice life here, but it does get monotonous. As harsh as the Crimea was, I sometimes miss it. I certainly don't miss the cold and the pain, but the excitement of riding into battle with the wind in your face and your comrades around you – it's almost indescribable."

"I know exactly what you mean. It's a feeling you can't get from anything else." There was a silence as they both got lost in their thoughts for a few minutes, remembering the past.

"Well," said Bull, "I better get back to it. I have to go down to the other mill this afternoon to make sure everything's running smoothly."

"You want some company?" asked Jack.

"That would be good," replied Bull. "I'm leaving at one."

"Okay. I'll meet you back here."

Jack left the mill feeling good that things were finally getting interesting again and headed back to the big house to get his coat for his outing with Bull. You could never predict the weather in Lancashire. Walking through the house to his room, he laughed at the irony. He realised that when he'd made his decision to go to America for Owens, he hadn't even considered the luxury he would be leaving behind. He found he didn't mind trading the comforts of such a grand home for a bedroll and a hard floor if it meant the excitement of a new adventure. Jack grabbed the things he needed, walked out of his room, and headed for the stable. While he was convalescing, Mr Owens had moved Skeiron into the stables at the main house, as they were better equipped and closer than the mill stable. This had made it much easier for him to keep an eye on his horse.

The main stable doors were huge, grand affairs. On sunny Autumn days like this, one of the doors was left secured open to allow the fresh air and sunlight inside. He paused to let his eyes adjust as he entered the dimly lit interior. There were twelve stalls in this area to house the two driving teams, several riding horses used by the family, and space for guests' horses. The family's two carriages were stored in an adjacent building. The place was kept immaculate by the hard-working stable boy. At the far end was a tack room, which was also where the stable boy sometimes slept at night. He was more fortunate than others, his father was head gardener for the estate, a job that came with a tenancy in one of the small stone-built cottages. This meant the boy had a proper home to go to, only staying in the stable when he was needed for late arrivals. Jack moved down the line of horses, admiring them. There were eight in total, not including Skeiron. Two matched pairs for pulling the carriages and four riding horses that looked to have some Arab blood in them. Compared to his Belgian Black, they looked small and fragile. Moving into Skeiron's stall, he checked her over.

"You're getting fat, old girl. I guess that's my fault, as I haven't been able to ride you too much not to mention all this rich food you've been eating. I think," he said, patting his stomach, "maybe I'm suffering the same thing. Well, I guess a ride to Liverpool and over a week on a boat will probably get us thinner. I'm sure I'll be throwing up most of my food on the boat too. Then, God only knows what the barbarians in the colonies will have for us to eat."

At his last statement, Jack heard a sharp intake of breath. He turned quickly around and saw Amanda across the stable. She was wearing a long blue dress with a shawl draped over her shoulders. She had clearly been spying on him again and had obviously heard his comment about leaving for America. Jack suddenly found he'd had enough of this silly girl watching him. He marched out of the stall so quickly Amanda was taken by surprise. There was only one exit to the stable, and Jack was going to block it. He took a step towards her. She took a step back. She now glanced around and realised she was going to be trapped. There was a momentary look of panic in her eyes, but then it was replaced by the defiance of being the Mill Owner's daughter.

"Leave me alone," she said.

Leave me alone, Jack thought. *That's rich.* She hadn't left him alone for the past two months, always spying on him. He was pissed and would have his say. "I'll leave you alone if you stop sneaking around following me. You need to decide exactly what you want. What is it about me that fascinates you so much?"

"I'm not fascinated with you," she said angrily, "and I haven't been following you."

"Bull ...shit," said Jack, taking another step towards her.

She continued to back up but was fast running out of room.

"Ever since you saw me naked that first morning, you've been after me. Are you a virgin?"

"That's not something a lady discusses, especially with the hired help." She stuck her chin in the air, folding her arms and looking past him as if he wasn't there.

"Hired help, am I now? I guess you're too good for me then. You should get back to whatever it is rich children do and stop bothering me."

Her face was beginning to colour, but with anger now, not embarrassment. Her gaze moved back to meet his, and her arms fell open, her hands balled into fists at her sides. "I'm not a child, and how dare you say those things to me? You know nothing about me."

"That's true," said Jack, "but I have met many silly girls like you before. Our commanding officers were always having their wives and daughters visit them. They were rich and thought the world owed them something. They looked down on the soldiers and didn't hide it either." Jack stepped to the side and purposefully leaned with exaggerated casualness against the end of one of the stall dividers.

"Leave," he commanded, jerking his head towards the open door.

She didn't move. "I will not be ordered around by a commoner," was her haughty response.

Jack had had enough. He had given her a chance to leave, which she hadn't taken. She needed to be taught a lesson. Striding forward, he grabbed her arms, slightly lifting her off the ground, and kept walking until her back was pressed up against the whitewashed stone of the stable wall.

"Try telling me that now, missy," Jack said, staring into her light brown eyes that had become huge with apprehension.

The anger seemed to leave her as they stood there in silence, the only sound their harsh breathing, and the apprehension changed to something else. Instantly, he became aware of the cleavage bared by her shawl being pulled away in the struggle. He looked down, drawn by an urge to expose more of that tantalising pale skin. Instead, he brought his mouth down on hers in a punishing kiss, pushing her body up against the wall with his as he set her down again, not caring at the dust or grime that must now be covering her fancy blue dress.

After a moment's hesitation, she began to kiss him back just as fiercely. His hands released her arms and moved to hold her waist, drawing her closer to him. At the change, Amanda seemed to come back to her senses. She pulled her mouth away and pushed against him, hitting his broad shoulders with her fists.

"Let me go," it came out first in a whisper and then louder. "Let me go! Release me at once!"

Jack looked into her eyes and saw the lie there and heard the conflict in her words and hesitated.

"I'll scream. I'll scream, and they'll all come running, and you'll be exposed for the brute you are!" Again, more lies, he could see she didn't even believe her own words, but he wasn't a brute. He let her go, and she stumbled from the sudden departure of his body and then ran out the door.

Jack stood for a few minutes staring after her, and then shook his head, grinning to himself at how the afternoon had started. Who would have thought Amanda would turn out to be so intriguing? He turned and walked back to Skeiron. Once she was saddled up, he led her out into the bright sunshine and swung himself up into the saddle. It felt good not to have his injuries slow him down and to be out again on his horse.

The ride with Bull to the other mill proved to be uneventful but enjoyable. A clear sky let the afternoon sun filter through the trees, almost completely bare of leaves now. Those same leaves carpeted the trail muffling the sounds of their horse's feet. The late autumn combination of sunny warmth and brisk air was invigorating. With Jack staying at the big house to recuperate, they hadn't seen much of each other in the recent weeks. As they rode, the two old comrades fell back into their familiar banter getting caught up on each other's news. Bull's mainly consisted of how much busier he had become with having to oversee two mills. Owens had increased his pay, which helped, but he felt he was certainly earning it with all the extra hours he was putting in. Jack's news was mostly about how his injuries had healed and what life at the big house was like. He also told Bull of his run-ins with Amanda and his last meeting with her just before their ride.

Bull just raised an eyebrow and shook his head. "Well you always did like trouble," he said grinning.

As it was after six o'clock when they returned to the mill, Bull offered Jack supper at his house. Jack gladly accepted. It would be nice to spend some time with Bull and Elly; their company was certainly more preferable than that of the landed gentry he had been surrounded with for the last while. They put their horses into the mill stable and walked to Bull's house. As they entered the house, Elly met them with a beaming smile.

"Look who I found wandering about looking lost," said Bull.

"Well I wouldn't exactly say lost," said Jack grinning, to his friend.

"Will you be joining us for supper?" asked Elly.

"Gladly," said Jack. "Wouldn't pass up a chance to enjoy some of your home cooking."

"Please, make yourselves comfortable at the table, and I'll bring us all some food." While Jack and Bull settled themselves at the table she disappeared into the back kitchen and came back through only moments later with steaming bowls of stew and some bread.

Elly's cooking always amazed Jack. She could make far tastier meals with simple fare than any meal created at the big house. They dug into their food hungrily, and it wasn't long until all the plates were clean.

"Like I said, you cook the best food, Elly. Thank you."

"It was my pleasure," Elly replied smiling.

As they were sitting at the table, a look passed between Elly and Bull. Jack saw it but stayed silent as it didn't seem to be anything to concern him. Elly was trying to get Bull's attention, but he wouldn't make eye contact with her.

"Jack" began Elly "There's something I want to ask you …"

"Elly," Bull cut her off, "Jack doesn't need to be bothered with that."

Elly looked down at the table.

"What is it?" asked Jack.

Elly kept her head bowed.

Jack looked over at Bull. "You might as well tell me. It's obviously quite important."

Bull looked chagrined. "It is to Elly." He nodded toward Jack while he looked at her fondly. "Go ahead, tell him."

Elly lifted her head. She looked very sad. "Sorry to bring this up, but there's a problem at the mill with one of my friends. Bull said we shouldn't interfere, but I just can't leave it alone."

"Tell me what's happening. There may be something I can do to help," Jack said, leaning forward attentively to encourage her to continue.

"I know it's not anything to do with your work as head watchmen at the mill, but one of the women who works with me in the carding room is being beaten by her husband. We were working together the other day, and the bodice of her dress got caught on a nail sticking out of the wall. The material ripped, and I could see bruises all over her ribs. When I asked her about it, she said she had fallen down some steps. After a few moments, she just broke down in tears and told me that her husband was beating her and forcing himself on her. As Bull says, it's not really any of our business, but she's a friend of mine and I can't stand by and do nothing." Elly paused and looked to Bull, hesitating.

Bull nodded encouragingly. "It's all right. Go ahead and tell him the rest."

She released the breath she was holding and started to speak again, "As hard as the beatings are to take, Jane would have just suffered in silence except she's worried she'll get pregnant again. Her last pregnancy was difficult, and the birth had dangerous complications. The midwife told her if she got pregnant again, giving birth might kill her and the child. Her husband won't listen and accuses her of not being a proper wife to him. But she's afraid for her life. I'm sorry to bring this to you, Jack, but I didn't know what to do. She asked me not to say anything to anyone, but I have to do something. It's not right what's happening. I was going to mention it to the vicar, but I fear he would then feel it was his duty to mention it to Mr Owens. As her husband also works in the mill, I didn't want to cause her any more problems. If her husband were to lose his job, they would be evicted and would lose the benefit of living in a mill-house. That would just make things even harder for my friend." She trailed off, looking at Jack hopefully.

"I see your dilemma," said Jack, sitting back in his chair again. "What would you like me to do?"

"I don't exactly know," replied Elly. "I've never been in this situation before."

"What would happen to your friend if her husband got fired?"

"I really couldn't say," replied Elly. "There are no single women who get to stay in a house on their own. There's a risk she could end up as a beggar."

"Okay, Elly. I'll see what I can find out and try to come up with a solution. I completely agree with you that this sort of thing just isn't right. As Bull will tell you, I really detest bullies, and this man sounds like a prime example. I'm going to be at the mill in the morning to see Mr Owens to go over the details of my trip to America. While I'm there, I can take a look around and get a feel for who these two people are. You'll have to give me their names."

Elly hesitated. "If I do this, Jack, you must promise me you'll go about it carefully. I couldn't stand to see her get hurt even more."

"Don't worry," said Jack. "I'll be careful how I handle the situation. Subtlety usually isn't one of my strong points, but there's a time and a place for everything, and this certainly is a situation that would require more finesse than I normally use."

He gave Bull a wry grin.

This seemed to put Elly at ease. She gave him the names and physical descriptions of the couple and also explained where in the mill they worked. With the discussion over and the hour starting to get late, Jack bid farewell to his friends. Bull walked him to the door while Elly cleared away the remains of their meal from the table. They paused at the entrance, and Bull handed Jack his coat.

"Damn shame to have a woman being treated like that, even more so with the Christmas celebrations starting up. Seems like everyone should be happy this time of year," Bull reflected as Jack put his coat on.

"Yeah," said Jack, "but hopefully we can do something about it. Thanks, Bull," he added as he made his way down the front path. "It was nice to be with friends. Thank Elly again for the fine meal too."

"I will," said Bull.

As Jack started up the road he put his arm in the air as a gesture of farewell and said over his shoulder, "See you tomorrow." He walked back to the mill stable to get Skeiron.

Nobody was in the mill stable at this time of night, so all was quiet as he saddled his horse and rode back to the big house. There was nobody in the stable there too. He had heard the stable boy's father was head gardener and remembered the big houses of his youth being decorated every year with miles of evergreen garlands. He imagined they would be made on the estate, and the lad was probably exhausted after helping his father with the chore. A servant's workload could double at this time of year. Rather than wake the boy, he tended to his horse's needs himself and went to his room to sleep.

Jack slept fitfully that night. Every sound seemed to wake him, and when it did Amanda kept creeping into his thoughts, the events in the stable replaying over and over in his mind. Despite his tossing and turning, he woke early as per his usual routine, dressed quickly, and splashed some water on his face to fully wake himself up. Making his way down the back stairs, he found he was still wrestling with the thoughts about what had happened with Amanda.

The house was quiet. It was early enough that none of the Owens family was up and about, and that suited him just fine. He wasn't eager to cross paths with Amanda until he'd had more time to think about things and get them settled in his mind. As was his habit, he stopped by the kitchen to grab some bread, cheese, and meat before heading outside.

When he entered the stable, he felt like he'd hardly been away. His night's sleep hadn't refreshed him as he'd hoped it would. Feeling annoyed by this, he pushed any more thoughts of Amanda out of his head and focused on the whinny of greeting coming from Skeiron.

"Hey, girl. Are you ready to stretch your legs?" He stroked her sleek neck as she nuzzled his jacket. When the stable boy heard him, his head popped up above the withers of the horse he was grooming in the adjacent stall.

"Is there anything I can do for you, sir?" he asked cheerily, if a bit bleary-eyed. The smell of evergreens was strong from his clothing, and Jack could see the telltale dots all over his hands from holly pricks. He smiled to himself in sympathy for the boy. That stuff was murder to handle.

"I think I have everything I need," replied Jack as he walked over to the rail where he'd left his saddle and bridle the night before. Picking them up, he noticed they were both spitting clean. "But I do appreciate the clean tack," he said over his shoulder.

The boy gave him a nod and got back to his chores as Jack finished saddling Skeiron, mounted, and rode out into the bright sunshine. He didn't hurry. He was busy thinking of the best way to handle the situation that Elly had asked him to help with. He was also enjoying the novelty of feeling the sun warm his bones, a sharp contrast to how wet this part of the country usually was. Back in the mill yard, Jack headed for the stable. He untacked Skeiron and put her into one of the box stalls. He expected his visit could take most of the day.

He left by the main stable doors and headed for the loading dock. Elly had told Jack that the woman, Jane, was working in the carding room and that her husband, Peter, usually worked around the loading area. Other than that, Jack had only a brief physical description of the couple he was looking for. He was hoping the information he had would be enough.

As he approached the loading dock, he saw three men unloading a wagon. Based on the description Elly had given him, any one of them could be Peter. Jack positioned himself unobtrusively at the far end of the wooden loading dock and casually watched all three in their work. From the manner in which these men interacted with each other, Jack soon had one particular man picked out in his mind as his quarry. There wasn't anything too obvious about him, but after a few minutes observation, he could see that the other two men were wary of him and gave him a wide berth when they could. With the load emptied, one of the other men got up onto the wagon and started to coax the horses into movement. Without warning, the man who Jack suspected was Peter walked up to one of the horses and slapped its rump. The startled horse tried to bolt away. The driver managed to get the horse under control but not before almost being thrown from the seat and exclaiming, "What the hell were you thinking, Peter?" confirming Jack's suspicions.

With the first person identified, Jack went into the mill. As he entered the carding room through a metal door, he saw several women working. With his eyes fixed firmly on them, he let the metal door slam heavily closed. Almost as one, the women turned their heads to see what had made the noise, all except one woman, who visibly cowered. Jack took note of this but continued walking through the room as if nothing had happened and walked out of the door at the far end. From the woman's reaction and how Elly had described her, Jack was sure he had now identified Jane.

When he'd been in the Crimea with the army, he had seen many women behave in this way. Soldiering didn't always make for the best husbands, and wives were sometimes 'ill tret'. However, it had been far easier for Jack to deal with this type of problem in the army than it would be now. As their commanding officer, he could swiftly discipline any man who was out of line, and wife beating certainly fell under that remit. The punishments that the army dished out could be quite severe and usually were enough to deter wife beaters from reoffending. Solving the problem in a civilian environment, however, was going to be much more complicated.

Needing time to think on how he wanted to proceed before he saw Mr Owens, Jack took a walk down the lane into the woods. There had been a frost the night before and shaded areas were still dusted with white crystals. The cool air held the promise of snow. As the constant clatter of the machinery started to fade, he was better able to concentrate on solving the problem. An hour later, he walked back into the mill yard with a plan of action. It would require Mr Owens's cooperation and Bull's help. Feeling confident, Jack strode up the steps to Owens's office and knocked on the outer door. A familiar, "Come in," was heard from inside.

Jack entered the outer office and kept walking until he got to Mr Owens's door that was partly ajar.

"Mr Owens," began Jack, pushing the door all the way open.

Owens looked up from his ledger. "Jack," he said with a beaming smile, "please come in and take a seat."

Jack entered and took a seat directly in front of the desk.

"Now to matters at hand regarding your trip. I've been looking at the sailings," Owens began. "There is a ship leaving for the Americas in eleven days. She leaves from Liverpool and arrives in New York about ten days later, depending on the weather. I've booked a passage to New York because most of the ships going to Charleston currently are cargo ships. Very few have private rooms for passengers or provision for taking a mount, and I feel Skeiron will be an asset to have in America. I also have some business for you to take care of for me in New York before heading south." He paused and regarded Jack closely. "This means you will be travelling over Christmas, but it was my impression that you have no commitments that will make that a problem?"

Jack nodded, and Owens continued. "With both mills running smoothly now, I think the sooner you are on your way the better?"

It wasn't really a question as Owens was the boss but being a decent man, he didn't like to order people around. Jack, however, was under no illusion that this was anything but an order.

"Before you leave, I will have legal papers drawn up giving you power of attorney to act in my stead and will secure your passage on the ship. I will also supply you with the plantation owner's address in America, as I'm hoping you will be able to do business directly with him and cut out the middleman in Charleston. I will, of course, send a letter in advance to tell him to expect your arrival. The actual Charleston suppliers I use, however, don't know I'm sending anybody, and none of them know you. This will give you the advantage of finding out prices and how they operate their businesses before you tell them who you work for. I will also give you travelling money and an advance on your wages, as you won't be here to collect them yourself."

"That all seems to make sense," said Jack. He paused for a moment. "I was wondering if I might speak to you about another matter that's been brought to my attention?"

Owens looked quizzically at Jack. "Go on," he said.

"I've been told that one of the women in your mill is being abused by her husband who also works in the mill. I'm guessing this isn't something that normally comes to your attention, but I've been asked to help in the matter and needed to ask you a question before I proceed. Hypothetically, as they live in one of your tied houses, what would happen to the woman if her husband suddenly stopped working here?"

Owens thought about this for a moment. "I am aware that a few of the houses my workers live in may have more occupants than they were originally designed to hold. If a house were to become available, I dare say there would be women who could share the house with her so she could stay working at the mill and have a place to live. Should I ask why this man would stop working for me?"

"You could, but it's probably better that you don't," replied Jack with a wry grin on his face. "What I will say, is from observing this man, if he were to leave, he certainly wouldn't be missed by the rest of your workers. In fact, I wouldn't be at all surprised if you never noticed he had left.

"Then I will trust you to handle this matter."

"I appreciate it, you won't regret it," said Jack, standing and leaving the office.

Once outside Owens's office, Jack went in search of Bull. He found him on the main weaving floor. The noise was horrific with all the machines clattering. It made any conversation impossible. Jack beckoned for Bull to follow him and led him outside.

"I've figured out who the couple are that Elly's concerned about. From the looks of things, she was right. To be sure that what I have in mind will be a fair punishment, I need to be certain that Jane is being beaten. I'm going to watch them for the rest of the day. If all is as bad as I suspect, I'll come find you in the morning and explain the plan."

"Fair enough," said Bull. "Need any help, you only have to ask."

Jack gave a nod. "Good to hear. For what I'm proposing to work, I'll be counting on your help."

With that, Bull went back into the mill, and Jack made his way back inside to continue his observation of the couple.

He spent the next several hours in and around the mill watching how Peter and Jane both interacted with their work colleagues. Neither came into contact with each other, but that wasn't unusual, as they worked in different areas. It was nearing dusk by the end of the shift. Jack made sure he was in the mill yard to watch them leave together and then followed them from a safe distance. To the casual observer, there was nothing unusual about their behaviour, but Jack noticed that Peter never touched his wife. Most of the other couples would walk home hand in hand after their long day or at least exchange informal touches as they talked, but not these two.

To Jack, it seemed as if Peter was openly making a statement about his disdain for his wife – that he never touched her except to beat her behind closed doors. Keeping his distance in the lengthening evening shadows, Jack saw the couple enter one of the mill-houses. These buildings were in a separate area from where Bull and Elly lived but were of similar construction. As it was now getting dark, Jack could easily watch the house without giving away his position. A few moments after the door closed, a light came on in the downstairs room, giving Jack a clear view of what was happening inside. Happy that he had a good place from which to keep an eye on things, he settled himself in to watch and wait. He didn't have to wait long, as no sooner had the lamp been lit than the curtains were drawn.

Shit, thought Jack to himself. Peter certainly didn't want anybody knowing what went on between them.

Seeing nobody on the street, Jack cautiously made his way to the now obscured window. It was close to pitch-black outside, as there was no streetlighting. Creeping up to the window, Jack could just see past the edge of the ill-fitting curtains. He had a pretty good view of the room, but he was also aware that he had to keep one eye on the street for anyone passing by.

As the minutes went by, Jack shifted his weight back and forth on his feet to keep himself warm. He was beginning to wonder if he had chosen the right window to watch through. He could see a few bits of furniture, but certainly neither Peter nor Jane had come into view. The house walls were thick enough, but the single glass pane didn't keep all the sound in or, for that matter, the cold out. With the noise of the mill a distant clatter and it being a still night, Jack was able to hear their somewhat muffled voices. From the intensity of them, it sounded like an argument.

Just then, Jane came into view. She was crying and holding her arm. Peter was right behind her. Grabbing Jane's shoulder, he spun her round and slapped her across the face. She fell to the floor in a crumpled heap, visibly sobbing. Jack's blood began to boil. He was about to move from his position and burst through the front door to square up to this animal but stopped himself. He had a plan to follow and couldn't risk alerting the man that they were onto him yet. He could see Peter standing over her shaking with rage. Jack couldn't help but hear his next words very clearly, as they were shouted.

"If I see you again before morning, I'll kill you! You stupid bitch!"

With that, Peter picked her up and pushed her out of the room. Jack quickly moved away from the window and back to his original observation post across the street. He was dismayed to see that the front door soon opened, and Jane came out, clutching her cloak against the cold as she left the house. After having witnessed her husband's rage, Jack was surprised he didn't see her get pushed out the door. But then again, Peter never touched her if there was the possibility someone could be watching. *He is a real bastard*, he thought.

Jack's heart went out to the poor woman, and he followed her to make sure she was all right and got to where she was heading. Jane made her way back towards the mill and entered the stable. Jack watched as she climbed up into the hayloft and lay down to sleep. Rather than scare this poor woman by approaching her himself, Jack went to see Bull and Elly and tell them of this latest development. He was ready to lay out his plan on how to get rid of Peter.

Jack knocked on Bull's door. He noticed a wreath hanging there as he waited. Looking down the row of houses, he realised that Mrs Owens must have provided them for each tenant's door. He was reflecting on the benevolence of that good lady when Bull answered, looking worried at what may have brought him back to their door so soon. He stayed silent as Jack was ushered in. Once they had all sat down at the table, Jack relayed what he had seen. The longer his story went on, the angrier Bull got. By the time his story was finished, Bull was getting up out of his chair to go and pay Peter a visit.

"Settle down, Bull," said Jack. "I have a plan for how we can resolve this."

"I know exactly how to resolve this, and it involves me inflicting lots of pain on Peter!" Bull pounded the table with his fist. Elly flinched and looked at Jack anxiously.

"Don't think I haven't already thought about that. When he first slapped her, I was so close to breaking the door down and doing just that I almost didn't stop myself in time. What I have in mind will involve some pain for Peter, though not as much as he deserves. But more importantly, it will get rid of him for good, so he never comes back and bothers Jane again."

Retaking his seat and calming himself with several deep breaths, Bull took Elly's hand comfortingly and looked to Jack. "Okay, so what's the plan?"

"Like you," began Jack, "my first instinct was to beat the man senseless, pack up all his belongings, and escort him out of here with the promise of more if he ever came back."

"And what's wrong with that?" asked Bull angrily.

Elly nodded in agreement.

"What's wrong is that it still leaves the possibility he might return and hurt Jane even worse than he is now. What I'm proposing is that Elly has a word with Jane."

At the mention of her name Elly looked up from where she had been tracing the rough wood of the table with her finger and gazed intently at Jack. "Elly will instruct Jane to provoke Peter into hitting her."

Elly gasped at this request but didn't interrupt him.

"Hang on a minute, it's a small sacrifice for the bigger picture," said Jack with compassion in his voice, patting Elly's hand as he continued. "She must do this tomorrow night after work when she is at home and alone with Peter before the curtains are closed. After he hits her, Jane needs to fall to the floor and lay motionless. In that instant, Bull and

I will burst in through the front door. Bull can restrain Peter anyway he sees fit."

Bull smiled at that.

"And I will go to Jane's side to check to see if she's all right. I'll then check for a pulse and fail to find one. I will announce that Peter has killed his wife and will surely hang. Bull, I'm sure, may hit Peter again at this point for good measure."

At this new information, Elly sat back in her chair, contemplative.

Jack relaxed a bit more too, seeing she was receptive to his plan, and went on. "Then to save any hassle for Bull and myself and not wanting to have the police around, I will suggest that Peter packs up his things and runs for it. I'm sure, being the coward that he is, he will jump at the chance and never be seen around here again."

There was a long silence when he'd finished.

"Apart from the bit where I don't get to hit him enough, I like it," said Bull.

"Elly?" asked Jack, turning to her.

Elly sat quietly for a few moments. Tears started to fall down her cheeks. "It's a good plan, Jack." she smiled. "It will give her the best chance to be permanently free from him. But what will happen to her afterwards? Where will she live?"

"That's already been taken care of," said Jack. "I spoke to Mr Owens this morning, and without giving any names or the full nature of my plan, he assured me that she would still have a place to live. She will have to share it with other women, but she can stay in her house."

"Oh, Jack," exclaimed Elly, getting up from the table and flinging her arms around his neck. "You're a genius!"

"I'm not sure about that, but I do have my moments," said Jack with a grin at Bull, who was now glaring at Jack being hugged by his wife.

"So as not to arouse any suspicions, I hate to say it, but Jane should probably still stay in the mill stable tonight. It will be warm enough with the proximity of the horses."

Elly and Bull agreed.

"If you could have a word with Jane in the morning and explain the plan, Bull and I can talk tomorrow to finalise a few details?"

Elly nodded in agreement.

"Well then," said Jack. "I'm going back to the mill to pick up Skeiron. I'm sure Jane will be well hidden, but I'll have a quick glance around to make sure all seems okay. Elly, tell Jane not to worry. Bull and I will have this all sorted before she goes to sleep tomorrow night."

With that, Jack left the house for the mill. As he'd expected, there was no visible sign of Jane in the stable. Still, just to be sure she was safe to be sleeping there, Jack made a cursory check around. Satisfied all was in order, he left the stable to ride back to the big house.

CHAPTER NINE

The next morning, Jack rode back to the mill and took a walk through the carding room where Jane was working alongside Elly. He was happy to see that Jane's night in the stable hadn't had any ill effects. Elly gave him a very slight conspiratorial nod to say that she had spoken to Jane, but Jane never looked up. Satisfied all was progressing well with them, he sought out Bull and finalised their part of the plan. Now that all the pieces were in play, Jack had some time to kill. He made his way back to the stable and went for a ride on Skeiron. He would be leaving Calder Vale soon, and this might be his last chance for a while to see this picturesque, if damp, part of the world. His afternoon passed pleasantly enough. He even shot a few hares for Elly to put into her stew pot. With the end of the mill shift fast approaching, Jack once again made his way back to the mill and stabled Skeiron. He then stayed by the stable, keeping himself busy tending to his horse until he heard the voices of the millworkers coming and going. He moved to the door to observe the passing workers and saw Bull coming out of the mill. Right on time, Bull strode up to the front of the stable to join him.

"Everything ready?" enquired Jack.

"As ready as it's going to be," replied Bull. "Elly explained everything to Jane. She's agreed to her part in the plan and expressed her gratitude for what you are doing for her."

"What *we* are doing for her you mean. However, I am now thinking it should be me who restrains Peter and not you?" Jack said, tongue-in-cheek.

"Aye, that'll be right," said Bull sarcastically, elbowing his friend in the ribs. "Just try and stop me. There's no way I'm giving up the chance to do some damage to that man."

"Well, all right, if you put it like that," said Jack laughing.

With the dull November dusk falling, they stood in the doorway for several more minutes before they saw Peter and Jane go by. Casually they fell in with the other workers filing past and began to follow the two of them. It was very much the same as it had been when Jack followed the couple the previous night. No contact between the two. This time, though, according to the plan, Jane was talking to Peter, or most probably nagging at him in the hopes of riling his temper. The idea was to get him so worked up that he forgot to draw the curtains. They needed him to snap as soon as he got into the house. Even from a distance, Jack and Bull could see it seemed to be working. Peter had glared at Jane on several occasions. Each time his face turned to say something to her, he was looking angrier and angrier.

After what seemed an eternity, the couple arrived at their house and walked up the path. As Jane opened the door, she reached out to straighten the Christmas wreath hanging there donated by Mrs. Owens. Seeing her pause Peter gave her a shove, sending her stumbling through the opening. He then slammed the door behind them hard enough to send the wreath flying. Jack and Bull kept up appearances of walking normally up the road until the moment the door closed. Then they doubled back to take up a vantage point in the shadows where they could clearly see in the front room window.

Right on cue, a lamp was lit. Peter came into view and moved towards the window to draw the curtains. For a moment, Jack and

Bull felt they were on the brink of their plan falling apart, but then Jane appeared behind him and said something. They couldn't hear what it was that she said but it stopped Peter dead in his tracks. He spun around to face his wife. Jack and Bull felt a burst of adrenaline and readied themselves to enter the house. The voices from in the house reached a crescendo. Jane was giving as good as she got. In an instant, Peter took one step closer to her and slapped her across the face. She staggered back against the wall from the force of the blow. As she bounced off the wall, he backhanded her again. This time, she fell to the floor.

Bull charged towards the house with Jack right on his heels. Without breaking stride, Bull hit the door with his shoulder, ripping it from its hinges. The door partly blocked their passage but didn't slow the pair down. They burst into the front room to see Jane lying prone on the floor and Peter standing over her. Without a second thought, Bull smashed his fist into Peter's face. Peter staggered back but stayed on his feet. Bull kept on moving and punched him in the stomach, doubling him up. The instant he was doubled over, Bull lifted his knee into Peter's head. The impact snapped him back upright. Bull took this opportunity to grab him by the throat and pin him to the wall. Blood was streaming from a cut above Peter's eye and from his nose.

"Don't. Fucking. Move!" ordered Bull.

Ignoring him, Peter started to squirm in his grasp. Bull leaned pressure on Peter's throat, cutting off his air supply. "I said don't fucking move!" Bull repeated, giving his throat an extra squeeze for good measure. Peter stopped squirming. Bull would have been happy to beat this poor excuse for a man unconscious, but they needed him to hear their next conversation.

"Jane," said Jack. "Are you all right?"

There was no sound from Jane. Jack knelt by her side and gently shook her shoulder. "Jane, Jane, can you hear me?"

Still there was no answer from Jane. She was so still that Jack was worried their deception might turn out to be the truth. Worried now,

Jack moved his hand to her neck. Relieved, he felt she was alive and continued with the plan.

"I can't find a pulse," he said aloud to no one in particular.

"Shit," exclaimed Jack, turning to face Peter. "She's not breathing. What did you do, you bastard?"

Peter said nothing.

"Check her pulse again," said Bull, frantically building the suspense for what Jack was about to announce.

Jack once again placed his fingers on Jane's neck and lowered his ear to her mouth to look like he was checking for her breathing.

Shaking his head, in a low voice, Jack said, "She's dead."

Standing, he turned to face Peter. "What did you do, you animal? You've fucking killed her! Let him go, Bull. I want a piece of him!"

The look of shock on Peter's face was plain for all to see. He started to struggle in Bull's grasp, more violently than before.

"Are you sure you want me to let you go?" Bull asked Peter, looking to Jack. "The man seems ready to save the hangman a job."

His words stopped Peter cold. You could almost hear his thoughts. He had killed his wife and was going to hang for his crime. At that moment, Bull released his grip on Peter's neck. It was the opening the desperate man needed. He made a vain effort to get to the door and leave the house but didn't even make it two paces before Jack's right hand exploded like a hammer, catching him squarely on the jaw. Peter crashed heavily to the floor. Jack was on him a second later and delivered two more punches to his head. Now Peter lay unconscious on the floor.

Not wasting any time, Jack ran into the couple's bedroom, grabbed the male clothes that were hanging in the closet, and stuffed them into a bag. He then went back into the front room, and with an arm each, Jack and Bull carried the still unconscious man out of the house, his feet dragging behind them. Continuing down the flagstone path Peter's legs ground the remains of the Christmas wreath into the mud on the path's edge. Jack sent a silent apology to Mrs Owens. This home clearly wasn't ready for any holiday cheer. As the cold night air hit him, Peter started to stir, but they ignored his mutterings. Half carrying, half dragging him along under the cover of darkness, they cleared the end of the row of houses keeping a vigil for any nosy onlookers. Their luck held, no one was about and they were well hidden among some trees when they unceremoniously dumped Peter onto the cold wet ground.

Seeing that he was beginning to come round, they encouraged Peter into consciousness by kicking him in the balls. The extra pain seemed to do the trick as he lifted his head and let out a loud moan.

"Shut up, or we'll shut you up," snapped Jack.

Peter, now fully conscious and beginning to realise the gravity of the situation, became silent, and sat up slowly, eyes on the ground.

"Okay, Peter, this is how it's going to work," said Jack. "You're in a world of shit with no real options. Don't think you can say this was an accident and get out of it. We both witnessed you hitting your wife through the front window."

Peter looked up at him in surprise at those words. He could see the minute Peter put two and two together and realized his mistake in not drawing the curtains and the implications. Any fight left went out of him.

Jack continued, "The hangman's waiting for you and rightly so. You killed your poor defenceless wife. The only thing that's stopping me from contacting the police and having you carted off to the gallows is that I have a responsibility to Mr Owens and the mill. He certainly doesn't need the scrutiny of the police or the embarrassment that would come with it from your poor judgement. Therefore, we're going to let you go."

Peter's eyes widened at this.

"However, if you ever show your face round here again" – Peter started to nod enthusiastically – "it won't be an arrest that you will have to fear from our testimony. You won't ever see the inside of a police cell or a courtroom. In fact, you will see only one thing – my face as I gut you for the coward you are and bury you on the moor."

At this last statement, Bull picked him up, and Jack threw the bag of clothes at him.

"Now get out of here before I change my mind."

With a total look of shock on his badly beaten face, Peter turned and stumbled away. As they watched him disappear into the darkness, Bull turned to Jack, "You think he'll be back?"

"I doubt it." Jack leaned up against a tree. "He seemed totally convinced he'd killed his wife. He's a coward, so he'll be shit scared of the hangman. He also got a pretty good reminder with the beating he just took that the hangman isn't the only thing he has to fear."

"I kind of enjoyed that," said Bull, smiling.

"I did get that impression," replied Jack with a grin of his own.

"It's the most excitement I've had in years. I half hope he does come back."

"Let's see if you feel the same way when Owens takes the cost of that door out of your pay," Jack quipped, laughing at the sudden look of consternation on Bull's face.

"Even if he does, it was still worth it."

Jack pushed away from the tree and started back toward the houses. Bull fell into step beside him.

"I'm going to go sneak Jane out the back door and take her to my house to see Elly. She'll be worn out with waiting. She's been nervous all day about how this would turn out. You get back up to the big house. The less you're seen down here after dark, the better. We don't want anybody getting curious. Tomorrow we can just spread the rumour that Peter left in the middle of the night and abandoned Jane. Nobody liked Peter, so they'll be happy he's gone and it's unlikely anyone will question it further."

"Sounds like a plan," said Jack, starting to walk away. Turning he said, "Hey, Bull." Bull stopped and looked back at Jack. "Felt good to be fighting side by side again. Reminded me of some of the scrapes we fought our way out of in the Crimea."

"Yes it did," said Bull with a satisfied grin on his face as he turned and entered Jane's house.

Jack made his way back to the mill feeling pretty good. Things had turned out just as they'd wanted, and the excitement of the last hour had got his adrenaline flowing. He entered the stable, saddled Skeiron, and made his way back to the big house.

As he rode, his stomach started to grumble. He realised he was hungry. With all that had happened that day, he'd forgotten to eat. Luckily, if past experience could be counted on, with the Owens entertaining a new visitor at the big house there would be some spare food in the kitchen. He'd grab something when he got back.

They were very generous in their hospitality. He had been treated like an honoured guest while he'd been convalescing and had eaten dinner with the Owens family most evenings. It wasn't always all three of the family, as Mr Owens was sometimes working, and Amanda would often be away socialising with friends. She'd been conspicioulsy absent since their last encounter. However, due to his evening's activities, Jack had missed his usual meal.

Distracted by thoughts of food, he dismounted and led Skeiron into the stable. Straight away, the stable boy came hurrying over to help him with his horse.

"I'm surprised you're still here," said Jack.

"I'm working, sir."

Jack could sense something off in the way he said he was working. He looked over the boy's shoulder and saw a pile of straw and a blanket.

"Were you resting over there waiting for me?" he asked.

With his head slightly bowed the boy nervously answered that he was.

"I'm sorry for keeping you working so late," said Jack.

"You didn't, sir," said the stable boy, quite shocked that somebody had apologised to him. "It's part of my duties to wait until all the guests are back and their animals settled in for the night."

"Well, as I'm not officially a guest, I think that means you don't need to stay."

"Are you sure, sir?" enquired the boy. "I'm not supposed to leave until everything's taken care of."

"As far as I can see, that's been done. You've more than carried out your duties. Now get along to your family. I'm sure they will be glad to have you home."

"Yes, sir. Thank you, sir," said the boy, not waiting for Jack to change his mind. He ran from the stable and over towards the gardener's cottage where he lived with his parents.

While he was finishing off bedding Skeiron down for the night, Jack's sixth sense picked up that he was not alone. Cautiously turning around, he felt a jolt of surprise to see Amanda standing across the stable in the exact spot where he'd confronted her a few days earlier. Though she was dressed in the glitter of finery like the lady she was, the black velvet cloak she wore almost blended her into the shadows. She was staring at him, and this time when their eyes met, she didn't look away. She continued to hold his gaze, but the defiant glare of before was gone, replaced by a softer, almost pleading look in her eyes. Jack left the stall and slowly crossed to where she was standing, giving her every opportunity to escape this time. He stopped and stood several feet in front of her.

"Has the evening's entertainment finished?" he enquired with a trace of sarcasm.

"No," she replied. "The men have retired to the study for brandy and cigars, so it now appears the women are surplus to requirements."

"I can't imagine you ever being surplus to requirements," said Jack, eyeing her up and down.

Amanda blushed slightly but didn't look away.

"You look very nice this evening," he said.

"Thank you," she said self-consciously, brushing the velvet, "but with this long cloak covering everything, I'm not sure how you could think that."

Jack stepped forward and undid the clasp at the top and pulled away the dark material, exposing Amanda's dress. She stayed motionless as if frozen to the spot as it fell from her bare shoulders. He caught it and draped it over his arm. She was wearing a full blue gown of expensive silk that exposed enough of her breasts and cleavage to excite even a blind man.

"I'm going to rephrase that," said Jack feasting his eyes. "You look beautiful."

Amanda's face coloured even more as she glanced sideways to avoid his intense gaze.

Jack's heart was now pounding out of his chest. The adrenaline that had been flowing through his veins from the earlier fight now surged back at her unexpected presence in the stable and the excitement he felt at being this close to her. It was making him light-headed. He could feel the extra charge flowing round his body. He knew the signs – fight or flight response they called it, your body getting ready for something. This something, he was happy to recognise, was neither a fight nor a flight. Not wasting any time, he threw the cloak over the side of a stall, reached down, and grabbed the bottom edges of her petticoats & skirt in one hand.

Watching her face intently, he slowly raised the gathered material. When his hand reached her waist, he stopped. He looked down at the pale skin of her thigh exposed above her stocking, tempting him to touch it. Leaning in, he kissed her softly on the lips. She gradually started to respond but seemed very unsure of herself.

"I'm … uh … not …" Her voice trailed off as his hand moved over the soft skin of her thigh and inside her undergarments.

Jack stopped and looked her in the eyes. "Is this what you want?" he said gently.

She seemed to get embarrassed and looked down.

"Hey, it's okay. I'm sorry I teased you before about being a child.

You're not. You're a very attractive woman but for your own good, you should know you can't follow men around and not risk getting caught."

"I think I secretly wanted you to catch me but didn't think you'd want me, as I have no experience."

Jack smiled at her. "One of the greatest gifts a woman can give a man is to share her body, but it should be saved for the right moments and not thrown away."

"This is the right moment. I'm giving it to you," she said, gaining confidence. "You are the most honourable man I have ever known. You saved my father, risking your own life in the process. You are a strong, handsome man and ..." Her voice started to falter. She raised her chin and looked him in the eyes. "I need you to take me."

This time when he looked, there was a fire there he hadn't seen before – a passion and also an urgency to experience the pleasure that could come from sharing sex.

Jack continued to move his hand until he found what he wanted. She gasped at his touch. He stroked softly but firmly. After a few minutes, he felt her knees give a little. He wrapped his arm around her waist to hold her up, pulling her body to him. He parted the folds of now moistening skin and inserted a finger. She was very wet, giving truth to her request. Well, he couldn't doubt her desires now.

As he continued to delve inside her, Amanda let out a moan. "More," she pleaded.

It was all he needed to hear. Jack was now overcome with the desire to have her, to make her his. With his other hand, he shoved aside her petticoats and opened her drawers. Unfastening his pants, he let them fall to the ground. Amanda, momentarily pulled from her daze by the loss of his fingers inside her, looked down and gasped.

"Will it hurt?" she asked.

"I won't lie to you. It might, as it's your first time. I'll go slowly and be gentle, but it may be uncomfortable in the beginning. Is this still what you want?"

She looked back to his face and gave the slightest nod. Freed from his role of gentleman by her permission, Jack moved to take what he wanted and placed his thigh against hers to spread her legs. Pushing his hard length against her opening, he slowly rocked back and forward going deeper with each thrust. Amanda kept letting out gasps and moans that Jack wasn't sure were pleasure or pain, but she didn't ask him to stop. When he was fully inside her, he used all his self-control to pause and put a finger under her chin. He lifted her face up to his and kissed her.

"You okay?" he asked.

"Perfect," she murmured, eyes half-closed.

With her body now pinned to the wall, Jack lifted one of her legs and held it at his waist. She moaned again as he started to ride her harder, but one look at her face, and he was no longer in doubt whether it was pleasure or pain. She felt so good, so tight. He could feel a tingling in his balls. Amanda started to writhe around against him, and Jack realised she was close to coming. *Well that was unexpected*, he thought. *What a hot little thing she is.*

Quickening the pace, he moved one hand down to stimulate her more. Her body tensed, and she grabbed his shoulders as the orgasm ripped through her. He had to adjust to hold more of her weight as she succumbed to the blissful feelings. Still, he didn't slow his thrusts. Surprising him again, Amanda grabbed his shoulders even harder as a second orgasm took her. Jack slowed his pace and thrust longer as his own orgasm built. He looked deep into her in the eyes.

"I'm close, I should pull out?" he said.

"No, please don't. I need this so much. I need to feel everything."

At her words, Jack simply nodded and let his body take over. Slowing his thrusts, he rode the edge of the pleasure until he finally exploded inside her hot wet tightness. He held her there for a few more minutes until their senses returned to somewhere near normal.

"I didn't hurt you, did I?" asked Jack.

"No", she paused looking at him with soft eyes. "It was amazing." Tears started to stream down her cheeks.

"Oh shit. I did hurt you, didn't I?" He lowered her leg and moved his hand to stroke her cheek.

"No." She laughed a little, pulling her undergarments back into place and straightening her dress as Jack buttoned his trousers. "I'm ok, really. I think I'm just overwhelmed with emotion. I've never felt anything like that."

Jack smiled at her and took her hand. They stood for a moment, quietly, hands clasped.

She shivered and he reached beside her to retrieve the cloak and draped it over her shoulders, securing the clasp. He kissed her lips softly and pulled her to him again. She leaned into his chest, content in his arms.

"Amanda?"

The call of her personal maid, Molly, broke the moment, and they both pulled away.

Amanda looked at him in panic. "Oh, I … You … We should …"

She was clearly having trouble forming a coherent thought. He couldn't stop the rakish grin that lit up his face. *That was what a man wanted to see after sex*, he thought. He moved quickly into the shadows as her maid stepped through the door.

"Oh, here you are, miss. Your mother was starting to worry when she didn't find you on the terrace after you stepped out for some air."

"Yes. I'm sorry. I just wanted to check on my horse. She seemed a bit off when I rode today."

Her maid looked to the stall, concerned. "Is she okay, miss? You seem flushed. Are you upset?"

Amanda pulled her cloak more tightly around her, concealing her rumpled clothing and wiped the last of the tears from her cheeks. She moved towards the stable door, placing a comforting hand on the girl's arm while also steering her outside. "All is fine. You know I enjoy a brisk walk sometimes after such a large meal. I just took the roundabout way to the stable, and with my corset so much tighter for this evening dress, well, you understand."

Molly laughed. "Oh yes, miss. I wonder how you are even still bearing it after we tightened it so much!"

Amanda smiled, seemingly in reply, but her face was turned to where Jack stood in the shadows. Although she couldn't see him, he smiled back. This had turned into a very interesting day.

The next morning, Jack woke feeling very happy, his thoughts full of everything that had happened the previous night. He was pleased, of course, that Jane would now be safe. It was certainly good that Peter was no longer a threat. But the main reason behind his happiness was that he and Amanda had finally connected. He now realised that, though they had never expressed it in words, there had always been a constant feeling, a tension between them that had exploded last night in the stable.

His mind still distracted by the intimate encounter, Jack quickly dressed and left his room. He didn't bother with the kitchen this morning. After the preceding night's party, the cook would be very busy preparing breakfast for any extra overnight guests and, he thought, wouldn't appreciate his usual visit.

He left the house, saddled Skeiron, and was already halfway way back to Calder Vale before he saw anyone. He was glad to be left alone. He didn't want all the pleasant thoughts of the night before with Amanda being disturbed from his mind. He actually caught himself whistling as he started to enter the village. He smiled to himself but stopped whistling.

Riding through the village, he shook his head to free his mind of thoughts of Amanda and focused on the situation with Jane and Peter. He wondered what the other millworkers were saying. Had anybody seen them? Somebody must have heard something. The way Bull had gone through that door had not been very subtle.

He didn't plan on being very long so passed the mill stable and tied Skeiron to the rail at the loading dock. Before he'd even had a chance to enter the mill, Bull came out to meet him. Without a word, the two friends walked to the side of the huge building so they could talk in private.

"Well?" said Jack, raising an eyebrow.

"Everything's good," replied Bull. "Actually, everything's great!" he exclaimed, slapping Jack on the shoulder.

"Go on," said Jack, now intrigued.

"After you left last night, I went into the front room of Jane and Peter's house. She was playing her part very well, still lying in the same place that she fell. I knelt down and quietly told her Peter had gone and that she needed to get some things and stay with Elly and myself for the night. She did as I asked and came to the house. I then left her with Elly, and I went off to sleep on the floor of the main room. I think they talked half the night. They're both working in the mill today as usual. Jane does have a slight bruise on her face from where Peter hit her. But as it happens, this worked out perfectly with our story."

"So nobody saw anything last night and is suspicious?" asked Jack.

"Nobody saw anything. They did hear the door breaking and the commotion, but it seems that wasn't uncommon. For all Peter's attempted secrecy about beating Jane behind closed doors, everybody knew. The walls weren't as soundproof as he thought. The whole street knew what he was doing, but people were too afraid to confront him, as he was very aggressive. They were also afraid that, if they got into any trouble, Mr Owens would hear of it, and they could lose their jobs. They all have families and couldn't take the chance. This morning, with the fresh bruise on Jane's face and what everybody already knew of the situation, they seem to be hoping it's all true. Certainly no one is looking for any other reason for Peter's disappearance."

"Then it appears it was a good plan." Jack gave a satisfied smile.

"Indeed," replied Bull. "It certainly seems to have put you in high spirits this morning."

"Mmmm." Jack gave a noncommittal answer and looked off

towards the hills. At his lack of reply and the ensuing silence, Bull started to grin broadly.

"Well, Skeiron needs some exercise, so I'd better get going," Jack said attempting to end the conversation and still not looking at Bull.

"Oh no you don't! You forget I know you too well. You're not getting out of here without spilling the beans. I know that look. Something happened last night, and I'm betting it involved a woman. C'mon, spill!" He nudged Jack in the arm with his elbow, hard enough to move him.

Jack laughed, recovering his balance. "There's nothing to tell. When I got back, I just stabled Skeiron and went to bed."

He moved around Bull and started walking towards his horse. Bull grabbed his arm and blocked his way.

"It'll go easier on you if you just talk now." He mimicked the words used in their many interrogations with enemies over the years.

Jack paused, a huge smile breaking over his face. "Okay, you win. You'd probably find out anyway."

He paused again, causing Bull to prompt, "And?"

"You must first swear to me none of this goes beyond us now – in protection of the lady."

At the use of the word *lady*, Bull's eyebrows arched in surprise. Jack could almost see the wheels turning in his head. There weren't too many women with that title around Calder Vale.

"It's Amanda," he bit out before he could help himself, his smile even wider if that were possible.

"You took Amanda to your bed!? With Owens in the house?!" Bull was impressed. "That took some balls."

"Not exactly," replied Jack, a rakish grin on his face. "The, um, encounter happened in the stable."

Bull whooped with surprise and slapped Jack's back. "In the hay, man, in the hay. Classic!"

"Okay, Bull." Jack raised his hands in surrender. "You got it out of me, but that's all I'm saying, and that's final."

Bull snapped to attention and mockingly saluted Jack. "Yes, Lieutenant Wolfe, sir!"

Both men laughed and walked back to the front of the mill, where Jack untied Skeiron.

"Let me know if anything changes," Jack said to Bull, swinging onto Skeiron's back. "I'm off for a ride to get this old girl fit for the trip. Too much rich food up at the big house stable has made her fat. I'm feeling it a bit myself," said Jack, rubbing his belly. "There's a party I have to attend tonight too. Some rich guy that's come to visit. Guess I'm being shown off as the man who saved Mr Owens."

Bull gave him a mock look of sympathy, making Jack laugh, and the two friends parted company.

The rest of Jack's day was mostly spent up on the moor. He rode for several steady miles. He didn't want to push Skeiron but needed her to start regaining her stamina for their long ride to Liverpool. He got back to the big house late in the afternoon. As he rode in, he kept a keen eye out for Amanda. He wasn't sure if he would see her but hoped he would. She had made quite an impression on him. Disappointed at still seeing no sign of her when he got back to the stable, he put Skeiron into one of the stalls and let the stable boy, who came running over, tend to her.

Jack then slowly made his way to his room, taking as long as possible. He was hoping he might finally bump into Amanda in the house, but she was nowhere in sight. When he could delay no longer, he went to his room to get freshened up and ready for the evening meal. Dinner parties normally didn't excite him but knowing he could be sure of seeing Amanda again did.

Once in his room, he was headed over towards the comfy chair in the corner when something on the bed caught his eye. It was a dark suit, a shirt, and a tie. He went over for a closer inspection and saw there was also a pair of polished shoes on the floor at the foot of the bed. Picking up the suit jacket, he turned it around in his hand. *Fancy*, he thought. A piece of paper fluttered to the floor. Jack laid the jacket back on the bed and bent to pick up the paper. It was a note from Judith Owens. "Jack, if it pleases you, you are more than welcome to wear this tonight." Jack smiled to himself. Mrs Owens truly was a gem. Heading back towards the chair, he plonked himself into the comfy material and stretched out to relax before the evening's events.

A good while later and feeling a bit less grateful to Mrs Owens, Jack made his way down for dinner, fidgeting in his new clothes. They fit him well enough but served only to remind him why he didn't like the confinement of suits or ties in the first place. As he entered the drawing room, he saw that he was the last to arrive. Mr Owens and the new house guest were over in the far corner of the room by the fireplace deep in conversation. Amanda was sitting with her mother on the sofa nearer the door. He was relieved to see there were no other, more local guests left over from the party the night before. He wasn't one for small talk. Jack had started towards Amanda when Owens noticed him and beckoned him over.

"Jack, I'd like you to meet Wilfred Caruthers. Wilfred, this is Jack Wolfe."

Jack held out his hand, and the two men shook. Caruthers was about the same age as Owens but looked harder. He had an air of arrogance, of somebody who had a lot of money and power and wasn't afraid to use either. He reminded Jack of the useless toffs who'd called themselves officers in the 17th Lancers.

"I've heard a lot about you. It seems you're quite a handy young man to have around."

"Well, thank you for saying, but I was just doing my job." Jack had to resist an urge to loosen his necktie. He felt uncomfortable in the man's presence.

"Yes. In the next few weeks, Jack's going to go over to the colonies and use his talents to see if he can get those ruffians to cooperate and increase my cotton supply."

"Then you'll miss the wedding," said Caruthers, leaning against the mantelpiece with a cocky attitude.

"What wedding's that?" asked, Jack feeling more irritated by the minute with the pompous man and the ridiculous turn the conversation was taking.

"One month from today, I will be walking down the isle of Blackburn Cathedral with the lovely Miss Owens."

Jack stared into the small coal fire, stunned, as he tried to absorb what the man was saying. The woman with whom he had been intimate with just last evening was to be married? To this, this old, arrogant, toff of a man? His mind raced. He couldn't imagine Amanda happily married to a man like this. He was totally confused and not sure if he was the butt of some sort of joke. The thought that he might be made him quickly regain his composure, and he was able to casually congratulate Caruthers rather than punching him. Just then, the butler announced that dinner was served, saving him from any further interaction with the man.

They all moved to the dining room and sat down at the table, with Caruthers, sitting next to a definitely subdued Amanda, opposite Jack. The dinner conversation was light and cheerful and moved along easily, but it was hard for Jack to keep his eyes off Amanda. He needed to find out what was going on but didn't want to arouse any suspicions and risk putting her in a compromised position. The richer classes didn't like their women to associate with the lower classes, and Caruthers was definitely from the elite class of society.

With the meal over, Jack went into the study with Mr Owens, while Caruthers stayed with the ladies. It looked like he would have to wait and try to speak to Amanda tomorrow to find out what was going on. After indicating a chair for Jack to sit down, Owens poured him a glass of whisky. Handing over the glass, he went behind his desk, opened a drawer, and pulled out a large leather wallet that Jack could see contained some documents. He placed the wallet in front of Jack. Owens then sat down behind his desk.

"Contained in that wallet," he began, "are the legal papers and power of attorney we discussed. There is also the information about your passage to America. Your ticket has been reserved, but you will have to purchase the ticket upon arrival at the docks in Liverpool. I have also included the plantation owner's address and, if you need it, the list of suppliers I have previously used in Charleston to transport my cargo." Owens then placed a smaller wallet in front of Jack. "This contains enough money for any eventuality you may have whilst representing me. Half is in American dollars."

Lastly, Owens unlocked a drawer to the side of his desk and pulled out an envelope with a large wax seal, tossing it on the desk. "Also, see that this gets delivered to the address written on the front before you leave New York." He sat back in his chair. "That should take care of everything, unless there's anything else you can think of?"

Jack took the letter and eyed the large crest embossed in the wax. "This is from Caruthers?" He looked Owens straight in the eye.

Owens nodded and looked slightly uncomfortable. Jack slid the letter into the larger wallet. Gathering both of the wallets in one hand, he paused, wanting to ask Owens what the fuck was happening with his daughter. Knowing he couldn't, he took a long sip of his whisky instead, the amber liquid burning its way down his throat.

"I think that covers everything." Jack stood, taking another hit off the whisky and trying to drown out the voice in his head that was still demanding answers about Amanda.

"Good," said Owens, standing also. He offered Jack his hand. "I probably won't see you again until after you get back from America. I will be leaving tomorrow afternoon to take care of some business that will keep me away for a few days."

Jack swigged the rest of his whiskey and took the offered hand.

"Good luck to you, my boy," said Owens.

"Thank you, Mr Owens," said Jack. "I won't let you down."

Picking up the two wallets he headed for the door. Once on the other side, he closed it behind him and let out the frustrated breath he hadn't even realised he'd been holding.

He went straight up to his room. The evening had been a bit of a blur. It was almost too much to take in. He sat on the edge of his bed and tried to make sense of what he'd learned. After a few minutes, he gave up, as it didn't seem to make sense at all. Lying down, he fell into a fitful sleep.

CHAPTER TEN

The next day, Jack went down for breakfast early as usual. He liked the early mornings and was most often alone when he ate. Today was no exception. After breakfast, he went over to the stables. Skeiron saw him come in and nickered. He absent-mindedly rubbed her nose while checking out the other stalls. The last two stalls that were reserved for guests' horses housed a matched pair of greys, meaning Caruthers was still at the house. With her fiancé there, he probably wouldn't manage to speak with Amanda, so it was no use hanging around. Jack saddled Skeiron and went down to the mill to carry out his duties.

Caruthers did finally leave that afternoon, but it was two days before Jack managed to speak to Amanda, and he could never have imagined the strange twist their meeting would take. As he was walking back to the house one evening after stabling Skeiron, he thought he heard a woman crying. He stopped and looked towards the large Lebanon cedar that stood on the manicured lawn to the side of the house. It was impossible to see under the tree, with its huge branches of green blue needles sweeping down to the ground. He walked over, and the crying got louder. Pushing a few of the smaller branches to the side,

Jack entered the hidden area under the tree. There was an old wooden bench encircling the trunk, and Amanda was sitting there with her head buried in her hands, sobbing uncontrollably. Jack moved over to her and sat down. He gently placed a hand on her arm.

"Hey, what's wrong?"

She hadn't heard his approach and visibly jumped. Seeing who it was brought more sobs. Jack just put his arm round her and said nothing. After a while, the sobbing subsided, and Amanda looked up.

"I suppose you hate me?" she said.

"Why would I hate you?"

"Because of what happened between us, and you finding out I am to be married like that. I should have told you myself."

"I confess to being a little confused, but I don't hate you."

His words seemed to ease her torment. With her emotions a bit more under control, she started to speak. "I've been promised to Caruthers for a long time. He's very rich, and our union will guarantee my father's estate for the next fifty years or more and elevate our family's status. I don't want to marry him, but it's a family obligation that I can't get out of. If I refuse to marry him, then he has enough power and influence to ruin my father. The man repulses me. When I was a little girl, I dreamed of marrying someone strong and handsome who I could love and be loved by and have a family," she paused. "Someone like you." She looked down, suddenly shy. "Nobody explained to me that's not how it works." She put her head in her hands, and sobs wracked her body again.

"I'm so sorry," said Jack, rubbing her arm to comfort her. "Is there anything I can do to help?"

At first, he didn't think she'd heard his question, but once she stopped crying and calmed down again, she answered, "It's so far beyond help. You must think I'm a whore. To be marrying someone and purposely have sex with you. What kind of woman does that make me?"

"A very unhappy one," said Jack.

"It was so selfish of me. I know I'll be spending the rest of my life with him. I just couldn't stand the thought of losing my virginity to a man I had no feelings for – someone who didn't look anything like the man I dreamed about as a little girl. You were everything I hoped for in a man. I'm sorry, but I just wanted one last bit of happiness, one last bit of something for me." She leaned against him, and Jack held her in his arms. Under the tree, they were in their own little world.

"What happens if you're pregnant?"

"I've thought about that," said Amanda. "It's so close to the wedding, a pregnancy won't be suspicious. People will just think it's his child."

"And what about me? If you are pregnant, do I have any say in what happens to my child?"

She bit her lip and looked up at him pleadingly. "Please don't make this any worse than it already is. If there is a child, it will not lack for anything. You know it will have a mother's love. I have to ask you not to say anything about this to anybody and for us to never meet again. I can't risk it. My father and mother would lose everything, and I would be in disgrace. If he even suspected anything Caruthers is so powerful he might hunt you down and do something horrible. Promise me you won't say a word."

Jack was silent for some time, thinking about what he was being asked to do. He could see the pain in Amanda's eyes, and he was a sucker for a woman's tears. "I give you my word to remain silent. I can't, however, promise to not come looking for you in the future. But if I do, I won't make any trouble. The only reason I'm consenting to your request to leave you alone is because I care for you, and I want to respect your wishes. If it were under any other circumstances, I would fight for you and I to be together."

Amanda started to sob again. "I've such mixed feelings. I'm filled with sadness that you and I will never be together but happy that I lost my heart and my virginity to a handsome and honourable man. Thank you, Jack."

They held each other under the tree until it was almost dark.

"I'd better go before somebody comes looking for me," Amanda said, starting to pull away. Jack reluctantly let her go.

They stood and with a final kiss and embrace, Amanda made her way back to the house. He watched her walk away until she was out of sight, full of very mixed feelings himself.

Jack left the next morning. It was a couple of days earlier than he'd planned. Truth was, he just wanted to get out of Calder Vale. The whole situation with Amanda wasn't sitting comfortably with him, but as there was nothing he could do, leaving it all behind seemed the best option. He had originally given himself three days to reach Liverpool, but the problems with Jane and Peter had meant Skeiron hadn't gotten the exercise she needed to be fit enough for such fast travel. Leaving a bit earlier would also allow them a more relaxed journey.

A day into the journey, Jack and Skeiron had been keeping an easy pace, and it looked like they were going to make good time. The weather was cooperating for once, and it wasn't raining. Rain seemed an almost constant feature of Lancashire. It was either warm and wet or cold and wet. He mused to himself that he shouldn't be surprised; the high rainfall and the damp conditions were why the mills had been built there in the first place. The rainfall filled all the streams and rivers, which drove the waterwheels and supplied the power for the looms. The constant damp conditions kept the threads that were being woven from drying out and snapping. Apart from having to journey there by ship, Jack was looking forward to being somewhere drier and warmer.

As Mr Owens had supplied him with ample funds for his journey, he was able to find lodgings along the way. It was not the time of year to be sleeping outside. On the morning of the fifth day, they reached the outskirts of Liverpool. It held no interest for him, with its buildings, people, and smog, it was just like all the other big cities he'd been to. Jack didn't like cities; he never had. Now, after his last few years of being in the Crimea and then the little village of Calder Vale, he liked them even less. They were dirty and smelly. The people were unfriendly, and he was forced to be constantly vigilant to make sure his horse and belongings weren't stolen. The nearer he got to the docks, the busier it got. There seemed an endless stream of horse-drawn wagons leaving and entering the port.

He finally found the offices of the steamship company and dismounted. Tying Skeiron to the rail, he went inside. Keeping one eye on his horse and gear through the window, Jack spoke to the man behind the desk about his reservation for passage to New York. After a brief conversation, he left the offices with his ticket purchased and all the other paperwork authorised. The ship wouldn't sail for another three hours, so he left the harbour area in the hope of finding somewhere that didn't smell. As he rode down along the riverbank, Jack was amazed at all the boats moving through the murky waters. There were ships bellowing smoke and others with sails. The traffic was constant, and so was the smell. It seemed like all the crap of the day was being washed passed. He did manage to find a slight promontory that afforded a little breeze that wasn't filled with the pungent smell of shit. However, this didn't last for long, so he gave up and made his way slowly back to the harbour and the ship.

By the time he arrived, it was only an hour until she sailed. Jack oversaw the loading of Skeiron and made his way up the gangplank to wait out the rest of the time onboard. The ship was very large and had a wooden deck, but the hull was made of steel. She had three funnels for coal smoke and also four masts, which the sails would be hung from. Whether the wind blew or not, this ship would continue on to her destination.

With 5,000 tonnes of cargo, most of the 357 passengers were in cramped conditions. Only the first-class passengers enjoyed fancy staterooms and elaborate dining quarters. Mr Owens, being a good customer of the shipping company with all his bales of cotton, had been able to secure Jack a single berthed cabin. Or, connections aside, the availability of Jack's accommodations was simply due to the fact that few people wanted to be on a ship on the Atlantic during Christmas. *Owens probably got it for a bargain*, he thought wryly. The cabin was still in the bowels of the ship, but it gave him the privacy and security he wanted. After finding his cabin and leaving his saddlebags in the small but comfortable room, he headed back up to the deck. Even in December, the bowels of the ship were uncomfortably hot from the steam engines.

Standing by the rail, he watched as people scurried around the harbour side. From where he stood, it looked like chaos. But he imagined there must be some sort of order to it all. Finally, the last of the passengers boarded, the gangplank was raised, and the thick heavy ropes, untied. They were on their way. The smoke billowed out of the funnels as the engines were engaged, and the paddle wheels dug into the water. Once the ship picked up speed, the air started to clear. Jack stood at the rail breathing it in, watching the land recede into the distance. When it became too cold to stand outside any longer, he took one last gulp of the fresh air and descended the ladder-like stairs to return to his cabin.

The days passed slowly, but he quickly settled into the ship's routine – breakfast at nine, lunch at 1, and an evening meal at six. Miss a mealtime, and you just had to wait for the next one. The only change to the daily routine was on one day, and one day only; in recognition of Christmas Day, the dining room had a few decorations on the walls, and there was a minor improvement in the food.

Once the ship had rounded the coast of Ireland and headed off across the Atlantic, there was nothing more to see – just lots of water. Being so far from land made Jack uneasy. He split his spare time between the deck, his cabin, and checking on Skeiron. The only time he really spoke to anybody was at mealtime. It was good to get information about America, and even more interesting was the other passenger's impressions of the now seemingly inevitable upcoming conflict between the Northern and the Southern states. The North supported maintaining the union of all states, while the South wanted to secede and form its own government. The whole situation had erupted around legislation ending the enslavement of black workers. It would seem that his trip might be even more eventful than he'd first thought.

It was at one of these mealtimes, in a rare moment while Jack happened to be sitting alone, watching the world go by, that his attention was caught by a steward bringing out food. He was walking away so Jack couldn't see his face, but there was something about the man that he thought he recognised. Curious, he went to get some of the food that had been laid out hoping for a better look.

While queuing, he spotted the same man at the back of the kitchen area. He still couldn't see the steward's face but kept watching him in the hopes he'd turn around. Unfortunately, he never did. By the time Jack had gotten to the front of the queue, taken his food, and returned to his table, the man had disappeared again. Sitting down, he tried to think of where he might have seen him. Was it on the street? Had he seen him at the harbour before the boat sailed? No, this was more. He had seen him somewhere, and the encounter had stood out enough for Jack to remember the man. He finished his food and headed back to his cabin. Lying on his bunk, he kept mulling over who this man was and where he had seen him. He fell asleep with these thoughts still unanswered.

The next morning, Jack went for breakfast and kept an eye out but there was no sign of the man. He liked to solve puzzles, and as there were two more days to go before the ship docked in New York, investigating this puzzle would help pass the time.

His first stop was the purser's office to try to get a name. The purser controlled the money on the ship. If anybody had a list of the crew, it would be him. Knocking on the door, Jack got no reply. He knocked again and tried the handle. The door opened, and he found himself in a small office. Cabinets lined one wall. Jack opened the first one. It was full of names and numbers relating to the cargo the ship was carrying. The second was full of insurance and legal documents. Looking through the third one, he hit pay dirt. It contained the crews' files. *Third times a charm*, he thought.

A quick rummage turned up a file with several copies of the master list of all the crew members' names. Slipping one into his jacket pocket, he made his exit. Nobody seemed to be around, so he made his way back to his cabin.

Sitting on his bunk, he surveyed the list. Somewhat dismayed, he saw there had to be over 300 names on the list. Reading them one at a time, Jack looked for any name that stood out. It took him over an hour to read the list and only two names caught his attention. They were fairly common names, and after a few minutes of searching his brain, he could put faces to these names. Both were men he had served with, but neither was this mystery man.

Jack studied the list again. There were letters beside each name. He tried to work out a meaning, but nothing seemed to make sense. His other option, of course, was to ask around the other members of the crew but he was reluctant, as they might not take too kindly to a stranger asking questions. When he had sailed back from the Crimea, he had spent a fair amount of time with the crew. They had told him that being a crewman on a ship was a great way to avoid the police. Some of the men he talked to were even wanted for minor offences. They just stayed aboard a ship and moved from country to country.

"If you ain't got a front door, they can't come knocking on it" was the motto. Jack could see their logic.

This thought brought him back to his present dilemma – how to ask the right questions without getting thrown overboard by a wanted man who mis-took Jack for the law! At the moment, his best chance was to see if he could figure out who the man was by simply observing him more carefully. It was nearing lunchtime, so Jack made his way to the dining room and positioned himself to get a good view of the room and kitchen area. But lunch came and went, and he never appeared.

With so many dead ends, his enthusiasm for his latest quest was waning. He decided to wander around the ship a few more times in the hope they would cross paths and to stave off the return of his boredom, and then go and see how Skeiron was doing.

After his two laps of the ship and no luck, Jack welcomed the time with Skeiron. This investigation was turning out to be a dud. He needed cheering up, and she always seemed to lift his spirits. He gave her some fresh water and started grooming her. His mind continued to puzzle over where he had seen the man before, but to no avail. While he groomed her, several crewmen came and went. At one point on a walkway above, Jack saw two of the men talking. With the rumble of the engines reverberating through the ship, it was difficult to hear what they were saying. What he was sure about was they were speaking Bulgarian.

The two men parted company, and Jack continued to groom. But there was something in the back of his brain that wouldn't stop nagging at him. While he he cleaned and checked her feet, his mind drifted back to the war and the Bulgarian fighters who had been stationed near his camp. Hearing the crewmen's voices had brought back images of the war. Jack shook his head to clear away the shocking images of the dead and dying strewn over the battlefield all his thinking had stirred up.

Finishing up with Skeiron, he went onto the deck. He was hoping the cold wind would clear his mind. As he stood against the rail, his thoughts went back to the war again. Frustrated with not being able to shake the memories, he went to the dining room. He hoped there would be other passengers there with whom he could engage in conversation to take his mind off his past.

It turned out he was in luck. Several people were milling about, and a few of the tables had people already sitting, talking together. Jack saw a man with whom he'd had dinner several days earlier. He was a likeable fellow with the gift of the gab, who was going to New York on business. He walked over and sat down. The man immediately started talking up a storm. Jack engaged him in conversation and managed to successfully push his nagging thoughts to the side.

The late afternoon spent chit-chatting about nothing in particular led to dinner being served, and the men ate together. The man then excused himself and left.

Jack stayed for a little while longer then he too left and went back to his cabin. The moment his door was shut, the memories came flooding back. To try to take his mind off it, he pulled out the crew list and glanced over it again. This time, six names jumped off the pages. They didn't mean anything to him, but they were all Bulgarian names. Against two of them was the letter *s*. He now wondered if the letters were job titles – *s* for steward? He decided to go and see the purser straight away and find out. The ship would be docking at lunchtime the following day, and the purser would then undoubtedly be too busy to see him. His progress stalled again when he got to the office. There was a note on the door saying the purser would be returning at nine the following morning. Frustrated at not finding the purser but happier now he had a plan, Jack went back to his cabin.

As it was the night before Jack was due to disembark from the ship, he decided to check his belongings and repack his bags. He didn't have many possessions with him, but they still needed to be organised into his saddlebags for his onward journey. Fishing out the two wallets from the bottom of one of the saddlebags, he laid them beside him on the bed. First, he opened the small wallet with his money, took out half the bills, and tucked them into his boot. He then took several more bills and put them into his jacket pocket. Money secured, he unfolded the larger wallet to check all the papers were in order. Satisfied all was there, he removed the letter he was to deliver for Caruthers in New York. As he set it down on the bed, the wax seal sprang open. The seal itself was intact but had come unstuck from the rest of the envelope.

Jack was now in a slight predicament. With the seal being open, the recipient of the letter would assume Jack had opened it and become privy to its contents. They would almost surely notify Caruthers, who would then probably tell Mr Owens that Jack had read the letter. This concerned Jack, as he had a good relationship with Mr Owens that he didn't want to jeopardise. Looking around his cabin for a solution, he saw the candle on his nightstand. He thought to himself that, if he could soften the wax without burning the paper, he could conceivably stick the wax seal back down, and nobody would be any the wiser.

Picking up the letter, he noticed it was addressed to a Mr Merris. It felt damp. The combination of the sea air and the warm temperature in his cabin must have moistened the paper and made the seal come apart. He would now have to carefully dry the paper before resealing the wax. Lighting the candle, Jack unfolded the letter so he could thoroughly dry the paper. With the letter unfolded, Jack couldn't help but read some of the words on the paper. With words like *military* and *blueprint* jumping off the page, it was no surprise his interest was piqued.

Being an honourable man, he wouldn't normally read what was written on a private letter, but these intriguing words and the fact he didn't like Caruthers prompted him to read further.

Jack read the letter three times to make sure he had fully understood what was written. Caruthers, it appeared, was happily offering his services to the Union Army should they go to war with the South. This was of no concern to Jack. If it came to war, he had no allegiance to either side. What did concern Jack as a British citizen and former soldier was that Caruthers was willing to sell confidential government blueprints of precision milling machines that would be used to manufacture new advanced weapons. Caruthers also pointed out that he was close to important British politicians, hinting that he would be willing to sell the recipients of the letter any useful information he came across and use his influence for a price. Both of these things would amount to acts of treason. And, if relations between Great Britain and America broke down again, as in 1812, these weapons could then be used against British soldiers in any conflict that erupted. For Jack, that was the ultimate betrayal.

He now faced a real dilemma. If he delivered the letter, he would be helping a traitor and possibly endangering British soldiers. If he didn't deliver the letter, he was sure Caruthers would exert pressure on Mr Owens to have Jack fired and possibly anybody associated with him. Leaving on bad terms would make it very difficult to have any involvement with the child Amanda could be carrying, and Bull and Elly might end up caught in the crossfire too. Jack decided, in light of the possible fallout, it was best to deliver the letter. But he would, upon his return to England, inform Mr Owens of what he had found out about Caruthers, in the hopes he knew the right people to speak to and have Caruthers arrested before he could do any damage. Of course, that would mean the arrest of Amanda's husband, but those hurdles would all have to be dealt with in future. Right now, he just had to get that seal stuck again.

As Jack dried the paper over the candle, he kept wondering to himself if he should just let it burn. With the concern for his friend and his possible child still at the front of his mind, he carefully, if not begrudgingly, completed his task. Once the paper was dry and folded, he warmed the wax and pressed the two surfaces together. A few seconds of pressure on the seal, and he was relieved to see the two surfaces firmly stick when he released it. Placing it back on the bed, he packed the rest of his belongings into his saddlebag, slid the letter into the outside pocket, and fastened down the cover. Ready to leave the ship, he lay down on his bunk and looked at the names on the crew list one last time and then went to sleep. He was going to make sure he was at the purser's office before nine and get to see him first.

Jack slept badly. The images of the war just wouldn't leave him.

He hadn't been this troubled for many years. The two overwhelming images were of Bull holding the bloody lifeless body of his wife and the man with his face covered in blood that he had shot after the attack on the girl in the farmhouse. Next morning, Jack woke and dressed quickly, glad to be getting off the ship. The claustrophobic conditions alone were starting to make him feel quite ill –never mind the constant rolling of the hull. The seas did seem calmer this morning, which he was grateful for.

After his night of fitful sleep, he somewhat wearily climbed the stairs up to the purser's office. He was quite early, but the purser's door was already open. Knocking, he walked in.

"Can I help you?" said a man in ship's uniform.

"I'm looking for the purser."

"That would be me," replied the man.

"I'm needing to talk to a couple of your crew members. I think they are stewards."

"That could be a problem," replied the purser. Jack steeled himself to hold his ground and demand to see the men. "They left the ship this morning."

"What do you mean?" asked Jack, confused.

"We made good time across the Atlantic and arrived six hours early. All non-essential crew were given permission to leave the ship."

Jack felt deflated. His mystery would seemingly remain unsolved. Thanking the purser for his time, he went back to his cabin to pack his belongings. No wonder the seas seemed calmer. They were tied to the dock!

Gathering his gear together, he went to the hold to make sure Skeiron was getting properly attended to. As he entered the livestock area, he saw another crewmember and decided to try to ask a few more questions before he left. At least if the crew threw him overboard now he wouldn't have far to swim.

"Excuse me," started Jack. "I was wondering if you know any of the Romanian or Bulgarian men who work on the ship?"

"What's it to ya?" came back the gruff voice.

"I'm sure I know one of them, possibly served alongside him in the Crimean War. I saw him the other day but couldn't get to speak to him."

This explanation seemed to put the man at ease. "Yeah, I know a couple of them. Weird little fuckers. Pretty much kept to themselves."

"How do you mean, weird?"

"They would have these religious ceremonies or something, sitting around rocking backwards and forwards and mumbling this weird language. They had these brown bottles they kept drinking from. One of our guys sneaked into their stuff when they were on duty and stole one of the bottles. He thought it was booze, but this reddy brown treacle came out. Strangest thing I ever saw. He was so disgusted he threw it overboard. We had a good laugh at that one."

"Is there anything else that stands out?"

"Not really, one of them walked funny …like he'd hurt his back or something, but that's it."

"Thanks," said Jack, making his way topside.

Standing on the harbour side in the chilly December wind, he reflected on what the crewmember had said. It didn't seem to help him identify the man he'd seen at all. He heard a nicker and saw Skeiron had been unloaded. Her warm breath made clouds in the air as she stamped her feet, in anticipation of her newfound freedom on land. It was time to go.

After leaving the ship, Jack asked one of the dockside workers if he knew of 22 Cortland Street, the address on the front of the letter. Luckily, the man was agreeable and knew the area. With directions in hand, Jack set off to the location. Making his way through the slushy streets of melting snow, mud, and horseshit, he soon arrived at his destination, as it was only several blocks away. He sat on Skeiron's back, looking over the property and trying to prepare for what might be awaiting him. The building was a four-storey limestone townhouse on a wide street and seemed well kept. Like most of the other buildings on the street, the windowsills were piled with snow and long icicles hung from the roof. He was relieved to see it wasn't down some dark alley with danger lurking at every turn. Jack dismounted. As he was contemplating his next action a street ruffian came up to him.

"Watch your horse, sir?"

Jack looked him over assessing him.

"Yes, "Jack pulled the reins away when the boy reached for them and watched his reaction. Seeing no cunning or avarice, and satisfied the boy was relatively honest, he handed the reins over to him along with a silver shilling.

"If my horse is here when I get out there will be a gold crown as your reward." The boy's eyes grew wide with surprise but he quickly recovered.

"Yes sir!"

"And, I may need to get away quickly so be alert and stay right here." The boy nodded eagerly. As further incentive Jack removed the the gold coin to show the lad and put it in his pocket so he could find it easily. Satisfied that the promise of a month's wages would keep his horse safe he made his way to the door.

At the right of the generously proportioned wooden door was a polished brass plaque that bore the number 22. Jack used the matching large brass door knocker to announce his presence. Alert for what might await him on the other side, he waited tense and impatient, keen to conclude this miserable business before heading south. He was pulled from his thoughts by the door opening.

A small man in a brown suit and round glasses peered out from behind the door, looking up and down the street before addressing Jack. His eyes met Jack's, assessing. "Can I help you?"

Jack started to relax as he took in this harmless-looking man. "I'm here from England to deliver a letter to a Mr Merris."

"Please come in," was the only reply.

The small man stepped back and opened the door, and Jack entered into the front lobby of the building. As his eyes adjusted to the gloom, he could see a wide staircase leading to the upper floors. The man in the brown suit walked towards a desk situated at the back next to the stairs. Reaching behind the desk, he pulled on a cord that produced the faint sound of a bell ringing somewhere above. Still cautiously standing just inside the door, Jack could hear footfalls approaching. He looked up to see two men coming down the stairs. Observing them, his senses went on high alert. Both of these men also wore suits, but they looked to be made of coarser wool. One of the men was thickset, with a drooping moustache and the physique of a fighter. The other man was slightly taller and thinner but carried an air of danger. This situation, Jack realised, was rapidly getting complicated. The men stopped at the bottom of the stairs and stared at Jack. The man in the brown suit walked back towards Jack with more confidence at having his goons close at hand.

"I'm Mr Glynn, Mr Merris's personal secretary. I'll take that letter," he said, holding out his hand.

Without taking his eyes off the two men at the bottom of the stairs Jack handed over the letter and immediately took two paces backwards until he could feel the cold door handle in his back. He felt no compunction to engage any further in what was clearly a dodgy situation. Jack was no coward, but his gut was telling him he could be in extreme danger. Knowing the contents of the letter, he suspected that these men were not here to be friendly. Discreetly feeling for the handle behind him he grabbed it and pushed down.

The two men sensing his intention to leave started to move towards him with purpose. Not wanting to find out what that purpose was, Jack whirled around, pulled open the door, stepped through, and slammed it behind him. He was relieved to see the lad with Skeiron right where he'd left them. Hurrying to his horse, he tossed the gold coin to the boy, mounted and rode away at a fast clip, quickly losing himself in the chaos of the busy city streets. He could see no signs of pursuit and imagined that they hadn't anticipated he'd have arrived on horseback. He patted Skeiron's neck; once again, she had given him a huge advantage in dealing with his enemies.

When he was sure no one was following him, he slowed to a walk to give his horse a much-needed rest. The journey on the boat hadn't been too kind to Skeiron. Her coat was dull, and she was much thinner than she had been when they boarded. They both were for that matter. He guessed horses maybe got seasick too. Not wanting to push her too hard but wanting to put as many miles between himself and 22 Cortland Street as quickly as possible, he set a slow but steady pace.

As the distance grew Jack relaxed his guard and began to reflect on the strangeness of what had happened. As far as the men knew, he was just a messenger. The letter was sealed and unread. Trying to make sense of it, Jack could come up with only two possible reasons for their aggressive behaviour. The first was that whatever business they were involved in was so secret and illegal that they viewed any outsider who knew their address or identities as a threat that needed to be eliminated. The second possibility was that Caruthers had told them to do him physical harm. And if so, why? Had Caruthers found out about what had happened between Jack and Amanda? Or, for some unknown reason, did he seek to weaken Mr Owens's business by stopping Jack from securing more raw cotton?

He shook his head in frustration. At the moment, without more information, he could make neither head nor tail of it. His dwelling on it wouldn't solve anything now and could prove a costly distraction, so Jack put the incident out of his mind but promised himself he would stay vigilant, especially when he returned to England.

He looked around, for what seemed like the first time. An involuntary shiver ran through him from the cold nipping at his face. With concentrating on finding the address to deliver the letter and then his subsequent rushed departure, he hadn't registered how cold it actually was. Lancashire got its fair share of snow and ice, but this was something else. Lancashire's snow was wet and soggy and melted quite quickly, along with the ice. The snow here blanketed everything and was at least four inches deep on windowsills, railings, and even the standing carriages. The covering of snow, along with all the icicles hanging from various places, reminded Jack of something he'd once read about in a Dickens book – although, if you looked more closely, you could see a fine layer of soot gathering on the surface that he imagined would only get blacker as the day wore on. If it weren't for the worrying encounter he'd just had at Cortland Street, he would be enjoying this temporary winter wonderland.

Other than its coating of snow, New York seemed like all the big cities across Europe he had travelled through, except, he surmised, the streets were wider, and the horse-drawn carriages were certainly much bigger. In fact, everything seemed much bigger. The one thing the cities did have in common was that they were all smelly, dark with smoke, and noisy. The exact opposite of what he loved – the open fresh skies of the countryside. Skeiron, he sensed had similar thoughts, as the moment they cleared the worst of the built-up areas, she gained a little extra spring in her step. They headed south. Jack had made up his mind that he was going to ride Skeiron to the plantation and not take the train. Just the thought of the train sent a shiver down his spine. The last time he'd been on one had nearly cost him his life and the life of Skeiron.

They had been on a troop transport heading across Europe to the Crimea when the train had derailed. The carnage that followed was something he had never forgotten. A heavy rain the night before had washed out part of the embankment that held up the rails. With nothing underneath to support them, the rails gave way as the train crossed over, and caused the heavy engine to roll onto its side spewing steam and smoke. This then had created a chain reaction in which each of the following carriages also rolled over. The carriages that housed the troops had come apart, their sides and roofs crumpling in on them as if made of paper. The carriage that Jack was riding in had split open along the seam of the roof. Fortunately, he had been sitting on what became the lower side of the carriage and so he had not been thrown far.

The not-so-fortunate soldiers on the top side had been flung violently sideways and smashed onto the roof of the now upturned carriage. Still, Jack hadn't escaped unscathed. Although not being thrown very far himself, he had been hit by the debris of the carriage and the falling soldiers. When he finally managed to extricate himself from the mess, he started to help the wounded. Being a military transport, the survivors managed to organise quickly and got all the men, dead and alive, out in pretty rapid time. The wounded were taken over to a makeshift field hospital the medical unit had hastily set up close by.

Having done all he could for the men, Jack had then gone back down the length of the train to the livestock cars in search of his horse. He could see that, being at the back of the train, they had faired a little better. Some of the cars were even still on their wheels.

His concern rose when he saw the one Skeiron was in had not been so lucky. Due to its more robust construction, it was practically intact, with only a few broken boards. But it was lying on its side. Now that he was closer, Jack realised no sounds were coming from inside. His mind filled with dread as he climbed onto the side of the stock car. After a few minutes of desperate effort, he managed to pull open the sliding door. Looking into the shadowy interior, he found it eerily silent and hard to make out anything. Once his eyes adjusted to the dim light, he could start to make out the various shapes of the horses. His dread increased when he saw none of them were moving. Jack could also see some were obviously dead, as they had parts of the broken train car protruding from them.

Looking towards the front he finally located Skeiron. She was lying motionless on her side. But his spirits lifted with hope that she had been only stunned by the force of the crash when he couldn't see any visible signs of injury. Filled with trepidation, he called out her name.

Instantly, her head lifted, and she looked straight at him. Jack couldn't believe it. She seemed totally fine. It was as if she had known he would come for her and so had decided just to wait until he arrived. Unsure of whether she could understand him, he told her to lie still and that he would be back.

Lowering himself back off the stock car, he rushed off to find some men to help get Skeiron out. Arriving back after a few minutes, the soldiers set to work pulling the boards off the car that had been broken and levering off the others. Once they had a big enough opening, Jack called Skeiron. After something of a struggle, she managed to extricate herself from the tangled mass and, on shaky legs, emerged from the hole. As she appeared, the soldiers cheered. They had a minor victory to celebrate – a moment of triumph in what had been a terrible day. Jack thanked the men and started to look over Skeiron more closely to be sure she was all right. She, like Jack, had escaped virtually unscathed.

Shaking his head to rid himself of the memory, Jack concentrated back on the present. He knew getting to the plantation on horseback would take him much longer, more than a month. But after being relatively inactive in Calder Vale while he recuperated and spending ten days on a ship, he was looking forward to the freedom of the outdoors and riding his horse. He had never seen this vast land before and wanted to experience the countryside as he rode. He also thought that he would get a better sense of how things operated here and how people thought on his more leisurly journey. This knowledge could give him an advantage handling Mr Owens' business when meeting the plantation owner and shipping companies.

He decided the first chance he got he would send Mr Owens a letter and explain that he may take a little longer to arrive at the plantation but that, in the interests of making sure this venture was a success, he would be taking the safer, more comfortable option and riding his horse and not the rails. That sounded believable to Jack, and as Owens wasn't there to argue the point and make Jack take the train, it seemed that was a reasonable thing to say. Besides, before he'd left, Owens hadn't specifically instructed him to take the train!

It's settled then, he thought. Feeling satisfied, he nudged Skeiron into a light canter, looking forward to the ride ahead.

CHAPTER ELEVEN

February 1861
Two months before the start of the American Civil War

Six weeks after arriving in New York, Jack finally crossed the border into Georgia. The weather had improved with every week that passsed and although it was still chilly in the mornings, they had left the serious cold and snow flurries behind. He'd enjoyed his time riding Skeiron. They had both been cooped up on the ship for too long. She seemed to enjoy the daily ride too, stepping out in high spirits each morning no matter how tired she'd finished up the night before. He'd slept where he could, often ending up in the hayloft of a farmer's barn, where there was room for his horse. A week into his journey, Jack had decided to head straight for the plantation rather than to the suppliers in Charleston. During his hours in the saddle, he'd reasoned that, if he could negotiate directly with the plantation owner, there was a chance he could cut out the middleman and save Mr Owens even more money.

The Jarrell plantation, where he was now heading, was about seventy miles south of Atlanta, just outside a little town called Juliette.

It was owned and operated by John Fitz Jarrell. He had thirty-nine slaves and shipped most of his raw cotton overland to Charleston, where it went by ship to England.

Jack was about a two days ride away when he ran into trouble.

"Get off the horse, Yankee," drawled the voice from somewhere in the trees.

He pulled Skeiron to a halt in the middle of the road and sat still, trying to figure out where the voice was coming from. The woods along both the sides of the road were so dense Jack couldn't see anybody.

"I said get off the damn horse."

"No," said Jack.

"Waddya mean *no*?" shouted the man. "I have the gun, and I make the rules. Now get off the fucking horse before I shoot you off it."

"No," repeated Jack.

For just a split second, he thought he could hear laughter. There was silence for several moments. Skeiron stamped her foot with impatience at the flies that had started to settle on her. Jack thought he had worked out where the voice was coming from but still wasn't sure whether or no the man was alone.

At that moment, a second man stepped out from behind a tree on the opposite side of the road from where Jack thought the voice had come from. He was dressed quite well and had a pistol in his hand but hanging by his side.

"I'd be much obliged if you would dismount so we can talk. My friend over there," said the man, waving his arm across the road, "might not be the best at conversation. But he can shoot a flea in the ass at 100 yards."

With his options running out Jack had to make a decision. This man was no more than twenty yards away and was armed with a pistol, well within killing range. His accomplice was almost certainly armed with a rifle. His adrenaline began flowing as he made his decision. Digging his heels into Skeiron's side he headed straight for the man with the pistol. Jack was counting on two things. The man with the pistol would be taken by surprise and not shoot, and the man with the rifle, not the quickest thinker Jack hoped, would be too afraid he might hit the other man to shoot. The plan was working. The man with the pistol quickly dove out of the way, and his compatriot didn't shoot. However, as Jack entered the treeline, a third man stepped out from behind a large tree and swung his rifle, hitting Jack square in the chest and knocking him clean off his horse.

That was when the plan fell apart. Lying there on his back, Jack was suddenly surrounded by about ten men. *So much for there being only two*, he thought as he was lifted off the ground.

They carried him off into the woods for several hundred yards before they unceremoniously dumped him on the ground in their camp. They then roughly took away his rifle and the knife at his belt. The man with the pistol came over and looked down at Jack.

"I did ask nicely," he said with a wry grin.

"It's not in my nature to do as I'm told," said Jack.

At this statement, a quizzical look spread across the other man's face.

"English?"

"Yes."

"Hey, Cyrus! You dumb fucker. He's not a Yankee. He's English."

"Well, I knew he wasn't from around here. He dresses funny," Cyrus yelled back from the woods, somewhere in the direction of the road. The man held out his hand to help Jack up. Jack took the offered hand and stood.

"What are you doing down here?" the man asked.

Jack was about to tell him it was none of his damn business but decided to hold his tongue now that the odds were ten to one. "I'm heading to Juliette to the Jarrell plantation. I'm needing to see the man about buying his cotton. I have papers to prove it in my saddlebags if you want to see them. Why are you interested?"

"Coffee?" the man said ignoring Jack's question. He walked away from Jack and sat down on a log.

Jack took the opportunity to survey his surroundings. He was in the middle of a well-camouflaged camp. After a few minutes, he walked over to join the other man and sat opposite the glowing fire. The man handed him a cup.

"I'm Jesse," he said.

"Jack," replied Wolfe.

"We've got trouble coming," he began. "The damn Yankees are trying to tell us how to live our lives and who we can and can't sell our cotton to. They have all their big fancy factories up north and don't want us selling our cotton to England because they want it all for themselves. This wouldn't be so bad, except they aren't always willin' to pay the best price. We say we'll sell it to whoever we damn well please, and they can go fuck themselves. They keep sending spies down here to get information about what we're doing and also to try to sway the opinion of the plantation owners. It looks like we're going to war to protect our way of life. We thought you might be a Yankee spy. You wouldn't be the first one we caught."

Jack relaxed a little. These were fighting men – the type of men he knew well.

"I came over from England about two months ago," he explained, "landed in New York. Rode my horse down here to see if I could make a deal with John Fitz Jarrell. Didn't expect to get caught up in another war."

"What do you mean another war?"

"I served in the Crimean War. I was a cavalry officer attached to the 17th Lancers."

"Believe it or not, I'm a cavalry man. I fought with the US Cavalry against the Mexicans. I've also studied cavalry tactics and read any papers or books on the subject I can get my hands on. Wasn't it the 17th Lancers who rode in the Charge of the Light Brigade?"

"Yeah, we were there. I'm not sure what the books you've read say, but it was a complete slaughter. We attacked the wrong target and got blown to pieces."

"From what I've read, it does appear to have been a foolhardy mission, but it did say the men showed great skill and tenacity in the face of overwhelming odds."

"We lost some good men that day," Jack answered, his voice a bit gruff from emotion.

Just then, Cyrus came walking into camp, leading Skeiron. Jesse looked over.

"That's quite some animal you have there. The way she took off at me I thought I was a goner for sure."

Jack smiled. "She's my pride and joy. She was with me through the war. We've ridden together for over ten years. We both should have been dead more times than I care to remember."

"Looks like I've got a horse to sell!" shouted Cyrus. "Gonna take her to ol' man Hendricks livery and get me some money. After that, I'm gonna get me a steak, some whisky, an' a woman!"

"I don't think you want to be doing that," shouted Jesse.

"I think I do. I'm sick of eating biscuits and squirrels," retorted Cyrus.

"Will you excuse me a minute?" said Jack, standing and walking over to Cyrus.

Jesse just shook his head and waited for the sparks to fly.

Jack stood in front of Cyrus, blocking his path. "That's my horse," he said, giving a nod towards Skeiron.

"Not anymore," said Cyrus, pulling a long skinning knife from his belt and waving the knife in Jack's face.

Jack just reacted on instinct. He grabbed hold of the hand holding the knife. Lifting the hand and knife in the air, he pushed against Cyrus. The momentum carried them both back until Cyrus's back was touching Skeiron's side. With his free hand Jack reached over Cyrus's shoulder towards his bedroll and found the hilt of his sabre. Pulling out the long blade, Jack stepped back. With the weapon pointed at Cyrus, he looked him in the eyes.

"Let's start this conversation again. That's my horse."

A little less certain now but not wanting to lose face in front of the others, Cyrus boldly retorted, "And I said not anymore."

"How do you expect to eat your steak with no teeth?"

A confused look came across Cyrus's face. "I've got tee—"

Jack flicked the sabre out of Cyrus's face so the point was facing straight up. Cyrus followed the movement of the blade and looked up. Thinking this was a sign Jack was giving up, his lips parted in a grin. The second that happened Jack powered forward and smashed the metal hand guard of the sabre into Cyrus's mouth. He howled in pain and fell to the ground. Jack stepped back and took up a defensive stance as Cyrus moaned on the ground. The other men who had been watching the exchange pulled a variety of weapons and advanced towards Jack.

"Leave him!" shouted Jesse.

The men stopped moving but didn't lower their weapons.

"I said leave him! He gave him fair warning of what would happen. It was his horse that Cyrus was wanting to sell."

The men looked at Jack and then Jesse. Then most of them laughed at the unfortunate Cyrus. Two of the men helped him up and took him away.

"Is it always this entertaining around you?" asked Jesse.

Jack just grinned and returned his sabre to his bedroll. Sitting by the fire again, Jesse poured more coffee.

"Where did you say you were heading?"

"I'm heading for a plantation just outside Juliette. The address was given to me by my boss. Do you know of it?"

"No, can't say I've heard of the plantation, only the town itself." Jesse took another swig of coffee. "I live about five miles away from here at a place called Covington. I'd say you're still forty miles shy of Juliette."

"At least I'm going in the right direction. What's the chance of running into more men like yourselves?"

"There are a few more groups like us scattered around, some more official than others. It's hard to say. I'd be more worried about the next few months. It looks like war's coming, and if that happens, suspicions will be even higher. If you're not in uniform, you're going to be a suspect."

Jack stood and offered Jesse his hand. Now that the confrontation was over, he was itching to get back on the road.

"I'm glad my horse didn't kill you," Jack said, giving Jesse a wry smile. "I've enjoyed our conversation."

"I'm just glad I was quick enough to get out of the way," was Jessie's sardonic reply.

They shook hands. Jack walked across the camp, picked up his rifle and knife, mounted Skeiron, and was gone.

It was mid-afternoon the following day when he entered the town of Juliette. It was small but not without some charm. New red brick buildings were interspersed with older faded wooden ones. Jack headed towards the general store. Tying Skeiron to the rail, he entered. The bell above the door jingled, and an elderly man wearing a white apron appeared from a back room.

"How can I help you, young feller?" he asked.

"I'm looking for directions to the Jarrell plantation."

"That's an easy one." The old man came from behind the counter and shuffled over to the door. Pointing into the street, he said, "You see the church on the corner with the tall white steeple?"

Jack nodded in the affirmative.

"Well you take a right there onto Oak Lane and follow that for about five miles. The plantation comes up on your left. Can't miss it."

"Famous last words," Jack said jokingly.

"Don't worry. You really can't miss it. He's got a sign and everything."

"Thanks."

"Can I interest you in buying anything?"

"No, I think I'm good."

"I see you don't carry a sidearm. I have some nice ones I could sell you. I've even got the new Colt Navy if you're interested."

"Are you just being a good salesman or do you think I need one?" said Jack good-naturedly.

"Most folks around here carry a sidearm of some description. I see you carry a long gun on your horse" he added with a nod to Skeiron. "All well and good if you need only one shot and your quarry is a long way away. But what happens if there's more than one, and you're in some drinking house?" The old man shuffled behind the counter and opened a glass display unit. "This is the Colt Navy 1861," he said, handing over a pistol. "It's just been released. It's a little shorter than its predecessor, the Navy 1851, and has lighter recoil. They tell me that, when they trialled it in the army, it was the cavalry guys who favoured it. Said the lighter recoil made it easier to fire while on the move."

Jack felt the gun in his hand. It was heavy, and he was sure it weighed over two pounds. He wasn't sure he wanted to be carrying this much weight around all the time. He did, however, see the need to protect himself and, after his meeting in the woods with Jesse and his cohorts, could see the merits of being better prepared. Also, the mention that cavalrymen preferred it piqued his interest.

"How much is it?"

"Twenty dollars."

"I'm guessing the ammunition is extra."

"Unfortunately, it is," agreed the man.

Jack considered it. He had money left from what Mr Owens had given him for travelling, and the money from his wages was still untouched. He was nearly at his destination and, according to Owens, would be housed and fed once he reached the plantation. He was tempted to spend the money.

"Who's the best shot in town with a pistol?"

"I'm proud to say my nephew." The old man beamed. "He's a good shot and a fast draw ... Why?"

"I'll make you a deal. I'll give you twenty-five dollars for your pistol, bullets, and a holster. I do, however, want your nephew to teach me how to shoot. If I'm gonna buy something, I want to know how to use it, and it seems like he's the man."

"I'm sure that won't be a problem." The old man beamed once more. "I have a gun range out back that you can use. We can do it right now if you like. My nephew's in the back, filling crates for a delivery."

The old man called his nephew in. He was a gangly youth, with a mop of blond hair, but had an air of confidence about him that Jack liked. The young man picked out a holster that would allow Jack to draw his pistol easily. He then showed him how to clean and maintain the pistol. They took the gun apart and reassembled it several times until Jack became familiar with its workings. Next the lad showed him how to oil the holster. This would keep the leather in good condition and, just as important, enable the gun draw to be smoother. He also suggested that filing off the front sight would make for an even faster draw, pointing out that, as pistols were really of use only in short distance shooting, the sight was almost redundant anyway.

With the maintenance side complete, Jack and the young marksman headed to the range. It was just the enclosed backyard of the store, but sandbags were piled up against one wall, alongside a series of life-size wooden cutouts of various animals and one fierce-looking Indian. They shot from a variety of different stances and also practiced drawing the pistol as quickly as possible and shooting a target. Jack seemed to be a natural at the shooting but perfecting the quick draw would take some more practice.

After they had finished shooting, they walked back into the store. As Jack entered, he noticed some clothing to the side of the store. With Cyrus's words about how he "dressed funny" ringing true, Jack decided a change to his appearance might also be a good idea and help him avoid trouble. With that in mind, he looked at the clothing available and bought a long, light brown, waxed leather coat; a brimmed hat;

and some gloves. He placed these items on the counter and paid what he owed.

Thanking the two men he gathered up his purchases and walked out to where Skeiron was tethered. Right away, it was clear the lump of iron now strapped to his right leg would take some getting used to but it was a small sacrifice considering the extra protection it would give him. As it was dry, he folded the coat and strapped it in with his bedroll. The hat and gloves he put on. Getting into the saddle, he headed out of town following the directions the old man had given him.

The countryside was pretty, even this early in the year. The sun shining on the split-rail fences and open fields made the riding quite pleasant.

Jack had been riding for only about an hour when he saw the sign for the plantation. Turning in to follow the tree-lined drive, he rode for another half mile along acres of empty fields. The previous crop had been harvested some time ago, and the bare earth was not yet sown for the new season. It would be another few months until the cotton was planted. Continuing on, he saw the plantation house come into view. Although not built on the grand scale of some of the other plantation houses with the big white pillars he'd seen on his journey south, it was still a good size and well kept. It was a wooden two-storey building, painted white, with a full balcony extending round three sides. As he approached the big house, he could see what looked like a long wooden bunkhouse behind and to the right. Outside it, several men were chopping wood. They were all black. This was something that had taken Jack by surprise the further south he had travelled. The black slaves did most, if not all, the work. The conditions that the slaves worked and lived in depended a lot on who the plantation owner was. Jack had seen the harsh way that some of the slaves were treated but had also seen many slaves that were happy where they were. It reminded him somewhat of the two mills near Calder Vale. At Mr Owens's mill, the workers were happy, while at the mill down the road, the workers had been ill tret. Struck him as the same shit, just a different country and colour.

Jack was looking at the house again when a black man came running from the side of the house.

"Can I take your horse, sir?" he asked.

"Yes, thank you," said Jack, dismounting. "Is Mr Jarrell at home?"

"Yessir, the massa is home. Please go on up and ring the bell. Miss Libby will see to ya'll."

Climbing the steps, Jack once again couldn't help compare the South and the slaves to many big houses in Britain. The slaves here, by the definition of the word, didn't get paid, but they also didn't have to buy food or clothing and were provided with a roof over their heads. Many people in Britain who worked on a big estate got a wage but had to buy all their own food, clothes, and rent a house. They had nothing left at the end of the week and were practically slaves in everything but name. They often had to move against their will as the landowner could let them go at the end of their hire year. This meant they had to rely on getting picked for hire at the yearly agricultural fair or become a beggar. He was just about to ring the bell when his thoughts were interrupted by the door opening.

"Can I help you, sir?" asked a tall black woman.

"I'm here to see Mr Jarrell."

"Is he expecting you? Mr Jarrell doesn't like unannounced visitors."

"Yes and no. The man who's interests I represent sent him a letter but couldn't be too specific as to when I would arrive. If you could tell him I'm a representative of Mr James Owens in England."

"Please follow me." She turned and motioned Jack to follow. They entered the house, and Jack was shown into a side parlour.

He had been waiting for only a few minutes when a tall distinguished-looking gentleman with a cheery face entered, wearing a brown three-piece suit and carrying a cane. His dark hair was peppered with grey. Jack guessed he was in his mid-fifties.

"Mr Wolfe?"

"Mr Jarrell?"

The two men shook hands.

"I received a letter from Mr Owens over a month ago. He informed me of the ship you were travelling on and said to expect your visit. He wasn't very specific about what business you wanted to discuss with me, but he did say it should be profitable for us both. How was your trip?"

"It had its moments. I hate boats, so that part of the journey was a necessary evil. The ride down here from New York however, was extremely pleasant. I enjoy riding my horse, and you have a beautiful country."

"I'm not sure how long it's going to remain beautiful."

"You mean with the possibility of war?"

"There's no possibility about it, young sir. With the North pressuring us like it is, we will be going to war. The only question is, whose side will England be on?"

"That's something I can't answer. The politicians will discuss it and make the decisions. The people will be told what to do and when."

"Who would you fight for, Mr Wolfe?"

"Please, call me Jack. And as to who do I fight for? It's not really a 'who' but a 'what.' I fight for what's right."

The answer seemed to amuse Mr Jarrell, but he said no more.

"I hope you will accept my hospitality and stay here until you're ready to return to England?"

"That would be very kind of you."

"Good. Please get yourself settled in. I have some things I need to attend to. Dinner will be served at seven tonight. I look forward to seeing you then." He gave a nod to Jack and strode off, leaving him alone.

As if by magic, and without any word from Jarrell, the same black woman who'd answered the door appeared and bid a young servant girl to escort him to his room.

"Will that be all, sir?" asked the girl after she had shown him to his room.

"Yes. Thank you."

With that, she gave a quick curtsy and left. Jack looked around at his surroundings. The room was expensively furnished. There was a large four-poster bed, heavy drapes at the windows, and lots of brass fixtures and fittings. Its ornate opulence, however, reminded him more of a whorehouse than a private home.

Leaving his room, he went down the wide staircase and back out of the front door to tend to Skeiron. Jack had been taught by his father to take care of the animals before yourself. Your horse could mean the difference between life and death. He had always followed this, and even more so with Skeiron. She was more to Jack than just a horse.

To his surprise, Skeiron was no longer out front. Anger was starting to rise in him at the thought that somebody had taken his horse. The men he'd seen earlier were still chopping wood, so Jack approached them to see if they'd seen anything. They were so engrossed in their work they didn't see him approach.

"Did any of you men see who took my horse?"

One of the men turned around. He was as black as night with an ugly scar running the full length of his right cheek. He was as tall as Jack but more muscular. "Your horse is in the barn, sir. Thomas took her there."

Jack thanked the man and headed over to the barn. The double doors were open, and he could see several horses' rumps protruding from the stalls. He stood inside the entrance for a few seconds to let his eyes get accustomed to the gloom. Halfway down the left wall was Skeiron. Walking over, he saw someone in the stall with her.

"Are you Thomas?"

The man looked up. He was more boy than man, tall and skinny but with a friendly face. "Yessir," he said, pulling his cap off his shaved head. "I was just looking after your horse."

Jack gave him a curt nod, "I can manage from here, thanks for bringing her in."

Thomas looked both confused and worried. He didn't move.

"I said I can manage but thank you."

Looking more uneasy by the second, Thomas nervously rolled his cap through his fingers. "Did I do something wrong, sir?" he asked.

Jack was now the one who was confused. "No. You didn't do anything wrong, but I make it a point to be the only one who looks after my horse. Why do you look so worried?"

"If Mistah Briggs finds out I didn't take care of your horse, he will punish me for not doing my work. It's my job to tend to the horses."

"Who's Mr Briggs?"

"He's the overseer. Tells us what to do and when. If something's not to his liking, we get punished."

"Doesn't sound like a nice man. How about this, you go and get water and feed for my horse, and I'll check her over and give her a rub down. Will that be okay? I don't want you getting into trouble."

Thomas's worried face broke into a smile. "Yessa. Thank you, sah!"

Jack brushed down Skeiron and checked her over while Thomas got water and feed.

"How long have you been here, Thomas?"

"Not sure exactly, sir. We've had two crops of cotton since I arrived, so I'd say a little over two years."

"Were you taken from Africa?"

"Originally, I was, when I was about twelve. But at first, I was on another plantation before I was sold to Mr Jarrell. He's a good owner, but Mistah Briggs …" His voice trailed off.

Jack felt for the boy. "Don't worry. I won't say anything. I'm just here from England to secure cotton for my boss. And I'm a worker, not a rich landowner."

"But you have such a magnificent horse. She must be very expensive. I could only dream about owning such an animal."

"She is pretty special. I bought her as a foal and raised her. We take care of each other."

At that moment, a man walked into the barn. He wore a long brown coat that was flapping open at the waist and a wide brimmed hat. His pants were tucked into knee-high leather boots. As he came closer, Jack could see there was a leather bull whip coiled up on his belt. Jack was hidden from view behind Skeiron, but Thomas was standing in the open.

"Now what the fuck are you doing, boy?" said the angry voice.

"Nothin', Mistah Briggs."

"That's what it looks like. You're supposed to be tending to the horses, not standing around doin' nothin' like the dumb nigger you are."

"He was helping me," said Jack, taking Briggs by surprise as he stepped out from behind Skeiron. "I asked him to bring water and feed for my horse. He had just finished when you walked in. He had also brushed her down," he added, which was a lie. "I was just finishing up. He's a very capable stable boy."

Thomas kept his head bowed during their exchange, unsure of what would happen.

"Run along, boy," said Briggs, looking Jack up and down with contempt.

Thomas ran.

After he had left, Jack came out from the stall and Briggs took another few steps towards him with a sneer. "You don't tell the niggers what to do. That's my job," he said in a menacing voice. "You should stay in the house with the rest of your rich friends. It can be dangerous out here. I wouldn't want you getting hurt hanging around with niggers."

The threat was plain enough to see, but Jack knew the danger was from Briggs and not from the slaves.

Jack didn't say any more. He left the stable but made sure he bumped into Briggs's shoulder on the way out. It didn't look like anything much, but it told Jack a great deal. The first thing it told him was that the man was soft and not well muscled. He bullied by intimidation, not strength. Also, the way he staggered back after the minor impact showed he wasn't particularly well balanced or light on his feet. The third was the way Briggs reacted. He spun around at Jack, and rage filled his words as he swore at him. Jack weighed up what he had learned. The man had a quick temper but wasn't much of a fighter, at least not a straight-up fighter. This cowardly man would sneak up behind you and attack. If it came to a face-to-face fight, Jack knew he had the other man beat. He also knew he would now have to sleep with one eye open. With a grin on his face at the new challenge, he went back to the big house to dig out his best shirt and get cleaned up for the evening meal.

Jack spent the next week being shown around the plantation while Mr Jarrell explained the growing and picking process. They spent evenings going over new shipment arrangements and discussing delivery amounts and frequencies and the supply route the materials would take. On one of the evenings, Mr Jarrell suggested to Jack that, for the right price, he would be able to also transport the raw material to Charleston Harbor. Jack was interested. It was a thought he'd had from the beginning. Common sense seemed to dictate cutting out the middlemen to get a better deal for Mr Owens. After much discussion, Jack was successful in negotiating a good price with Mr Jarrell for the additional service. By the end of the week, they had a deal that both men were happy with.

With their business concluded, Jack began planning to head to Charleston to inspect the freight company that would be handling the delivery of the raw cotton to Lancashire. He expected it would take him the best part of two weeks to travel the 250 miles, but he was eager to get started on the journey. While he was grateful for the generous hospitality that Mr Jarrell had shown him during his stay, these weren't his people. They were the upper classes, and he didn't belong. In search of some camaraderie, he had taken to wandering the grounds in an evening and talking to the slaves.

The last evening before he left, he saw one of the field hands carrying a large heavy sack as he came round the corner of the house. From his encounters with the slaves, Jack knew not to help. If he did, they would get into trouble. He felt uncomfortable not lending a hand but at least the slaves knew he wanted to help, so that made it a little easier. He recognised the man as Samuel, a slave Jack had spoken to on a few previous occasions.

As Samuel struggled with the load, Jack fell into step beside him. Samuel was in his late twenties. His last employer had taught him how to write, so he could keep basic records of the crops. The man had, unfortunately, died and Samuel had been sold to Mr Jarrell. His life here was far removed from the one he'd lived with his last owner. Mr Jarrell never came near the slaves and left everything up to Mr Briggs. As long as everything ran smoothly, he chose to be ignorant as to how they were treated. Little did the man realise that events were about to unfold whose outcome would mean he would have to take an interest.

Samuel and Jack were just approaching the bunkhouse when two more slaves appeared. They nodded their greeting and then went to help Samuel. The sack was dumped on the ground and its contents emptied. It was an assortment of harnesses and other metal shackles and buckles. These were for the horses that worked the fields. They needed to be cleaned and prepared for the coming planting season. The men sat down, and each picked up a piece. They had just started cleaning and oiling the leather when the crack of a whip was ominously heard coming from behind the bunkhouse. The three men started mumbling to each other in an agitated tone. The crack of the whip was heard again.

"What's happening?" Jack asked. There was silence. He crouched by the side of the men. "Samuel, what's happening?"

"Thomas took too long doing his chores. Mistah Briggs is teaching him to be quicker."

Teaching him to be quicker, thought Jack. *That could mean only one thing from Briggs – punishment. Just like Briggs to pick on the weakest.*

Jack had grown quite fond of Thomas. They had spent a fair bit of time together, talking and exchanging knowledge about horses while Jack was taking care of Skeiron. Young Thomas had even taught Jack a thing or two he didn't know. There was no way the boy deserved the punishment he was getting. Jack decided to go around the back and see exactly what was happening.

Making his approach quietly, he saw that Thomas was shirtless and had his hands tied together with a rope. The rope was then thrown over a branch to keep them in the air while exposing his back, the back that Briggs was whipping.

"You need to learn to be quicker, boy!" shouted Briggs. "Taking care of Mr Jarrell's horses is an important job. Maybe a dumb nigger like you isn't up to the job?"

"I am, sah," countered Thomas. "Please give me another chance?"

"I'd worry about getting through this whippin' first before asking for another chance. You should be thanking me for takin' the time to make sure you do the job right."

"Yes, sah. Thank you, sah."

Jack's blood started to boil. The young lad was having to thank the man for whipping him.

"Maybe it's not you I should be punishing. If that feller on the fancy black horse were here, I should be whippin' him. He's making you take too long tending to his damn animal."

"N-n … no, sah. His horse is easy taken care of."

"Don't answer me back, boy," screamed Briggs with violent rage.

Briggs pulled back his arm, and Jack could see he was about to strike again at the helpless Thomas.

"You should be careful what you wish for," said Jack in a loud voice.

Briggs whirled around with a murderous look in his eyes. "What do you mean?"

"Did you not just say you wanted me to be here so you could whip me instead?"

Briggs just stared at Jack, an evil grin starting to crease the corners of his mouth.

"Well here I am."

Briggs started to approach him, the long whip trailing on the ground behind. "I see you left your pistol and knife in your room," he gloated. "Bad move."

Lightning fast, Briggs whipped out his arm, the end of the whip snaking through the air. Jack had just enough time to turn his head before the whip made contact with his face. Instead of raking across his eyes, it caught him high up on the cheekbone, splitting the skin. Blood started to freely flow from the wound.

"You're pretty quick, for a coward," Jack said putting his hand up to his cheek to wipe away some of the blood. Looking at his red fingers, he then looked over at Briggs. "I'll give you that one," he said with a mischievous grin.

"You didn't give me anything," said Briggs. "I took it, and when I'm finished with you, I'm gonna whip this nigger and then that fucking horse of yours as well."

"Have you ever read the Bible?" Jack asked.

"What the fuck has that to do with anything?"

"Did you ever read about the four horsemen of the apocalypse?" Jack was counting on the fact that he had but didn't remember all the details.

"Yeah, so what?"

"Well you may remember," said Jack, taking three quick strides towards Briggs, "that one of them was called Death."

Too late, Briggs realised that Jack was now standing too close for him to use his whip. He had distracted him long enough to step inside its deadly arc. Taking two more steps closer, Jack threw a vicious punch to the overseer's face, breaking his nose. Briggs staggered back. Jack kept following him, jabbing out more punches to his face. He wanted to mark him so that all the slaves could see that this man, who had terrorised them, was not invincible. Once this happened, he would be useless and have to leave. Fear was the overseer's greatest weapon.

Each time he threw a jab, Briggs stumbled back. Taking another step back, Briggs tripped over a bucket and landed on the ground. While he was down, Jack turned to Thomas and untied the rope holding his arms. He collapsed to the dirt and was immediately picked up by Samuel who had followed Jack. Turning his attention back to Briggs, Jack was surprised to see the man was already back up on his feet and was also intrigued to see he had a knife in his hand.

"I'd recommend you put that thing down. It's dangerous out here and I wouldn't want you getting hurt," Jack taunted.

Briggs grew more enraged, realising his own words from their first confrontation were being used against him, "You cocky sonofabitch! I'm gonna gut you like a slaughtered hog."

He started to circle around Jack, flashing the knife to try to make him jump back. Jack decided this had gone on long enough. The next time Briggs flicked out the knife, Jack would make his move. Briggs was rapidly gaining confidence, thinking once again he had the upper hand. He was enjoying the feeling, and he also had an audience, as more slaves had now come from cleaning the harnesses and were watching. This was Briggs's moment to put the fear back into them. He lunged, the blade aimed at Jack's torso, but Jack had been waiting for this and easily sidestepped the blade. At the same time, he stepped in, so the blade was now behind him and Briggs's arm was level with his side. He clamped Briggs's arm in the crook of his own arm and his side and then levered upward, straightening the arm until he heard Briggs's elbow pop. The colour drained from the overseer's face, his mouth opened as the pain ripped through him, and he started to scream. Jack needed to silence him quickly, as to not alert anybody in the big house, so he clamped his hand over Briggs's mouth and drove him backwards against the bunkhouse wall. Sweat was starting to break out on Briggs's forehead.

"You're going to get your horse and ride out of here tonight. If I hear you came back, I won't stop at breaking your arm. Is that clear?"

Briggs nodded.

Jack removed his hand and stepped back. "Now go!"

Briggs stood there for a second and then decided to scream for help. Jack beat him to it and punched him straight in the throat. Briggs grasped his throat with his good hand and crumpled to the ground like an empty sack. His breathing was coming in short wheezy gasps.

"Some people never learn," Jack muttered as he stepped away from the beaten man and turned towards the watching slaves. Samuel approached Jack.

"Thank you for saving Thomas. He didn't deserve his punishment."

"You don't have to thank me. I was just doing the decent thing and standing up for someone who needed it." Jack eyed the moaning man on the ground.

Turning back to face Samuel, he added, "As Briggs doesn't look capable of much right now, I'd be grateful if you would have his horse saddled, put on it and send him out of here. I'm going to wash up and then go back to the big house. I'll tell them I've just seen Briggs riding hell for leather down the drive. That way, you won't get into any sort of trouble when he doesn't show up in the morning."

"Thank you again," said a relieved Samuel. "That man is an animal."

CHAPTER TWELVE

5 April 1861

The following morning, Jack packed up his belongings and headed out for Charleston. There had been some confusion as to who would take charge of the slaves after Briggs failed to turn up for work, but with no mention of foul play, everybody was in the clear. He, himself, was glad to be on the road again with Skeiron. As he rode, he mused on whether he would ever be happy to settle in one place. He also mused about the slaves – sold in Africa by their own tribes, traded like a commodity, and then worked without freedom. Part of his conscience rebelled against the situation, while another part of him wondered, with the right plantation owner and overseer, could their lives actually be better here?

He was roused from his thoughts by a a column of about fifty mounted men wearing grey uniforms coming towards him. He kept his eyes directed straight ahead as they kept riding past, until one man peeled off the column to speak to him.

"What's your business here?" he asked abruptly and with some menace, eyeing Skeiron.

Jack tensed for a possible confrontation, quickly and calmly replied, "I'm from England. Here to secure a cotton supply from the Jarrell plantation. I'm now on my way to Charleston to speak to the shipping company."

The man, who was obviously in a hurry, seemed satisfied with Jack's unhesitating reply and, possibly his English accent. With a terse nod, he rode off to rejoin his comrades. Jack let himself relax again. He presumed he'd just encountered a detachment of cavalry from the Confederate Army. They looked ready to take on anything. Jack had been reading in the papers how seven slave states whose economies depended on cotton had broken away and formed the Confederacy. It seemed war was now inevitable. Jack just hoped he would get to Charleston, finish his business, and be on a ship before that happened.

The closer he got to Charleston, the more troops he saw. Most people he spoke to simply wanted the North to leave the South alone. They were proud to have declared their independence and taken a stand. Some were even quite optimistic, reminiscing about the earlier Wars of 1812 and Independence, figuring if they'd beaten a great empire twice, trouncing the Northern states shouldn't be a problem.

Jack was still one-day short of Charleston when he heard the Confederate Army had declared war on the Union Army by firing on Fort Sumter. The engagement was to last for only two days, with no loss of life, but the line in the sand had been drawn. The Northern President Lincoln called for the Northern states to provide 75,000 troops to put down the rebellion. In response, four more Southern states joined the Confederacy.

As he entered the outskirts of the city, people were milling about everywhere. The opinion seemed evenly split. Some citizens were packing wagons, leaving in fear the North would attack Charleston in order to keep its hold on the fort. Others were boarding up their windows, fortifying their homes in preparation for the fight. Jack continued on towards the harbour. His first stop would be the freight company and then the steamship offices to buy his passage back to England.

He entered the docks area but was stopped by the harbour officials before he had a chance to make contact at either business. He was informed that few ships were leaving for England, as the Union Navy had quickly moved to blockade the port in response to the attack on Fort Sumter. Passengers were allowed to leave relatively unhindered, but any merchant ship carrying cotton had to run the blockade and risked being fired upon. Jack thanked the man and made his way to the freight office.

Upon entering the building, he asked to speak to the manager, who appeared from the cargo warehouse and ushered him into his office. After much negotiation, with the manager stressing how difficult it would be to get a ship full of cotton through the Union blockade, a deal was eventually struck. Jack was sure the man had known all along that he could deliver the cotton but had wanted it to seem impossible in order to drive up his price. The manager knew of a sea captain who was prepared to run the blockade for the right price. Once the cotton arrived from the Jarrell plantation, it would be loaded up and sent on to England. Jack and Skeiron would also be able to catch a ride on the same ship.

Jack left the offices pretty pleased with himself. Even with the high prices of the blockade he would be delivering the cotton that Mr Owens wanted and for less money than Owens had been prepared to pay. Indeed, saving money through making the process more efficient seemed the point of Mr Owens having his own man on the ground on the American side. Jack could see the value of his personal review of the process the cotton shipments were following to get to England. Now he just had to find something to occupy his time over the next two days until his ship departed.

Back out on the street, he mounted Skeiron and headed towards the mouth of the river. He had been told that it would give him a view of Fort Sumter and the skirmish that was currently going on there. He rode at a relaxed pace, enjoying his last few remaining days on dry land before he had to board another damn ship. He certainly wasn't looking forward to that.

Two hours later, he arrived at a small settlement on James Island. It was a rural community that happened to be the closest settlement to the fort – so close that the Union troops would occasionally come ashore and buy provisions from the general store. He decided to stop at the small hotel, one of the only commercial buildings on the short main street, besides a bank and the general store. Once inside, he made his way to the bar. The bartender came over, and Jack ordered a whisky. Standing at the bar, he struck up a conversation with the man regarding the battle for the fort and what he thought the outcome would be.

"The silly buggers are cut off," the barman began. "Their supply route is now through Confederate territory, so they have no chance. Some of their soldiers were here last week drinking. I think there's only about fifty of them in total. My guess is they'll sneak onto a ship in the middle of the night and beat a hasty retreat."

"You don't think they'll keep fighting to hold the fort?"

"Not likely. They've been under a sort of siege for a while now. The men who came ashore last week were complaining of lack of food and no ammunition. Their supply boats aren't being let through."

Jack looked contemplatively at his whisky and took a swig. "Do you think the war will escalate?"

The bartender responded by wiping the already clean bar with extra vigour before answering, "Without a doubt. Those damn Yankees think they can tell us who we can and can't sell our cotton to. I say we can sell it to whoever we want, and they won't stop us."

Just then loud sustained cannon fire could be heard coming from the fort.

"Doesn't sound much like they're short of ammunition to me," said Jack.

They both pondered that for a moment. No more shots were heard.

A young man came running into the bar.

"They've surrendered," he shouted excitedly as he hopped from one foot to the other. "The fort surrendered. They had already agreed to surrender this morning, but their commander wanted a 100-gun salute as he lowered the flag. That was what all the ruckus just was. We've won." He ran out of the bar to spread the news.

"Well it appears you arrived too late to see the fight," the bartender said with a shrug of his shoulders.

"Yeah, it does. I wasn't too bothered about seeing anything anyway. It was worth the ride just to get out of town for a while, and this seemed like as good a direction to travel as the next. I don't suppose you have anywhere I could stay? And somewhere to put my horse. I've got a ship taking me back to England the day after tomorrow."

"Sure thing. There's a barn out back, and I keep three rooms upstairs. The rooms cost 75 cents a night. Room and board is a dollar. I can rustle up some food if you're hungry?"

"Certainly am. That all sounds great."

Once the bartender had shown Jack his room and the stables for Skeiron, Jack went for one last short ride out to the promontory overlooking the fort before turning in for the night. It was quiet, but the ravages of the earlier battle could be seen clearly. Several walls were destroyed, and black palls of smoke drifted skyward. The sight brought back thoughts of the Crimea. War never seemed to bring the solutions people thought it would. Would this one be any different?

As Jack rode back to the hotel, images and memories from past battles kept his mind occupied. Once there, he put Skeiron into the barn and bedded her down for the night before going up to his room. It was very simple, with a washstand and single bed resting on bare floorboards. He had a quick wash and went back downstairs for some food. After ordering at the bar, he sat at one of the small round tables. He was all alone as the owner had gone out back to take care of some chores. Casting about for something to pass the time, he picked up a discarded newspaper. He saw it was the *New-York Daily Tribune*. As it was a Northern paper, he assumed some of the soldiers from the fort had left it. The front page was dedicated to the continued aggressive stance of the South and how the Southern states were wrong to break away from the Union. As he turned the pages, he read the odd article but skimmed through most of them. As he was nearing the back of the paper a headline grabbed his attention. "Animal Attacks on Freed Slaves."

Focusing on the article, he read that former slaves were being found dead and animals were being blamed, more precisely wolves. The hairs on the back of his neck stood up as a chill went over him. The victims were almost all women. They had been attacked in rural areas, their throats ripped out. The horrific details brought back the grisly scene of Mary's death. The images filled his mind. Jack sat bolt upright.

"Mother fucker," he swore under his breath. The similarities to these deaths and the deaths in the Crimea couldn't just be a coincidence. Jack felt sick. How could this be happening again? The attacks had started on the outskirts of New York, but from the reports coming in, he could see that the attacks were heading south. He felt his adrenaline kicking in.

He spotted several more newspapers, from different places, on a nearby table and grabbed them to see if he could find any more details on the attacks. A quick scan revealed there were other stories relating to similar deaths. One even had details of a reported sighting of a small man with a strange gait leaving the scene, but somehow this lead was never followed up.

Then suddenly it hit him like a ton of bricks. Why hadn't he been able to make the connection before? The strange steward he had glimpsed on the voyage ..... he stood abruptly causing the chair to go flying backwards and slammed his palms on the table in anger. He hung his head and drummed his fingers against the wood in frustration.

"Fuck...fuck.... FUCK," why hadn't he made the connection

on the ship? The timing fit perfectly. This was no coincidence. The despicable little fucker had been within his reach twice but was still alive. It was unacceptable. He must have done some damage when he shot him, but only enough to maim. *Damn*, he scrubbed one hand across his stubbled jaw, *so he now had irrefutable confirmation that his shot hadn't killed the predator in Romania.*

He grabbed the chair and sat down again. Rereading the articles, Jack started piece it all together. The first reported attack was at a place called Woodbridge Town. Then there had been two more out in the middle of nowhere, before a fourth just outside Princeton. The most recent newspaper, the *Daily Richmond Examiner*, had also reported three animal attacks.

It suddenly struck Jack that maybe nobody else was making the connection. The victims were always strangers to the area, with no families to kick up a fuss. The locations of the attacks were far enough apart that different sheriffs would be involved. Also, with war imminent, nobody would be paying too much attention. Was he the only one to see the similarities between the cases and suspect what was really behind them? If this was the same man who had killed Mary, then he wasn't going to let him escape again. He contemplated leaving straight away to investigate further, but it was already late evening, and he still needed to think through what he was going to do. He had to be sure that this time the little bastard met his end.

His food arrived, but he found he had lost his appetite and just hurriedly shovelled it in without really tasting it at all. He then went back to his room and lay on his bed. Hands behind his head, legs crossed, his mind raced, running through all the different scenarios. Several hours later, he had his mind made up, and had decided on a plan of action.

He went down to the bar to borrow pen and paper. Bringing them up to his room he sat down and first, drafted a letter to Bull. He wrote of what he had read in the papers and his certainty that this was the same man who had killed Mary. He also told him about the strange man he had seen on the ship from England. He then laid out his plans to head off to track down and kill the man and said that, if Bull wanted to join in on the revenge, he should take the first available ship to Charleston. Once there, he was to go to the main telegraph office and collect any messages from Jack that would detail where he was and how to find him.

As he would also now not be travelling back with the cotton to Calder Vale, Jack drafted a second letter to Mr Owens, detailing his business meetings and all the relevant details of his new cotton supply from the Jarrell plantation and inform him that he would be staying on in the States to attend to some personal matters. His mind drifted briefly to Amanda and how she was faring in her new marriage. If she was pregnant she would be close to delivering. He had been looking forward to seeing her but any life he had in England would have to wait.

With all his communications complete, he fell into a fitful sleep.

Waking early the next morning, he saddled Skeiron and headed back to the Charleston docks. After seeing the letters safely put aboard ship for delivery to England, Jack went by the freight office to inform the manifest clerk he wouldn't be travelling on the ship, but all the other arrangements still stood.

His next action was to buy provisions for his journey north. He estimated it would take him nearly three weeks to get to Richmond. Supplies secured, he was finally free to head off to eek out some revenge for poor Mary. He wasted no time in setting off. In each town he rode through, he scoured the local papers and asked around to see if anybody had heard about any "wolf attacks." Nobody seemed to know anyting, but at this point, he wasn't too surprised to be finding no information. He was still several hundred miles from where the last reported attack had taken place.

As Jack progressed, his investigations were becoming somewhat hindered by the fact that asking too many questions was turning out to be more dangerous than he'd anticipated. In the last town he'd passed through, he had been surrounded by several men who'd accused him of being a spy for the North. Luckily, he had managed talk his way out of it, get to Skeiron and leave town in a hurry without a fight. The war with the North was making people nervous. They weren't wrong to be on guard with him; there were undoubtedly real Northern spies around trying to find out their own information. He would have to be more careful about who he spoke to and the questions he asked. Most of the people in the areas he was riding through were Southern sympathisers, and he didn't want to risk being accused of spying again.

The further north he travelled, the more soldiers he saw. People were also becoming more and more wary of him, as any man who wasn't wearing a grey uniform and was of military age stood out as a possible enemy. He had just left the town of Chester, Virginia, when he heard shooting up ahead. He rode off the trail and into the trees. There was still sporadic shooting, but it was diminishing. He slowly rode on, keeping a watchful eye on his surroundings.

The trees started to thin, and in the distance, Jack could see several bodies on the ground. They were all wearing the uniform of the Confederacy. He scanned the area to see if he could see who had shot them. The whole area was quiet, but smoke from the shooting still drifted among the trees. Jack spotted movement from behind a large fallen tree. It seemed to be a soldier in a grey uniform, trying to stay hidden from whoever had shot his comrades. He then spotted movement in front and to the right of the lone man.

"Hey, Reb," somebody shouted. "You gonna throw down your gun? Or you gonna die like the rest of your Southern scum?"

The only reply was a bullet fired in their general direction by the lone survivor.

"Is that the best you got?" came the same voice. "If everybody in the South shoots like you, this war's gonna be over by Christmas."

Laughter followed.

Jack could now see that there were three men in the woods. This didn't seem like much of a fair fight to him. He dismounted Skeiron and tied her to a tree. Putting his sabre on his belt and pulling his rifle from its scabbard, he started to move stealthily in their direction.

The three men were also on the move. They were splitting up and hoping to circle their victim. With one man in the middle continuing to throw insults at the soldier in the hopes of distracting him, the others continued their approach. Jack decided his first target would be the man in the middle. He was stationary and wouldn't be looking out for attack. Jack got to within twenty feet of him and stopped. He was so quiet the man was still unaware he was being stalked. Jack laid down his rifle and drew his sabre. He wanted this manoeuvre to be completely silent. Very slowly, he halved the distance between them. The man must have sensed something as he started to turn towards him. With no time left and ten feet to cover, Jack leapt at the man. He swung up his arm in a lazy arc and then powered it down. The only sounds were the swish of the blade as it severed the man's head from his shoulders and the consequential bump of the head hitting the earth. Quick, quiet, and painless – a good death. Jack caught the rest of the body and lowered it to the ground so as to not make too much noise. *One down and two to go*, he thought.

Retrieving his rifle, he surveyed the area once again. From this new position, he could see the fallen tree where the Confederate soldier was hiding; it was about seventy yards away and slightly downhill. He could also see the man on the left circling around. The man on the right was now nowhere to be seen. The situation was fairly desperate. The soldier was being approached from both sides and seemed unaware of his plight. Jack decided on his course of action. He took aim at the man on the left. He still couldn't see the other man but hoped, once he heard the shot, he would stop his approach until he figured out what was going on. Jack also hoped that, before the man on the right fully figured it out, he would be dead. Regulating his breathing, he settled the bead of the rifle on the man's head. He squeezed the trigger.

As the burnt gunpowder exploded from the end of the barrel, obscuring his view, Jack was already reloading. He was supremely confident in his own abilities and, therefore, knew the man was dead. Once reloaded, he began scanning for his last target.

"Not even close!" shouted a voice. For a split second, Jack thought it was the man on the left who he had been aiming at. He then realised the voice had come from in front and belonged to the Confederate soldier. Just as he was piecing this together, he heard a different voice.

"Let me know if this one's any closer." A man stepped out from behind a tree less than five yards from the soldier and fired a bullet into the ground no more than six inches away from his head. He then continued to point a pistol straight at the helpless man.

"Throw down your weapon!" he ordered.

The soldier complied.

"Paul, Allan, come on down. I got the sonofabitch!"

Jack realised that, when he had shot the man on the left, causing the Confederate soldier to shout that the shot wasn't even close, the man had presumed one of his comrades had taken a shot at the Confederate soldier. He was now standing in the open, unaware that he was the last man left.

"Drop your pistol!" shouted Jack. "I've got a rifle pointed straight at you. Your two friends are already dead."

The man gave a slight glance in Jack's direction. He couldn't fail to notice Jack standing there pointing the rifle at him. He looked back at his target. He seemed to be weighing up his options. His thumb moved and started to cock the hammer. Jack fired. The instant the weapon discharged, he was running through the trees. He wasn't sure how badly the man was hurt, as he'd had to rush his shot. Leaping over the fallen tree the soldier had been hiding behind, he approached his target.

The man was still moving, but his pistol had flown out of his hand. Turning him over, Jack was surprised at how young he was.

At that moment, the soldier who had been hiding behind the fallen tree came up to stand by Jack's side, pointing his pistol at the fallen man.

"Why did you attack us?" asked the soldier.

The wounded man said nothing.

Taking a step closer, the soldier placed his boot on the bullet wound in the man's chest. The man screamed in pain.

"Why did you attack us?" he repeated.

"Fuck you," said the man.

The soldier pressed harder with his boot.

"We know who you are," croaked the man in a pain-ridden gasp.

"But why me? There must be more valuable targets."

Frothy red bubbles began to appear at the man's lips. "We knew where you'd be. You were an easy target."

The soldier released the pressure. "How did you know where to find me?"

The man said nothing. The soldier started to lift his boot to apply pressure again.

"He's dead," said Jack.

"Are you sure?"

"I've seen enough dead bodies to recognise the signs."

There was silence for a few moments.

"It appears I owe you my life," said the soldier, offering his hand.

Jack took the offered hand. "It looked like you could use some help."

"Are you English?"

"Yeah."

"What brings you … I'm sorry. I'm forgetting my manners. I'm James Stuart. My friends call me Jeb." They shook again.

"I'm Jack Wolfe."

"It's nice to meet you, Jack. Very good timing. It was starting to look a little grim."

"I'm sorry I didn't get here sooner. Looks like you lost some men," said Jack, nodding in the general direction of the dead soldiers. "Why do you think they attacked you?"

"Well it appears they thought I was somebody worth killing."

"And are you?"

"That depends. I'm only a lieutenant colonel, but I am friends with Robert. E. Lee, commander of the Army of Virginia. Maybe they were trying to capture me for information and not kill me? Anyway, what brings you to this neck of the woods?"

Jack started to explain about being sent to America to secure cotton supplies for his boss in England. He mentioned the newspaper articles he had come across and how people believed wolves were killing former female slaves. He then went on to tell him about the Crimean war and the attacks there and that he thought they were linked, especially after having seen the Bulgarian on the boat ride over.

"I'm now headed over to Richmond, where the last reported attacks happened, to see if I can find the man and kill him."

Jeb was silent for a few minutes. "I don't think I've heard of any of these attacks, although it could be because I'm from the southern part of the state and the attacks seem to be further north. The only reason I'm out this way is because I'm heading to Harpers Ferry to report to Colonel Thomas Jackson. It seems we have a bit of a disagreement going on with the Yankees."

"Before the man died, you asked him how he knew where to find you. How do you think he knew?"

"We've had a few minor indications that the North was getting sensitive information. It appears there's somebody quite high up within General Lee's command that's giving information to the North. They set an ambush for me and my men."

"What do you want to do with your men?" asked Jack.

"If we can round up the horses, I'd like to take them to Richmond and give them a decent burial."

Jack nodded. "I'm headed that way myself." He went back to Skeiron and they both rode off in search of the horses. The mounts of the Union sympathisers were long gone, spooked by the gunfire. But the horses belonging to Jeb's men were hobbled nearby, so Jack took those. They tied Jeb's men to the horse's backs and set off together.

On the ride, Jeb told of his service with the US Army and fighting the Indians. Jack told of his exploits during and after the Crimean War. It seemed that, as a cavalryman, Jeb knew of the Charge of the Light Brigade and was suitably impressed that Jack had been one of the men who took part.

It took two days to reach Richmond. Once there, they parted company, Jeb to see to his men and Jack to find the reporter who had written the latest story about the animal attacks.

CHAPTER THIRTEEN

7 May 1861

Jack headed straight to the offices of the *Richmond Examiner*. He wanted to talk to the reporter who had written the original story and also see if there had been any new attacks. Entering the large brick building, he walked up to the reception desk, his dusty boots echoing off the polished stone floor.

"I'd like to speak to Thomas Welby please," he said to the overweight man behind the desk.

"What's your business with him?"

"I'm needing some more information about a story he wrote."

"Which story?" asked the man.

Jack was starting to get annoyed. This fat officious bastard didn't need to know his business.

"That's between the reporter and me. Now, do I have to go search myself or are you going to do your job and tell me where he is?"

"Second floor," was all he said, ignoring Jack to look back down at the paper on his desk.

Jack took the wide stairs up to the second floor two at a time. At the top, he found one long dimly lit corridor with doors leading off it. He knocked on the first door and entered. A man sitting behind a desk looked up.

"Thomas Welby?" asked Jack hopefully.

"Last door on the left," the man replied.

Closing the door, Jack made his way down the corridor. The last door was a half-wood, half-frosted glass affair with the words "Press Office" stencilled on the glass in black letters. Knocking and entering, Jack found himself in a room of about eight desks. Most were unoccupied but all were piled high with papers.

"Thomas Welby," he said.

A young man looked up and nodded. Jack walked over and, without waiting to be asked, sat in the empty chair opposite the reporter. He had decided that he needed to be careful with what information he shared. He didn't want this reporter joining the dots himself, linking the cases, and going to the police. The last thing Jack wanted was the law getting involved and trying to arrest the sick, crazy bastard alive. His death at Jack or Bull's own hand was the only suitable punishment for Mary's murder and that of the countless others.

"You wrote a story about slaves being killed in animal attacks," Jack began. "I wondered if any more had been reported on that."

"Why do you want to know?" asked the reporter, alert for any possible leads on the story.

"I'm a hunter by trade and figure there might be a decent bounty to kill this animal," he easily lied.

"I heard of one more incident, but my editor said not to bother with it as nobody wanted to hear about another nigger dying."

Jack winced inwardly at the slanderous term, remembering Samuel and the other slaves he had become friendly with on the Jarrell plantation. "Can you tell me where it happened so I might go there and see if I can track it down?"

"Yeah. It was a little place called Hopewell, about twenty miles from here on the bay."

"What happened?"

"Another slave girl was attacked and killed, same as before – throat ripped out."

Jack had what he needed and stood to leave.

"What's your name?" asked the reporter.

Jack turned and left without answering.

As he left the building, he saw the night was drawing in, and he didn't have anywhere to stay. But before he did anything about his lodging, he decided to send a quick telegram to the Charleston office to await Bull's arrival and inform him of his progress and where he was heading.

At the small telegraph office, he sent his telegram and also asked directions for Hopewell. Leaving the building and crossing the sidewalk he mounted Skeiron and headed in the direction the clerk had pointed. The weather was improving, so Jack decided a night under the stars wasn't such a bad thing.

At that same time, 3,600 miles away in the mill office in Calder Vale, Mr Owens took delivery of a letter. He opened it to find another letter inside addressed to Ian Mathews. He set that to one side and began to read the note addressed to him. It was from Jack. It went into great details about where the cotton would be coming from, the shipment sizes, and the frequency with which they would be dispatched. It also explained the cost of the loads, noting that, with the outbreak of war and the blockade of the ports, there would be some disruption to supply. But Jack had found a freight operator and a ship's captain who were willing to run the blockades. The letter also recommended that Owens buy up all the raw cotton he could get his hands on that was already in England, as the price was bound to escalate quite considerably.

Owens put down the letter. He smiled to himself. He had been right about Jack. He was an astute and conscientious man. With this new information, he would be able get ahead of his competitors.

Leaving the office, Owens went in search of Ian to give him his letter. Finding him in the loading area, he passed over the letter and went back to his office.

Letter in hand, Bull took a break and went outside of the mill for some privacy. He sat on some dry boulders, opened it, and began to read. The more he read, the more his hands shook and the rage built within him.

Once he'd finished reading it, he stood with a new purpose and went to find Elly. She was working in the weaving room. Bull took her outside, where it was quieter.

"What's happened?" she asked. "You look really angry."

Bull explained the contents of the letter he had received from Jack. He then told her that he had to go to America to avenge the death of his first wife.

Elly smiled up at Bull. "And that's why I love you so much," she said.

Bull's look of anger was replaced by one of confusion. "I'm not sure I follow?"

"You are a very passionate, loving man who would protect me with his life. I cannot love that about you and then not understand why you have to go and avenge the death of Mary. I don't want you to go because I will miss you but I support you going. I'm sure it will be very dangerous so just make sure you come back to me safely." She put her arms around him and leaned her head on his chest. She was scared and sad that he had to go away but understood it was something he must do.

"I will," he said quickly, before his throat caught up with his emotions and he couldn't speak. He hugged her tightly to him. They held each other for some time before she reluctantly released him and went back to work.

Bull next went to see Mr Owens. He explained what had happened in his past and what had come in the letter from Jack. He then asked Mr Owens for his permission to take some time off and go to America to seek out the man responsible for Mary's death. He didn't mention to Owens that he was going with or without his boss's permission. He also didn't mention that he was going to kill him if he found him. Mr Owens, being the fair man that he was, granted Bull his leave of absence and promised to have his job waiting for him when he got back.

Expressing his thanks, Bull left the offices and made his preparations to leave for Liverpool the following morning.

Outside of Hopeville, Virginia, America

After his night camped out under the stars, Jack woke early and continued towards Hopewell. Entering the town, he made his way to the church. He hoped that the reverend wouldn't be so suspicious of his questions about the death and also that he might have been involved with the burial of the unfortunate girl.

The church was empty, but the little house to the side showed signs of life. He opened the wrought iron gate and walked up the brick path. He knocked on the door, and a middle-aged man wearing a priest's collar answered. Jack told him he was a hunter and explained he was looking for some information about recent animal attacks. The reverend seemed to believe his story and gave him all the details he had, which unfortunately were sketchy at best. He did learn of the location of the attack and decided to go there to see if he could learn anything more. He bid the reverend farewell and rode out of town.

Arriving at the location of the attack, he looked around. The area was fairly secluded. A narrow cart track wound its way between the fields from the plantation to the road. The area was sparsely inhabited, but he rode to the nearest home, which was a small run-down one-room shack. He enquired of the man inside if anyone had witnessed the attack or anything else that was unusual, but nobody had seen anything that could help him.

He was wound up with frustration, once again he had run into a dead end. Feeling somewhat discouraged, Jack decided to slowly head south. His quarry seemed to be heading that way, and he hoped it would put him closer if and when the next attack occurred.

Over the next three weeks, with sporadic attacks still happening, Jack found himself once again working his way slowly south while chasing a ghost. He would arrive at the attack site sometimes only a day or so after it had occurred. But each time, the story was the same; nobody had seen anything.

He realised Bull would now probably be on his way and would need to know where to meet. Breaking off from his quest, he headed to Norfolk, the nearest telegraph office, and found himself some lodgings at the edge of town. It was an old but clean clapboard two-story house. The paint was starting to peel a bit all over, other than that, it was tidy and well kept. The place was ideal. A separate staircase to the upper floor where Jack had his room afforded him the privacy to come and go as he pleased. As soon as he'd settled up with the proprietor, He went to the telegraph office and sent a telegram to await Bull in Charleston. The message simply said:

> Meet me at St Pauls Church in Norfolk, Virginia.
> 6 June at noon

At that same time, in Charleston Harbor, a ship from England had docked. Soon after, a large powerful man with dark, shaggy hair disembarked and headed for the local telegraph office.

Jack used the week he had left before Bull arrived to figure out if they could get ahead of their quarry. He scoured the papers in Norfolk with the hope of getting more information but there seemed to be nothing more about any similar attacks. However, he wasn't convinced that the lack of reporting meant no new attacks. It was simply possible the newspaper editors felt the same as Thomas Welby's editor and didn't always consider the killing of former slaves by an animal worth reporting.

Frustrated at the lack of information and not sure of his next move he kicked up his feet and resigned himself to just browsing the papers to pass some time. The main headlines were all war related. He started reading an article about a minor skirmish between Union ships and Confederate artillery batteries at a place called Sewell's point. The two had shelled each other with no gain by either side. There were reported to be only ten casualties. The article gave details of the battle, noting that the Confederates had built a new gun position overnight and, the following morning, had taken the Union gunboats by surprise, forcing them to retreat.

It also reported how the Confederate casualties had sustained their injuries. Most were from shrapnel due to the cannon fire. But there was a strange report about one of the casualties. He had been in the rear collecting more gunpowder for the cannons when a stray cannonball fired from the Union gunboats had exploded near him. He had been blown off his feet and knocked unconscious. When he regained consciousness some time later, he found a man kneeling over him. He gave details of the man as being quite small with sharp features. When the soldier had regained consciousness, he had asked the other man what had happened. The man had simply stood up and limped away. The man wasn't in uniform and nobody had seen of him before. The soldier had also been robbed of his personal possessions.

Jack came to his feet. Here was the missing piece he had been looking for. His nemesis was clearly back to his old tricks of preying on wounded soldiers. This lucky soldier had regained consciousness just in time. However, acting on this new piece of information meant trying to predict where the next battle would take place. As an outsider, and with Union spies everywhere in the South, his task seemed nigh impossible. To make matters worse, everybody seemed to have a different opinion about where or when the next conflict would happen, further adding to the confusion.

The only sure way to get any information was to talk to a military commander, and that seemed like even more of an impossibility. Without any proper leads or information about where the next military action would occur, Jack was at a loss. His only possible course of action would be to now head north, towards where the fighting was happening, and hope his adversary continued his pattern of attacking wounded soldiers. He would, however, have to wait for Bull first.

In the meantime, Jack read everything he could possibly find about the conflict between the two sides – paying particular attention to where people thought the battles would be fought and who would be the victor. These predictions were mostly guesswork, as the generals wouldn't have divulged their tactics to the papers. But Jack did learn more about the current state of the war and got a better perspective on how things were done in the colonies.

When the sixth of June finally arrived, he made his way to the church in Norfolk still unsure whether Bull had managed to get to America or, if so, whether his telegrams had even been waiting for his friend in Charleston.

Jack arrived at the church just before noon. He found some shade, tied Skeiron to a rail, and sat on a nearby bench.

He didn't have long to wait. He had just sat down when the sound of an approaching horse made him look down the street to see the unmistakeable shape of Bull riding towards him. Jack stood and walked to where his friend was now dismounting. He held out his hand in greeting, but as per his custom, Bull ignored it and enveloped him in a big bear hug.

"Good to see you." Jack gave him a wide smile. "How was your trip?"

"It's good to see you too," said Bull. "The trip was too long. I threw up most of the way to Charleston. I'm not made to be on a boat."

"I feel your pain. I hate fucking boats too. By your punctual arrival, I'm guessing you had no trouble getting here?"

"It wasn't too bad. Once I found the telegraph office and read your messages, I asked the clerk how far it was. He said about 400 miles. You can imagine my response to that?" said Bull with a grin.

"You thanked him kindly with a cheery smile?"

"Not exactly," replied Bull

"I hear ya. This country's too damn big," quipped Jack sardonically. "So how did you get here?"

"I asked the guy in the telegraph office the best way to get here. Well to cut a very long, and sometimes painful, story short, I ended up riding on the back of a wagon for a while and then took the train. I knew you'd taken Skeiron, so figured I'd better get myself a horse. Luckily, the man at the stable knew where this church was, so here I am."

"Painful?" asked Jack with a quizzical look.

"I thought riding on the wagon was bad enough, being thrown around with every hole in the road, but the train was worse. Crammed into a railway carriage with too many passengers and sitting on a hard plank of wood that they call a seat. My arse was numb within the first hour. I kept getting up and walking to the back of the train to work out the numbness and get some fresh air. My fellow passengers didn't seem to appreciate when I kept pushing past them, but I gave them one of my winning smiles, and they calmed right down."

"By winning smiles, I'm guessing you growled at them?"

"Maybe," said Bull with a glint in his eye.

Jack laughed. He'd been among strangers for so long. It was good to have his friend back.

"So, what's the plan?" asked Bull, getting back to business.

"Well," said Jack, "despite my best efforts, frustratingly, so far I've only managed to follow his trail of death. Initially, he seemed to be heading south and preying on former slaves in isolated areas. However, now that the conflict has started, he is back to his old tricks of trying to kill wounded soldiers. There haven't been any more slave attacks reported in the papers, but he was sighted by a wounded soldier just after a skirmish a few miles away from here. I'm going on instinct, but I think he'll be heading north to where the fighting is to find some easier prey."

"Despite? Despite what?!" said Bull. "You found the bastard on another continent, for Christ's sake. I think you've done a hell of a lot. What you've pieced together all makes good sense. North it is then."

Bull changed his horse at the local inn, and they rode for the rest of the day. During the long ride, Jack brought Bull up to date on the investigation. Filling him in on the details of how he had put the pieces together and realized Mary's murderer was now in America, the steps he had taken so far to find the man, and the close call he'd had in one town after asking too many questions.

"It seems you haven't lost your knack for finding trouble," said Bull.

"I don't go looking for it," Jack said in defence. "It just seems to find me. And I'm not sure you're exactly immune from finding trouble yourself after all the scrapes you got into in the Crimea."

"Yeah, good point," said Bull, grinning.

"By the way, how many horses have you had since you've been here?" asked Jack, trying to keep a straight face.

"Just this horse and the one I bought in Charleston, so I'm getting better at keeping them alive. To be fair, nobody's been shooting at me though."

They kept up the enjoyable banter for the next few miles. They had both missed the camaraderie. Jack regaled Bull with stories of his adventures in America and Bull brought him up to date on the news from Lancashire. Ellie was doing fine and spending more time with her friend Jane. Thankfully Peter had never shown his face again. It seemed their warning had worked. Amanda had not been seen in months and the rumour was that Owens' might be expecting a grandchild. This gave Jack pause, and he wondered if it was his. And, if it was, what would the implications be for the future? However, the demands of their search for a murderer in such precarious times soon pushed those thoughts out of his mind.

While travelling north for several days they managed to learn, from very carefully asked questions, that a high number of troops had been seen heading towards a place called Big Bethel. This was a rural community near Hampton. They set off with high hopes of finding the man they were after.

They were still two days away when the battle took place so arrived in the aftermath, with the medical operation to help the wounded in full swing. Seeing an opportunity for information, Jack went to a wooden building that looked like it might have once been an old school but was now a makeshift surgery. Finding a doctor, he asked about the casualties and their wounds, in particular any that had had animal bites. It seemed there were three dead Confederate soldiers with animal bites to their necks. Jack slapped his gloves against his thigh in frustration. Once again, they were too late.

This pattern continued for the next few weeks. Ever moving northward, they always just missed their quarry. But they kept on; their luck had to change sooner or later.

It was midway through July when they finally got some good news. The last doctor they spoke to reported more animal attacks but also spoke of a medical orderly he suspected of robbing the dead.

"He seemed to be very hard-working. Always around the operating theatre willing to help when there are no more casualties to bring in. The sight of blood didn't bother him either, which is a handy thing. I've had far too many orderlies who fall over when the blood starts to flow."

"What made you suspect him of robbing the dead?" asked Jack.

"Every time a body was brought in, the personal belongings were inspected to try to identify them – so the next of kin could be notified. All the bodies he brought in had no personal possessions, which raised my suspicions."

"What did he look like?"

"He was surprisingly small for being able to lift the bodies so easily. He had sunken cheeks and very dark eyes, definitely foreign. Oh, and he walked sort of crooked."

"Do you have any idea where I can find him?"

"As a matter of fact I do. The outfit he was working with has just marched up to Manassas."

Feeling more hopeful than he had in a long time, Jack thanked the doctor and went to tell Bull the first real promising news they'd had in weeks.

With renewed purpose the two friends once again travelled farther north.

When they reached Manassas four days later, the place seemed to be in complete chaos. General Beauregard's Army of the Potomac, with over 21,000 men, had encamped just outside the town. With such large forces ready to do battle, it seemed the war had really started. Jack and Bull rode carefully round the large camp, in the hopes of finding any of the medical units.

They had completed a full lap of the camp when Bull saw some more tents being erected away from the main camp. They decided to investigate these new arrivals.

"Are you the medical unit?" enquired Bull.

"Part of it anyway," replied the man.

"What do you mean part of it?"

"We've been split up to go with different units. Rumour has it there's a big battle brewing."

"Can you tell me if you have any Bulgarian orderlies working with you?"

"No. Sorry. We came from West Virginia, all local boys." The man seemed to think for a few seconds. "The other medical units that are here are coming from different areas. Maybe they have foreigners helping them."

"Any idea where they're camped?"

"No. Sorry again. We just arrived and were ordered to set up our tents over here. I haven't seen much of anything else."

Bull thanked the man, who quickly got back to his work.

He and Jack sat their horses for a few minutes, dismally surveying the mass of white canvas tents.

"It's like looking for a needle in a haystack," said Bull.

"At the risk of getting in trouble, I think we should try to find somebody in command and ask them. We seem to be getting nowhere."

"Well, Jack," said Bull, "you were never that bothered about getting into trouble before. So why start now?"

"You make a good point. Let's go see what trouble we can find."

"Not that I'm complaining," Bull said, "but before we get into trouble, and to satisfy my curiosity, how come we haven't been shot or arrested yet? We could be enemy soldiers or spies. We aren't in uniform."

"Yeah, that is a good point," Jack agreed. "We never would have been able to move this freely about a military camp in the Crimea. I think it's down to how this war came about. The escalation of the war happened so fast and there were so many volunteers pouring into the camps that there just weren't enough uniforms to clothe everybody. The ones you see in full grey uniforms would have been the first to enlist. The rest just have to make do with their own clothes. Some smaller groups are wearing the colours of their local militia. If the Union Army is dressed as haphazardly, this is going to be one confusing war!"

Leaving the newly arrived medical unit, they rode into the main camp looking for any indication of some sort of headquarters. If the Americans were anything like the British, then the commanders would be camped away from the main body of men.

Seeing a sergeant, they asked him where his commanding officer was. He eyed them suspiciously but waved in the general direction of the eastern edge of the camp. Continuing in that direction, they got to the edge of the tents but once again couldn't see anything they recognised as a command centre. Asking another soldier, they were told to keep riding across the open field towards a stand of tall trees a hundred yards away. They were halfway there when a group of horsemen approached.

"What's your business here?" the leader asked them.

"We're looking for someone in charge."

"Why do you need to see someone in charge?" came back the retort.

Not wanting to give any details, for fear of word spreading and the man they were hunting escaping, Jack kept things vague. "We have some information that your commanding officer needs to hear."

"Where are you from?"

"England."

"Likely story. Easy to fake an accent. Can you prove you're not actually Yankee spies?"

Things were quickly starting to go from bad to worse. Under his breath, Bull mumbled to Jack that they needed to get out of here. Jack weighed up their options. He had heard that the justice was very rough for anyone suspected of being a spy. Such men were usually locked up, given a short trial, and shot. Even if they were eventually found innocent, being locked up would seriously bugger their pursuit of Mary's killer.

Jack turned to Bull. "Remember the Light Brigade and that screwed-up order we were given?"

Bull nodded gravely. He would never forget the charge into the valley of death. "Yes. I do."

"The head of that valley looked a lot like those trees over there," Jack said, hoping Bull was getting his hidden meaning.

"What the hell are you fellers talking about? Not a time to be standing about shootin' the breeze!" The irritated voice of the leader cut into their conversation.

"Yeah, those cannons were quite something close up," said Bull, ignoring the man.

Jack now knew Bull had got his meaning. "Looks like we found that trouble after all."

With that, Jack dug the heels of his boots into Skeiron's side and charged into the mounted men around them. Skeiron was heavier than the American horses and easily crashed through them, with Bull hot on his heels. They took the soldiers completely by surprise and had covered thirty yards before the latter started shooting.

The first volley of shots missed completely. They must have composed themselves before shooting again as the whine of the bullets on the second volley could be heard as they flew past. They had almost made it to the trees when, true to form, Bull had his horse shot out from under him. Jack didn't realise it straight away, but as he entered the trees, he looked over his shoulder. He could see Bull slowly getting to his feet backing away from his horse as it thrashed on the ground in pain, unable to stand.

Without a second thought, he wheeled Skeiron round in a tight circle and pounded back towards Bull. He could see the other cavalry soldiers closing the distance from the other side. He wasn't going to make it. Undeterred, he urged Skeiron into more speed, not about to abandon his friend. She seemed to sense his urgency and sped up. The other horses were closing in on Bull, but so was Jack. He was going to get there first.

Unfortunately, there was no way he would get Bull onto his horse in time. Instead, he rode past Bull and straight at the approaching men. He needed to make enough confusion to allow himself time to get back to Bull.

His tactic seemed to work. The three horsemen who were charging at him realised what he was doing, but it was too late. Jack aimed between the two horsemen on the right. They were riding so close to each other that, when they started to veer apart, the middle one and the one on the left collided into each other, unseating the rider on the far left. The rider on the right veered off only enough to miss Jack's horse but not far enough to avoid the fist that Jack threw at him on his way through their line, making this rider fall to the grassy field. Whirling Skeiron round in another tight turn, Jack went after the last rider. He was still regaining his balance after impacting with the other horse, so he didn't hear Jack's approach until it was too late. Jack rode alongside and kicked him out of the saddle. With all three soldiers off their horses, he galloped to where Bull was making his way towards the trees. He slowed and hauled Bull up behind him.

They were pounding towards the treeline and freedom when several men stepped out from behind the trees, all pointing their rifles at them. Jack slowed Skeiron to a stop. There was no escaping this time. They sat there dejected and slowly raised their arms in surrender. The soldiers with the rifles approached from the front, while the three cavalry soldiers, who Jack had unseated, now mounted up again, closed the net on them from the rear.

"I ought to shoot you right here," said one of the cavalry soldiers, blood trickling down the side of his face.

"Well if you do, I hope you're a better shot than you are a horseman," Jack mocked.

"Fuck you," said the man as the foot soldiers started laughing.

The hoofbeats of several fast-approaching horses could now be heard. They reined in next to the group, and the man with the blood-streaked face looked over.

Snapping a salute, he said, "Colonel Stuart, sir. We've captured two Yankee spies. They were asking questions around camp, and when we approached them, they tried to escape."

"Thank you, Lieutenant," said Stuart, starting to turn away from the man and looking at the two captives. "Fancy meeting you again, Jack," said a surprised but amused Colonel Stuart.

"It appears the shoe's on the other foot this time," Jack replied wryly but with some relief at the fortunate turn of events.

The faces of the soldiers surrounding them were of total confusion.

"Good work, Lieutenant. I'll take it from here," said the colonel.

"Very good, sir," said the man hesitantly.

"Jeb, one thing before they leave," Jack spoke up quickly. "My friend's horse was unfortunate enough to be shot as we tried to evade the soldiers. Would one of them be kind enough to spare a bullet to end its suffering?"

Jeb gave a nod of agreement to the lieutenant and the man departed with the other soldiers, leaving only Colonel Stuart and his two aides.

"Let's get you boys to camp. I'm guessing you have something to tell me."

Following Jeb, Jack and Bull rode into camp and dismounted, leaving Skeiron tied to a rail in front of the large tent serving as Jeb's headquarters. Jeb's aides continued on. Bull winced at hearing a gunshot, thinking it could the one ending his horse's life. It was a kindness but never easy to lose your mount. Once they were all inside, Jack introduced Bull and explained how Jack and Jeb had come to meet.

"Please sit," said Jeb, waving his hand at a couple of canvas and wood chairs. "Now tell me, gentlemen, what brings you this far north?"

Jack explained how he had tracked the slave killer down to Norfolk. He told how he'd then heard of soldiers being attacked at Sewell's Point and Big Bethel and also that he'd sent for Bull and the reason behind the summons.

"I'm sorry for your loss," said Jeb, casting a look of sympathy at Bull.

Bull nodded his acceptance.

"I'm not going to second-guess you. It seems you've done plenty of research on this fellow and know what you're talking about. As he's now killing Confederate soldiers, it becomes my problem too. How can I help?"

"We're here because we talked to a doctor at Big Bethel after the battle, and he said one of his medical orderlies was acting strangely. From what he told me and his description of the man, I knew it was the guy we were after. He told us he was headed to Manassas, so here we are. I guess we aroused too much suspicion with our questions, but this is the first time we feel we may be ahead of him. We need to know where your medical units are situated so we can check them out for this guy."

"I can certainly get you their locations. You will have to be quick about your task, though, as General Beauregard is planning an attack in the next few days."

Jack nodded. "If you can get us the locations, we'll do the rest."

Jeb went over to his desk, scribbled a note onto some paper, and stamped it with a seal. Walking back, he handed the note to Jack. "This is a letter of instruction from me to anybody you encounter whose assistance you require. It details that you are under my command, and they should comply with any wishes you have."

Jack put the note in his inside pocket.

"If you see Captain Jenkins over there, he will be able to give you the locations of the units you seek. Good luck, gentlemen."

"Good luck to you too, Jeb. Stay safe."

With that, Jack and Bull shook hands with Jeb, left the tent, and walked over to see Captain Jenkins and get the information they needed.

After a brief discussion, the locations of the medical units were secured, and they headed over to where the cavalry horses were tethered. Walking down the line, they spoke to the sergeant in charge.

"We'll be needing one of your spare mounts for my companion," said Jack, handing the sergeant the papers from Jeb.

The man glanced over it, handed it back, and then showed Jack several of the spare horses. They chose a horse for Bull, saddled it, and headed out to the nearest medical unit on the list.

There were four units in total – the one they had seen earlier and three others. But with dusk approaching it was quickly becoming too dangerous to continue their search. Travelling around in the dark out of uniform with so many armed men, even with the papers from Jeb, was inviting trouble. They decided to see one more unit before camping for the evening.

The next medical unit also proved to be basically fruitless, except that one of the orderlies knew of the man they were seeking and said that he had indeed made the trip to Manassas.

Feeling a bit more hopeful, Jack and Bull rode their horses over to the wooded area where they had tried to escape capture earlier in the day and set up their own camp. They planned to make an early start the following day.

CHAPTER FOURTEEN

21 July 1861

Jack and Bull woke at about five. The sun wasn't yet up, but daylight was starting to arrive. A slight dew lay on the grass, and the air smelled sweet. The coolness of the early mornings was a welcome contrast to the hot days. Jack walked over to the edge of the trees, stretched, and smiled to himself. He liked this time of day. Looking down on the camp and seeing all the tents laid out before them, he was momentarily transported back to the Crimea and some good memories of army life. Unfortunately, the tents made him also remember the carnage that he had endured and the loss of poor Mary. Pulling himself back from his thoughts, he looked to his left. Bull was standing next to him, looking down on the same scene.

"Brings back memories, doesn't it?" said Bull with sadness in his voice.

"All kinds," replied Jack.

Without another word, they both turned around and went back into the trees and their impromptu camp. Jack grabbed food from his saddlebag and passed some to Bull. It wouldn't do him any good to dwell on the sadness the scene had brought up in him –not when they were so close to claiming vengeance for Mary.

After eating a cold breakfast of biscuits and water, they saddled their horses and went to find the third medical unit. The rest of the camp was slowly coming to life, with wisps of smoke rising from the first fires being lit. Starting off down the hill, they circled the main body of tents. They were just riding past the quaint colonial house commandeered by General Beauregard as his headquarters when several cannon balls crashed down around them, with one smashing through the very front of the house. The battle had clearly begun. Jack and Bull now rode on faster to reach their destination.

With the explosion of those cannonballs, General Beauregard's plan to attack first lay in tatters. The Confederate Army was now reacting to what the enemy had done and not the other way around as planned. This meant the area was in complete chaos, which, in some ways, helped Jack and Bull move around more easily, as everybody in the encampment was too busy scrambling to respond to pay them any attention. The downside was the medical unit would now be active and its members dispersed, engaged in their duties on the battlefield. There was also the risk of being hit by bullets or cannon fire while they searched for their quarry.

After fifteen minutes of hazardous riding, they finally arrived at the third medical unit's camp. It had been set up as a field hospital, but the big central tent for operating on soldiers had not yet received any casualties, leaving the smaller tents for their aftercare empty. They spoke to some of the orderlies and were able to confirm that this was the unit the Bulgarian was attached to. Satisfied they had now closed in on their man, they walked back outside and listened to the sounds of battle.

"Do you want to wait here for him to come back?" asked Jack.

"It's tempting," replied Bull. "But can we live with ourselves if he kills more injured soldiers while we wait?"

"Probably not," said Jack.

"Then let's go find this bastard and finish it!"

They walked back to their horses and swung up into the saddle.

"Which way do you want to go?" asked Bull.

"I'm thinking to where the fighting sounds heaviest. It's the most likely place for casualties and our man. I was wondering if you wanted to go by the cavalry sergeant first and see if you could borrow a spare mount," Jack paused with a grin, "well, you know, just in case ..."

"You're a funny man, Jack." Bull, gave him a grin of his own, as he dug his heels into his horse's sides to spring forward. Jack quickly followed and they once again headed off into the midst of war.

Cresting a small rise, they paused to survey the carnage before them. Cannons were firing from both sides. The Confederates were holding a small hill, with the Union soldiers trying to push forward and take the high ground. In spite of it looking like the Confederates were outnumbered two to one, they were holding their position. The Union soldiers would make a charge up the hill and, depending upon the accuracy of the defenders' fire, would either gain a bit of ground and dig in or be pushed back. The death toll was rising on both sides.

"It looks like we're in the right place," said Bull grimly.

"It certainly does. It's been only five years since the end of the Crimean War, but by the look of things, we've found a more efficient way to kill each other."

"Yeah, nobody wants to be the weaker side. It's an arms race for sure."

As the battle gained momentum, the areas where the fighting was fiercest changed location. These changes meant the stretcher-bearers could start to extricate the wounded soldiers from the now abandoned areas and bring them back to the field hospitals. Confident this was where their quarry would be lurking, they moved down the slope and into the carnage.

The sounds and smells were all too familiar to Jack and Bull – gunpowder, guts, and death. It just smelt like hell. They picked their way through the dead and dying, ever vigilant for the evil little man they sought. Scrutinising every medical orderly transferring bodies to stretchers and carts, they observed that there were no suspicious injuries. Most of the wounds were from either bullets or shrapnel.

"It looks like sabres have gone out of fashion," said Jack. "There doesn't seem to be any slash wounds on the men."

"I guess nobody wants to get that close anymore. Just kill from a distance. It's safer, easier because it's less personal."

"Talking of safer, have you seen what's over there?" said Jack, pointing to a rise at the side of the battlefield.

"What is it?" asked Bull, his mouth agape in disbelief. "It looks like horses and fancy carriages …"

"You're right, that's exactly what it is. We're not far from Washington, and if I'm not mistaken, that's some of the rich folk coming to have a gander at what war looks like. They think it's an afternoon's entertainment. Reports in the local papers say their mighty Union Army will stomp all over the rebels. The papers up north have been full of how this war will last only about six weeks. I think they're in for a shock. From what I've seen of these Southern boys they ain't gonna lie down so easy. We can't forget, they were a key part of the fighting force that kicked our English butts off this soil not so long ago."

Carefully making their way through the sea of wounded and dead bodies, they continued on towards where the fighting now sounded the most intense.

"Where the fuck is he!?" exclaimed Bull, standing in his stirrups and looking around in frustration.

"I've no idea, and its really starting to piss me off. We have gotten ahead of him at last and are still having no luck." Jack reined in Skeiron to have a better look at the battlefield around them.

Bull pulled up beside him. "What if we head back to the medical unit he's assigned to? He may be there, or at the very least, we can find out if anyone's seen him or even if there are any more of his victims."

"It's as good a plan as any."

With that decision made, they rode back to the field hospital.

When they arrived, they were able to talk to a few of the orderlies and one doctor. Unfortunately, the answers were very brief. The medics were all busy and not very impressed at having been interrupted to answer questions. From what Bull and Jack gathered, the good news – or bad news, depending on how you looked at it – was that the man they sought had been seen but only on the battlefield, and two casualties had been found with their throats ripped out. With this new information, they rode back into the fray, determined to not return until he was dead.

Heading back towards the battlefield, they could see that the action had shifted yet again. They stopped at the first rise. Jack surveyed the area with a small brass telescope.

"Can you see anything?" asked Bull.

"There are several orderlies down there but none that match our guy's description."

Sitting on their horses they continued to study the battlefield below.

"Wait a minute. Three hundred yards, down and to our left. It looks like an orderly tending to a casualty. There's something not right about him," said Jack, lowering his telescope to collapse it and put it in his pocket.

They set off slowly so as not to spook their quarry. The battle was raging on just over the next rise. It was hard to tell in the ever-changing battle exactly where the two sides were.

They were within about a hundred yards when the orderly looked up and seemed to stare right at them. He was covered in blood, but that wasn't unusual. What stopped Jack in his tracks was the sight of the same red death mask he had seen in Buzau, Romania, the last time he was this close to the man – the time when he'd thought he'd gotten rid of him for good.

Pulling out his rifle, he took aim. He regulated his breathing and ignored everything that was happening around him to focus on his target. He had just started to squeeze the trigger when the rifle was knocked out of his hand. Jack pulled back quickly and looked around to defend himself, but no one was there. Luckily, he saw the sling of his rifle had caught on the pommel of his saddle, preventing it from hitting the ground. He grabbed the barrel, quickly inspected it, and saw to his relief it remained intact. There was scuff mark on the top of the barrel where a musket ball must have grazed with enough force to knock the weapon from Jack's grasp but not strong enough to break the rifle. It seemed they both had battle scars now. Realisation dawning, he looked to the direction the shot must have come from and saw the battle had shifted yet again and Union troops were quickly bearing down on them. It must have been a musket ball from these troops firing on Jack and Bull that had knocked the rifle from his grasp.

With no possible way to reach their nemesis before being overrun by the Union soldiers, they swung their horses away from the advancing soldiers and set off at a full gallop. At their fast pace, the two horses ate up the distance, and they had soon outridden the danger of the troops on foot. They now, however, had a river to the front blocking their path. Jack and Bull turned their horses to follow the bank of the river in the hopes of eluding the advancing Union soldiers. What they didn't realise was that these weren't advancing troops but retreating troops.

Reinforcements to the Confederate ranks from the Shenandoah Valley had arrived in the form of two brigades. General Beauregard had thrown both straight into the fray. The new overwhelming numbers tipped the balance of the battle and forced the Union soldiers into a full retreat. After following the riverbank for a bit, Jack and Bull now found themselves well off to the side of the movement of troops and so began to circle back to where they had last seen their quarry. The area was full of Union troops who they now realised were retreating towards the bridges over the river and freedom. Stopping to look through his telescope, Jack once again scanned the area.

"The miserable little bastard!" he exclaimed. "He's now helping the Union soldiers. He must have recognised me and realises he needs to escape. He's retreating with them!"

"Then what do we do?" asked Bull.

Jack sat his mount, watching the proceedings unfold. It was a fairly orderly retreat, until Confederate artillery fire started raining down on the fleeing soldiers. Total chaos then ensued, and in the mad rush to escape, a wagon was overturned, partially blocking the bridge over which most of the retreating Union soldiers were trying to pass. Panicked, soldiers started running off the battlefield in all directions, throwing away the extra weight of their rifles and equipment in their haste. Some had made it to the river and were moving toward the bridge while trying to find places shallow enough to cross.

"I say we get over there and find the motherfucker. Hopefully with, the soldiers more intent on saving their own skins we may get lucky and not arouse suspicion by just joining in the retreat."

Bull surveyed the scene before him. "I'm in."

Riding their horses among the retreating men, they were in the greatest danger so far. If the soldiers suspected they weren't from the North, they would shoot them. Southern artillery was also still raining death and destruction all around them. And as if that wasn't enough, their ultimate goal, Mary's killer, was now aware he was being hunted and would be ready the next time he saw them.

It wasn't easy to tell who anyone was. The blue sea of retreating men before them seemed endless. Luckily, the one identifying factor they had was the man they were hunting wasn't in uniform. Jack rode Skeiron off to the side of the melee with Bull in his wake and, once again, scanned the scene. He swung his telescope from the bridge at the front and then to the rear of the mass of retreating troops. As he scanned the rear, he saw that there were advancing Confederate soldiers in the distance.

Looking back towards the river, he had almost given up when he finally spotted him. He was right at the front, about to cross the partially blocked bridge. Time was now running out. Once the Confederate soldiers arrived, everybody who was left would be taken prisoner, and that would include Jack and Bull. By the time they'd explained who they were, their enemy would be long gone.

He slammed the telescope closed and pocketed it. "The fucker's just crossing the bridge. We'll have to find another, quicker way across. We can't afford to get stuck on this side of the river with the Confederates closing in from the rear." There weren't many options to get to the other side. Besides a few fords, the only crossing for miles was the bridge, and that was now choked with troops.

"Looks like were going for a swim," said Jack.

"Well I hope this fucking horse can swim, 'cos I can't," said Bull. With no time to waste they dug their heels into their mounts and headed down the steep bank into the river.

"Just keep hold of the saddle and let the horse do the work. We'll make it. Also make sure you keep your rifle and powder out of the water. Their fuck all use wet. If you do fall off get clear of the animal. Drowning is the least of your worries. If you go under, your horse will most likely kick you to death long before that happens."

"Now that's a cheery thought" said Bull grimly. "Good idea on the powder and rifle though." Both men made sure anything that needed to stay dry was kept well out of the water.

Apart from the fear of drowning, or being kicked to death, they found the water almost pleasant after the heat of the dusty battlefield. The horses waded through the water until their hooves were off the riverbed and then began paddling their way across. They snorted and spluttered but eventually got Jack and Bull to the other side. Some of the Union soldiers actually cheered, thinking two of their own had escaped. Bedraggled but on the far bank, Jack and Bull set off back towards the bridge. The fast-flowing muddy river had swept them a few hundred yards downstream.

"You think he'll try to blend in with the crowd or go off on his own?" asked Bull once they had squelched up the muddy slope.

"It's hard to say." Jack stood in his stirrups as Skeiron shook off the water. "But if he wants more blood, he'll stick with the crowd. He'll probably feel a bit safer there too, as he thinks we're still on the other side of the river."

Jack was right. Making his way along the road Casper Bogdan tried to blend in. The blood on his clothes wasn't a problem; many of the soldiers were wounded. He kept looking over his shoulder for a sign of his pursuers. There was nothing. Not many people could cross the bridge at once. By the time they crossed, if they crossed at all, he would be long gone.

Feeling his confidence return, his bloodlust started to rear its ugly head. He'd managed to kill a few soldiers on the battlefield and taste their blood, but he'd been thwarted from enjoying his last victim when that man on the black horse had raised his rifle at him.

Bogdan remembered him. It was the man who had shot and nearly killed him after he'd satisfied his needs with that peasant girl in the farmhouse all those years ago. An evil smile crept onto his face. He liked to kill the women more than the men. He liked to rape the women too. The fear in their eyes was what he lived for. Finishing off the wounded soldiers wasn't half as much fun.

The smile disappeared as he remembered the pain he'd suffered after his pursuer had shot him. He half thought about going back and making the man suffer pain in the way he had.

The one problem with this plan was that Casper Bogdan was a coward. He liked his victims weak or injured. Shaking his head as if to remove the memory of being shot, he continued to trudge up the road.

He neared the edge of a settlement, where there were some old abandoned buildings. There was also an upturned open-topped carriage. The horses had long since bolted, but the basket that had held the picnic was open on the ground, its contents picked up by the retreating soldiers. Bogdan stopped. He sniffed the air. He could still smell the perfume of the women who had been riding in the carriage. He smiled again, picturing the women in their fine clothes being thrown out when the horses bolted. He could picture it in his mind – how they'd landed on the ground, their skirts flying up. He could see their exposed pale legs. He was pulled from his pleasant reverie by a whimper from under the carriage. Getting down on his knees, he peered under. There, trapped underneath, was a woman. Her companions had run away and left her in their rush to escape. He couldn't believe his luck.

"Don't worry. I'll help you," said Bogdan, smiling at his easy deception. He took hold of the small carriage door and pulled. It was stuck. He pulled harder and it twisted and opened.

"You hurt?" he asked.

"My leg's a bit sore, and I banged my head," replied the woman in a small voice. "But I think I'm okay."

"Come," said Bogdan, offering the woman his hand. Gratefully, she took it, and he pulled her out. Bogdan noticed how nice she looked dressed in her finery, a long yellow flowing dress with a bonnet. She also had a string of pearls around her slender neck. He'd never been this close to a rich woman before. He uncontrollably licked his lips.

"Can you stand?" he asked.

"I think so. I'm a bit wobbly, and my knee hurts. I don't think I'll get very far."

Bogdan looked round. "I will help you over to that cabin. You can rest there until help arrives."

"Thank you," said the woman as she hobbled beside him.

"Yes, look," said Bogdan. "There's a bench on the porch."

Putting most of her weight on him, Bogdan helped the woman to the cabin. He could see that it was abandoned by its smashed windows and general dilapidated state.

"I'm not sure I can make it," she complained. *Rich kuchka*, thought Bogdan. *Never done anything hard in her whole life.*

"Try. We are almost there," he said with feigned kindness.

She looked up and saw the seat ten yards away. It seemed to give her spirits a lift, and she made more of an effort to get there. They stepped onto the porch. It creaked, but the rotten boards held.

Surreptitiously, Bogdan looked over his shoulder. Nobody was paying them any attention. All those around them were too wrapped up in their own misery. He helped the woman take one more step onto the porch, but instead of assisting her in sitting down on the bench, Bogdan took all her weight on his shoulder, turned, and pushed through the front door of the cabin. Once inside he threw her onto the floor and kicked the door shut behind them, a confused expression crossed the woman's face, quickly turning to fear.

"What's happening!?" she shrieked.

In response, Bogdan walked up to her, leaned down, and punched her in the face, temporarily knocking her out. Standing, he looked down and smiled in anticipation.

Half a mile back down the road, Jack and Bull were making steady progress. They had ridden back to the bridge crossing and were now riding parallel with the road. Their wet clothes were starting to dry out already, giving off traces of steam in the hot sun with every movement. They scrutinised every face as they passed, getting more and more disillusioned with every one that didn't belong to Mary's killer. Most of the soldiers never gave them a second glance back.

"Do you think we missed him?" asked Bull. "Should we retrace our steps?"

Jack shook his head decisively. "No. He's here somewhere; the sneaky bastard hasn't avoided capture for all these years without being able to blend in. We keep going."

They started to enter the outskirts of a town. The first few buildings they passed had been abandoned long ago – the rotting structures falling in on themselves. Jack and Bull continued to scour the faces of the soldiers, hoping to see the man they were after, while also keeping an eye out for an ambush. Luck was still with them, as nobody had paid them much attention so far. But as they were not Union soldiers, they risked being attacked as suspected spies or even Southern sympathisers.

The cabins they were now passing seemed to be newer or at least abandoned more recently. This little town wasn't that far from Washington. It was likely the people had moved here in the hopes of making their fortune in the nation's capital. Well, it wasn't quite the nation's capital anymore, as the Southern states had now named Richmond as their capital.

Onward they pressed. Jack becoming more and more uneasy the farther they went from the relative security of the Southern battle lines. He had made some friends with the Southern officers and felt safer there. This was the Union Army. If they were captured, it was likely there would be no fair trial for them, especially with the letter they carried from Jeb. It was more likely they would be summarily shot.

They were passing an overturned carriage, with Jack keenly looking for possible ambush sites when he thought he saw movement in one of the abandoned buildings. He got Bull's attention, and they reined in at the side of the road.

"I think I saw movement in that cabin over your right shoulder," said Jack.

Bull made no move, not wanting to look, for fear of alerting anybody inside that they had been seen. "Any idea what it was you saw?"

"Looked like a man, but I couldn't make out more than that. For all I know, it might be a soldier needing a rest. But it seems strange. These soldiers look like they want to get as far away from here as they can and as quickly as possible."

As if to make the point, gunfire could be heard from the direction of the bridge. The soldiers on the road looked in the direction of the noise. Fear was written all over their faces. They all seemed to quicken their pace.

"Sounds like there's a rearguard action going on."

"Do you think they'll try to regroup and attack the Southern troops?" asked Bull.

"I doubt it, but you never know. I do think they'll try to defend the bridge to slow the Confederates down. That's what I'd do. If I were a Southern commander, I'd be trying to get over that bridge and push my advantage. From what I've seen, if they can get over the bridge in any significant numbers, there's not much to stop them. This army's in full retreat." Turning in his saddle to look back towards the cabin, Jack still couldn't see any more movement. "You up for a little breaking and entering?"

"Absolutely!" replied Bull.

"Okay, you see the small barn behind the cabin. I think we should tie the horses up round the back so nobody on the road can see them and possibly steal them. We then approach the back of the cabin on foot."

"Sounds like a plan to me."

Veering off the road, they rode in a wide arc to bring themselves up behind the barn then dismounted and tied the horses. Jack peered around the corner of the building. The back of the cabin was right in front of them. It had a central door and a window at either side covered by a dirty, tattered curtain.

"It looks like, from the size of it, there are four rooms – two at the front either side of the front door and the same configuration at the back. I say we take a closer look." Bull nodded his agreement. Before they moved both men removed their boots and emptied out any water that remained inside. The last thing they wanted was a watery squelch to alert whoever was in the cabin to their presence

Stealthily, the two men approached the silent derelict building. Once at the back door, they quieted their breathing and listened for any sign of movement within. After two minutes, all was still quiet.

"Were gonna have to go in," said Jack in a low voice.

"How do you want to do it?" asked Bull equally quiet.

"If you stay here and count to sixty, I'll go round the front. When you get to sixty, open the back door and go in, I'll do the same at the front. That way, if he's still in there we'll have him cornered."

With a thumb's up from Bull, Jack started to make his way round the side of the house. He glanced at the road. The Union soldiers continued trudging forlornly past. No one looked their way. Stepping onto the porch, he carefully made his way to the front door. Moving cautiously, he walked as close to the cabin as possible to avoid the inevitable creak from the centre of the sagging boards. He arrived at the door with a few seconds to spare, drew his navy colt and thumbed back the hammer. As his count hit sixty, he turned the handle and pushed open the door. He went in with his weapon up, sweeping the small sitting room for any sign of the man he had seen through the window. Not seeing him immediately, he looked around. There was a door on the right and another door at the rear. He thought he heard sounds in the room to the right so he moved silently past the closed door and positioned himself at the door to the back rooms to wait for Bull to emerge. Getting impatient when Bull didn't appear after a few minutes Jack crouched low and slowly pushed open the door.

Meanwhile, Bull, too had hit is count of 60 and opened the back door, entering into the kitchen. Aiming his rifle, he swung it across the room and saw it was empty. He now had two doors to choose from, one to his left and one in front. He was about to move towards the left door when the door in front of him started to open. Taking a knee and steadying his aim, Bull waited.

Oblivious to the impending confrontation, once inside the cabin Bogdan had dragged the semiconscious woman into the other front room. He shut the door behind them and his eyes lit up as he entered the room and spotted a bed. It was old, but it had a mattress. *What luxury*, he thought. Better than the ditches he was used to raping these women in. He unceremoniously dumped her onto the mouldy mattress and straddled her body. The woman was starting to regain her strength and began to fight him. Bogdan punched her again and again until she couldn't fight him anymore. Breathing hard, he was hot and sweating after their struggle. He got off the bed and leaned against a wall to survey his work. She was sprawled out, bloody and bruised. Her dress had ridden up with the struggle and he admired the exposed stocking clad legs. The pure white skin underneath made him want to leave a mark.

He moved back to the bed and knelt over her for a few moments fingering the lace on the neckline of her dress and contemplated tearing it off of her. He thought he heard a noise at the front of the cabin and was about to go look out the window to investigate when she whimpered and tried to move her hand to her now rapidly bruising face. Not wanting to risk drawing any unwanted attention by having to subdue her again he desperately looked around the room for something to gag her and tie her up with. The only suitable material was the shabby curtain partly covering the window, but he didn't want to remove it for fear of someone outside seeing in and stopping him. He took out his knife and sliced two strips of material off her dress. He secured her hands in front of her with one strip and then tore the other strip in half roughly stuffing part of it in her mouth and tying the other around her head to hold it in place. Satisfied she was silenced he decided to have a quick look out the front door to make sure they hadn't drawn any attention from the retreating troops. The woman still wasn't moving much, so he thought it would be safe to leave her for a few minutes. Climbing off the bed, he walked to the door, opened it, and stepped through.

At the same time, Jack was continuing to open the door to the rear room. Hearing a slight creak of a floorboard, he flattened himself against the wall, so as to make a smaller target. He cautiously pushed the door open the rest of the way with the barrel of his pistol. Once it had swung back to the wall, his eyes made contact with Bull's on the other side of the opening. A grin creased his face as he recognised his friend until Bull fired his rifle. Jack sensed the bullet pass within inches of his body. The burnt powder that spewed from the end of the rifle stung his face and temporarily blinded him.

The next thing he knew, Bull was charging straight at him while Jack's mind was still trying to work out what was happening. He was disoriented with the deafening noise of the rifle being fired in such a confined space of the room and the plumes of smoke. As Bull ran past, Jack thought he heard him shout, "He's here."

No stranger to gunfire and the smells of battle, Jack soon regained his senses and turned and followed his friend. Bull was standing by the door that Jack had passed on his way in.

"The fucker's in here!" Bull bellowed.

"What happened?" asked Jack.

"As you opened the kitchen door, I saw you grin when you spotted me. I started to lower my rifle when the door to the side room behind you opened and the devil himself walked out. I took a snap shot, and he stepped back inside and slammed the door. I'm not sure if I hit him or not."

"Did he have a weapon?"

"I didn't see one, but that doesn't mean he hasn't got one."

While they were talking, Bull reloaded his rifle.

"One way or another, we're going to have to go in there. I say we do it now, fast and hard. We've come too far to not to," said Jack.

"Sounds about right to me," replied Bull.

"Just in case he's got a gun, I'll go in first. You have a wife and more to lose than me."

"Mary was my wife, so I should be the one in first."

"Then let me do this for you and Elly."

Bull reluctantly nodded his acceptance.

"On three," said Jack. "One … Two … Three!"

They burst through the door. Jack went in first and to the left. Bull, straight behind him, went right. Bogdan was there, holding a knife to the throat of a dazed, badly beaten woman. He had her positioned in front of his upper torso with only his legs showing to shield himself from their attack.

"Put down the knife," said Jack.

Bogdan moved his head slightly from behind the woman's head to peer at Jack with one eye.

"Put down the knife and you can walk out of here. Nobody else has to die." Jack knew it was a lie, but he hoped the tone of his voice might convince Bogdan to let the woman go. There was no way the man was leaving here alive.

"No," said a guttural Slavic voice. "*You* drop weapons, or I slit the bitch's throat."

Jack ignored his threat, thinking, *the longer you talk, the more time your enemy has to think about how to get out of the situation. You need to keep him off balance with actions.* He decided to take the initiative.

Making as if to lower his weapon, he shot Bogdan through the right knee. He was very satisfied to see it did have the desired effect of distracting him and putting him off balance. The impact of the .36 calibre bullet hitting the kneecap and then the joint almost tore the Bulgarian's leg off. As Bogdan swayed sideways, Bull fired. The bullet caught Bogdan high up on his chest throwing him back onto the bed and over the other side in a spray of blood. The woman fell sideways, her gag loosened and she started screaming as she hit the floor. Ignoring the screaming, Jack vaulted onto the bed and over the other side. Bogdan was in complete shock. His right leg was useless, and his chest was a red mass of bubbling blood. He looked up at Jack and sneered.

"I make one request?" he said.

"No," was all Jack said as he raised his pistol and shot him in the head.

Time seemed to stand still. Everything that had driven Jack for the last several years was over. This monster was dead. It was finally over. They had won.

The screaming that was coming from the other side of the bed dragged Jack back to the present. Bull was crouching by the woman's side talking to her, but nothing seemed to calm her down.

Jack walked round the bed, holstered his pistol, and bent down in front of her.

"Are you hurt?" he asked.

The woman kept screaming.

"Are you hurt?" he repeated.

Nothing apart from the screaming

Jack slapped her across the face. The screaming instantly stopped.

"Thank fuck for that," said Bull. "I thought she'd never shut up."

"Are you hurt?" Jack asked again.

The woman seemed about to answer when a noise outside the cabin drew Jack's attention. He stood and peered out of the window.

"Oh, shit!" he exclaimed. "Looks like we've got trouble coming, Bull. About ten of the soldiers are getting curious and are headed this way. I'm guessing the shooting and the screaming got their attention.

"Look, Miss," said Jack. "There are men coming who will help you. We have to go."

With Bull in the lead, the two men left the room just as the front door burst open on their left and two Union soldiers entered the cabin. When they saw Jack and Bull, they started to raise their rifles.

Jack reached for his holstered pistol in a blur of speed that would have made the storekeeper's nephew proud. In one fluid motion, he pulled the iron from its holster, cocking the hammer as he did so, and shot the lead soldier in the chest. As the man was falling, Jack thumbed back the hammer again, took aim, and shot the second soldier. This wasn't the time for being careful or regrets. Just find the biggest part of the target and pull the trigger. The chaos of war didn't leave time for questions or explanations. They couldn't risk being shot or taken prisoner.

"Run!" Jack yelled as he turned towards the back of the house.

He and Bull both exited the back door like it was a jailbreak, running fast until they reached the back of the barn to retrieve their horses. Untying their mounts, they swung into the saddles. Leaning over the necks of their horses to make as little a target as possible, they galloped away from the barn, keeping it in between themselves and the pursuing soldiers.

They had covered thirty yards when bullets started flying all around. Jack got nicked on his upper arm, but that was all the damage they took.

"Let's swing back around and get across the river. These Northerners don't seem to like us!" Jack shouted over the gunfire.

Bull yelled back, "Do we head for the bridge?"

"If it's available. I don't want to get back in the river if I can help it."

Once they were safely out of range, they reined in to let the horses cool off, slowly heading towards the bridge. When they reached the crest of a ridge, they stopped to get their bearings. In front and slightly to the left was the bridge, now empty of Union soldiers. Across the bridge, Southern soldiers were milling about. Nobody seemed to be in charge, and they certainly weren't pushing their advantage and coming across the river.

Like all good soldiers, Jack and Bull looked for any sign of the enemy. As the left was devoid of anything but the now advancing Confederates, Jack and Bull scanned to the right. They could almost see to the edge of the town, where they had killed Bogdan. The last of the retreating Union soldiers could just be seen, but there was no danger from them.

"Looks quiet enough," said Bull. "You think we can manage to cross the bridge without the Southern boys shooting us as Yankees?"

"Crap," said Jack. "I hadn't thought of that. I'd forgotten we aren't in uniform."

"I don't suppose we have anything that could be used as a white flag?" said Bull.

"Not unless your underwear will do the trick," quipped Jack.

"After today's activities, I'm not sure it's all that white anymore." Bull grinned.

They both sat there, trying to work out their next move while watching the troops on the far bank.

"We may not have to cross the bridge after all. Looks like a column of Southern cavalry heading straight for it."

"That's what I like to see," said Bull, "a welcoming committee."

They stayed where they were and watched as the column neared the bridge. Movement in the distance off to their right caught Bull's eye as he watched the progress of the Southern cavalry.

"What's that?" he said, pointing towards the treeline above the bridge on their side of the river.

Jack took out his telescope and scanned the area. "Jesus Christ, its Union cannons! They're gonna wait till the cavalry crosses the bridge and then pound the shit out of them. They won't be able to get back across quick enough to escape. They'll be cut to ribbons."

Bull sat back on his horse with a resigned air. His horse stamped in impatience. "I hate to sound too cold, but is it really our problem? This isn't our war."

Jack lowered the telescope, thinking for a few moments as he collapsed it and tucked it way in his saddlebag. He looked across at his friend. "It's a good point, and I might have agreed with you, except for the fact that Jeb Stuart is at the head of that column. He's the guy who came to our rescue when the Southerners thought we were spies. He's a good man."

"Okay then. I'm in. What are we going to do?"

"As we're cavalrymen, there's only one thing to do … Charge." Jack gathered up his reins, his gaze steady and serious.

"You mean the cannons?" Bull looked incredulous as he did the same.

"Yes. They aren't pointing this way, and the artillerymen certainly won't be able to move the cannons around quick enough to shoot at us. That means we'll just have some lightly armed troops to deal with. Are you still with me?"

Bull gave him a nod. "I go where you go, Jack. I wouldn't have it any other way."

"Okay then. The first horses are about onto the bridge. The cannons will wait to fire till most of them are across, so I say we go …now!"

"Looks like we found trouble again!" said Bull, digging his heels into his mount.

Jack spurred Skeiron into action, and both men were soon racing across the open ground towards the cannons. The range was about 500 yards to the treeline. They were eating up the yards when the cannons opened up. The ground shook, but nothing came their way. It appeared their calculation was proving correct. Jack glanced over his shoulder and saw the cannonballs exploding all around the advancing cavalry. He and Bull were now only 50 yards away when the cannons spewed their death again.

Bull's horse spooked at the noise, but he held on as they entered the trees. Pulling his pistol, Jack began shooting the soldiers manning the cannons as he rode through them. On hearing his first shot, they looked over in dismay to see the enemy among them already and began scrambling to raise their rifles.

Still moving fast, Jack was picking the men off as he rode through them. He couldn't get them all, as he was moving too fast but knew Bull was behind him to get what he missed. Bull didn't have a pistol, only his one-shot musket, so he reined in and shot the last remaining soldier on the first cannon. He then turned his rifle in his hands and held onto the barrel. Digging his heels into his horse, he sprung forward after Jack. Most of the soldiers were so shocked to have two hostile riders suddenly in their midst they didn't even get off a shot. Bull was now using his rifle like a club, finishing off any soldiers who had been fortunate enough to survive Jack's first onslaught. Jack's pistol was now also empty, so he holstered it and pulled his sabre from his bedroll.

As he charged on, his mind was momentarily back in the Crimea. It felt like déjà vu. Unrelenting, he continued down the line. The Union soldiers had only managed to set up three cannons in their hurried attempt to stop the advancing Confederate Army, so Jack was through the line more quickly than he'd expected.

He wheeled Skeiron round and was about to start back through the line but stopped as Bull came charging through with a grin on his face.

"Man, it's good to be alive!" he shouted as he reigned in next to Jack. "Feels like we're back on the peninsula!

"And you still have your horse," said Jack wryly.

"Well, how about that? Maybe my luck's finally changing." Bull's silly grin just wouldn't leave his face.

"Seems to me you've always been pretty lucky, Bull, but I'd say your horses are getting luckier."

Bull laughed in agreement.

They left the treeline and headed cautiously towards the approaching cavalry. They could see Jeb Stuart was out in front.

Jack and Bull reined in, watching them warily and raised their hands in a show of surrender, hoping to not get shot by some trigger-happy trooper before Jeb was close enough recognise them. Jack knew the minute he did, as he raised his hand to halt the column and trotted forwards with another officer to meet them.

"It appears I'm back in your debt," said Jeb, removing his hat and bowing in an elaborate show of gratitude, "Did you leave any for my boys?"

"There should still be one or two staggering around up there," Jack said, looking pleased.

Without a word, the captain next to Jeb turned his horse back towards the rest of the waiting men and signalled several to ride with him up the hill to see what was left of the Union artillerymen.

"It could have got pretty nasty if we'd ridden into those cannons. I know it's not your fight, so I'm indebted to you both."

"I'd like to think you'd have done the same for us."

"That you can count on."

The three men watched as the small cavalry detachment rooted out the rest of the Union artillerymen. Jeb turned back to Jack. "Tell me, how did your own private mission turn out?"

With everything that had happened since they'd killed Bogdan, it hadn't yet sunk in. They had finally got him. Jack and Bull grinned at each other with satisfaction.

"We caught up with the bastard," Jack replied. "He won't be hurting anybody anymore."

"I'm glad you succeeded. That sort of thing can eat away at a man. What are your plans now?"

"We haven't really given it any thought. I'd say we'll probably head back to England."

"Well if you boys ever find yourselves back here, I'd happily sign you up to ride with me. We can always use good men."

"We'll be sure to keep that in mind," Jack responded and Bull nodded his agreement.

They shook hands all round.

"Stay safe, Jeb." Jack started to turn Skeiron down the road.

"You too boys," he replied.

Jack and Bull spurred their horses to trot towards the bridge and through the Southern lines. Jack looked around at all the men in grey uniforms. He looked at the open countryside and wondered if he would ever see it again and also what it would look like after suffering the ravages of war. He was sure the countryside outside Sevastopol still showed the scars of battle from the Crimea all these years later. He hoped that wouldn't happen here.

"So what *are* we going to do?" asked Bull.

"I guess we ride to Charleston and see about catching a ship back to England."

They rode in silence for a few miles.

"Is there something wrong with me?" asked Bull. "I seem to enjoy being shot at! I have a beautiful wife who I adore but …" He let the sentence hang there.

"Well, if there is, then I've got it too. I think once you've experienced the high of surviving an extremely dangerous situation, everything else seems pale by comparison. It's just the way it is. We do still have to manage to survive one more highly dangerous situation though ..."

Bull looked confused. "What?"

"Sailing across the ocean in one of those smelly creaking death traps."

"No. Don't remind me!" said Bull with a groan.

With that, they picked up their speed and headed for Charleston and England.

AFTERWORD

The events, battles, places, and historical people of the Civil War are all true. I have just woven Jack's narrative among them. The train crash in the Crimea did not actually happen, but the battles of the Crimea are also real, and I have created characters to participate in them. All weaponry described and used is also factual, along with army units and names. Calder Vale is a real village in Lancashire. The Lappet Mill and village were founded by Quakers Jonathon and Richard Jackson in 1835. You can see the mill-houses there today, along with the mill and millpond. The Lappet Mill is still producing textiles. The description of the charge of the Light Brigade is factual based on documents in the British National Archive (www.nationalarchives.gov.uk) under British battles.

Jack's use of *ill tret* to mean "badly treated" in chapters 7 and 10 is not a typo. It is correct for his time and place. This expression continues to be a commonly used colloquialism today in Lancashire, England.

Other books by John Saxxon:
Jack Wolfe On the Trail of a Traitor

ABOUT THE AUTHOR

John Saxxon grew up in Lancashire, England. His writing is inspired by his love of the history of the British Empire, the American Civil War, and his English roots. John currently lives in Aberdeenshire, Scotland. Jack Wolfe: On the Trail of Murder is his first book.

For more information on John Saxxon and his books go to www.johnsaxxon.com

CPSIA information can be obtained
at www.ICGtesting.com
Printed in the USA
LVHW081645231118
597954LV00042B/1582/P